THE LAZARUS IMPACT

By Vincent Todarello

I will knock down the Gates of Hell,
so that man will mix with those from the lower depths.

I will smash the doorposts, leave the doors flat down,
and I will let the dead go up to eat the living.

And the dead will outnumber the living.

-The Epic of Gilgamesh, Tablet VII

PROLOGUE

"I can't believe it. An entire city?" Professor Strauss asks as he is lead through the thick, hot jungles of central Mexico.

"Bigger than all the others too, as far as we can tell. Sprawling," says Dr. Blough.

"Chichen Itza? Tikal?" asks Strauss.

"Bigger. Just goes to show you we're only now just scratching the surface of the ancient Mayan civilization's expanse. Imagine what else could be hiding in these jungles?" Blough remarks. "Just covered up. Swallowed by the jungle, reclaimed by nature. It's incredible."

"How tall are the structures?" Strauss asks.

"Well the one that prompted the discovery seems taller than Coba. We haven't officially measured it yet. Like I said on the phone, you're the first person I contacted once we made the discovery," Blough explains.

"I appreciate that…"

"But there's something I neglected to mention," Blough interrupts.

"Oh?"

"Here. Come this way." Blough takes a hard turn off the freshly cut path through the jungle, leading Strauss through the brush. He occasionally hacks down the foliage with his machete as they push forward. "Now, the structures are all impressive. But the real reason I flew you down here is because of a burial site we unearthed on the edge of the city. It's like nothing we've ever seen. It flies in the face of every burial custom we know about the Mayans."

Strauss swats at mosquitoes as they walk. "Well it could depend on the time period this city was active. Burial customs varied between…"

"No. I know. I know all that. You'll see what I mean when we get there," Blough explains.

A few minutes later they enter a clearing in the jungle, and several archaeologists crouch on the ground around a cylindrical structure made of ancient, hand-carved stone blocks. It stands about six feet high. The archaeologists carefully remove leaves and natural rocks from the area without disturbing the ruins. They use brushes to sweep away dirt and screen sifters to parse through the gravel. Some are on top of the structure, removing debris from inside it.

"You see the glyphs on the stones?" Blough asks.

Strauss is in awe at the craftsmanship and detail preserved in the stone. Even the paint remains in some places. He begins to translate the pictograms on the stones, mouthing words to himself as he circles the structure. As he goes around, his demeanor changes from awe and excitement to confusion and fear.

Blough notices. "What is it?"

"These symbols. I…"

"I know a few things here signify death. I thought maybe the afterlife too, but it seemed a little confusing to me," Blough interrupts.

"It's not the afterlife. It's after death," Strauss corrects him. "Or alive with death. It doesn't make sense, because then there's some stuff about the heavens, falling stars, or coming from the stars."

"And the others?" Blough asks.

"They seem to be about disease or illness, and warnings. This was a place that was totally forbidden. Forbidden to everyone. Dangerous, even. Not just off limits." Strauss notices a large circular shaped stone with a diameter that roughly matches the size of the cylindrical structure. "Was this on top?" he asks.

"Yeah. We needed a pretty massive military helicopter to help lift it off," says Blough.

"So it was like a lid?" Strauss asks.

"Yup."

"And what's inside?"

"Still excavating, but we found some human remains near the structure," Blough answers.

Just then there is commotion from the archaeologists on top of the cylinder. "There must be hundreds in here," a man calls out from down inside.

Strauss rushes to the nearest ladder and climbs up to the ledge as a skull is handed up from the archaeologists within. They place it directly in his hands.

"It looks charred, like it was burnt," Blough remarks from beside Strauss' ladder. Strauss steps down to examine it with him.

"Yeah. There's a hole in the skull here," Strauss says.

"Could it be from the burning? Or maybe trephination?" Blough asks, craning his head to get a better look.

"This is ragged, like trauma; not drilled out like a medical procedure," Strauss explains. "No, this was done before the burning. I'd need to confirm at a lab, but my gut tells me this was a wound."

"They're all like that. All the skulls have holes in," one of the archaeologists says from up on the cylinder ledge.

"Ceremonial? There are myths of sacrifices, right?" Blough asks.

"No. There's nothing here that would indicate a ceremonial or religious aspect to this. It's like it was done out of safety. An ancient quarantine. This might be the earliest evidence of such a practice. It's like they rounded up the diseased people and put them in here," Strauss suggests.

"And they burned them. I assume they killed the sick people with a blow to the head, threw them in here, and then torched them." Blough says.

"I wonder. What's the significance of the wound to the head?" asks Strauss.

"Could be that it was a painless way to dispatch of the ill," Blough offers.

Strauss ponders. "Could be…"

"So what do you think about these meteors coming? Think the Mayans had it mapped out and knew about it given their skills at sky watching?" Blough asks.

"Not unless the meteor shower is cyclical. And then only maybe," Strauss says.

"Well, you know we *are* standing at the edge of one of the biggest meteor impacts we know of on Earth. This whole area was hit, right?" Blough laughs.

Strauss chuckles. "That's true."

"Alright let's call up some press already, shall we?" says Blough. "Maybe we can steal some of the spotlight in tonight's news reports."

CHAPTER 1

"Are we rolling? You got the police there behind me? Yeah? Okay." Wolf addresses the camera in his unmistakable Australian accent, sweeping strands of his wavy silver and gold hair out of his eyes. He puts on a baseball cap and a heavy wind breaker. Steam escapes his mouth with each breath out in the cold. Police barricades block a road that bends through the moonlit fields behind him. He shields his eyes from the harsh camera lights. "Folks, as you know, our own scientists have calculated the location that the meteor shower is likely to hit. Despite the official secrecy and the warnings to stay clear of the area, despite the barricades you see behind me, I'm going to get it on camera for the viewers. Tonight's episode of Extreme Naturalist is live. As always I'm your host, Wolf Camden. Don't change the channel. You don't want to miss this." Wolf looks up over his shoulder and signals to someone. "Off we go then, JT."

The cameraman backs up and catches one last shot of Wolf putting a flight headset on his ears. He sits with his legs dangling out the side of the helicopter with one hand up, grasping a handle on the side of the chopper door as it lifts off the ground. A policeman runs over as they take off.

"What the fuck is going on here? Where are you going with my chopper?" The officer sticks a stiff hand at the camera lens, knocking it to the ground and shattering the lens. The image goes black.

"Jesus Christ, man. That's a nine thousand dollar camera," the cameraman complains.

"You told me to jab my hand at the camera," the cop says.

"Yeah, but I didn't expect you to smash the fucking thing!"

Wolf speaks loudly over the beating pulse of helicopter blades into a hand held camera. "I've heard your complaints, folks. The show started to come apart as we got more sponsors, more money, more fame. We became comfortable, lazy. Instead of just editing together some carefully shot footage of me climbing vines in the thick of the jungle, or trekking through icy mountains with nothing but a goat skin and a matchbook, tonight I'm going to get right in the thick of extreme danger, and be the first man to encounter a meteor as it strikes the earth. This could potentially be life threatening. Depending on the size of the meteors, the impacts could be something similar to small nuclear explosions. We're told that there won't be anything that large, and that many will burn up in the sky as they enter our atmosphere, but our scientists think otherwise. In any case there could be some potentially damaging after effects, like a dust cloud or debris suspended in the air, or disruptions to power and satellites." Wolf gets a signal from the pilot over his shoulder. "Now that we're well beyond the police barricade, JT is going to let me out and fly back to a safe place."

Wolf takes the flight cans off his ears and puts a hand on his head to stop his hat from flying off in the wind. He hops out of the chopper as it hovers a few feet from the ground. He stands in a field of tall grasses that shimmer emerald and amber as they catch beams of light shining down from the helicopter. The moon is bright, lighting up the night sky and the ground beneath.

Wolf films the chopper as it lifts up and starts to fly away. "Aww fuck!" he exclaims. "Aww fuck! Fuck!" Wolf struggles to focus the camera on a nearing object in the sky. A flaming ball soars through the air behind the helicopter, heading right toward it, trailed by a tail of fire. He sets the camera down on the ground, aiming it up at the sky. He flails his arms around frantically, trying to get JT's attention up in the chopper. It's no use. A meteor, no bigger than a third the size of the chopper, rips right through it at lightning speed and continues to sail overhead. The helicopter is obliterated in a huge explosion; Wolf feels the fireball warm his face even at a distance, and the ground quakes violently from the meteor impact. The camera is knocked onto its side, and Wolf is thrown to the ground. Bits of flaming debris and twisted metal rain to the earth. Wolf gets up and runs toward the crashed helicopter, dodging the wreckage. "JT! JT!" he screams.

Several moments later he returns to the camera. He falls to his knees in front of it and puts his head into his hands, tossing his hat off to the side. He gathers himself as streams of smaller meteors streak through the night sky above, shaking the ground again as each hits the earth.

He would want me to keep going. He repeats it in his head again and again, wiping the tears from his eyes. Wolf approaches the camera, picks it up, and continues the show. "Uhh. I don't know if this is still airing. But JT's chopper was struck by a meteor. It's just been completely vaporized. There's nothing left but this debris you see here. He's gone. JT… JT was a close mate. A very dear friend of mine for a long time. He's been there with me, with us, on every adventure for the past five seasons of the show. I think, to honor him, his dedication, I should continue on. I have no radio. No cell phone on me, uhh, no way to communicate back to the crew behind the barricade. I can either go back, or go forward. After a moment of silence and a prayer for JT, back there, I decided I should push on and examine these meteors, which, as you can see are still raining down from above. The one that hit the helicopter was only about a meter or two in diameter. That, and all these others you see overhead, are relatively small in comparison to what our scientists say is coming with this shower." He looks up into the sky. "Lots of them aren't even reaching the ground. They're just burning up. But let's go take a look at the craters some left behind. Then we'll get out of here, back to safety."

A massive crater glows with a low orange flame in the field up ahead. The ground seems to sizzle as streaks of smoke rise up from the cold earth.

"The ground is literally steaming. The debris is so hot that it's turning all that night time winter frost on the ground directly into water vapor." He winces in disgust after breathing some of it in. "Awful. The smell is disgusting. Like a sulfur smell, mixed with the smell of burnt packing foam or plastic." He feels a burning sensation inside his body. Agony and pain overtake him, and a stiffness forms through his muscles that feels like soreness from the day after a rigorous workout. Wolf coughs uncontrollably as a waft of the steam blows up against him. He falls away, out of the gusts to where he can breathe.

CHAPTER 2

Twenty feet below ground, Brandon Jessup watches Extreme Naturalist on a small tube television that he managed to rig up to his parents' cable service. He lounges on a homemade bean bag chair, vacuum sealed and filled with rice. Tonight's the big night; the end of the world, or so he hopes. His parents think he's crazy. Unlike other kids who want new baseball cleats, or who save their money for a car, Brandon stockpiles apocalyptic comic books, first person shooter video games, survivalist books, and canned goods.

"Alright. That's as close as I'll get," Wolf says. I don't know if this is toxic, but it certainly doesn't smell healthy," he says between coughs, standing on the edge of a sloping crater the size of a baseball field in diameter. He has another fit, ending with a throaty vomit. He spits up a stringy mucus and breathes heavily, trying to calm himself. "Well. There goes supper." He chuckles, making light of the situation. "Happy Christmas everyone. And if you're ever stuck out there on your own, just remember: there's always tomorrow." Wolf says his catch phrase with a bit of hesitation, wondering whether there will even be a tomorrow. The confused look on his face speaks volumes to Brandon.

Brandon flips through the channels for a bit. He lands on a news report. They show aerial images of a new archaeological find with narration.

"Thousands of years ago a great civilization thrived in these jungles. Today we know them for their incredible accuracy in star gazing and sky mapping, and their mystical prophecies regarding celestial events. They were the Mayans. The jungle here is thick, but not tall, so archaeologists have had good fortune finding the ruins of their ancient cities. One recent find, here in central Mexico, is ironically on the edge of a large crater basin that was later grown over. In fact that's why the jungle doesn't grow very tall; it sits atop a ground made of almost solid limestone and underground rivers. This ancient location is the same place where scientists believe a great meteor once collided with Earth millions of years ago and perhaps wiped out the dinosaurs, well before the dawn of the Mayan civilization or even mankind."

I'm not deep enough. Brandon shuts the television and makes his way through piles of canned food and boxes of bottled water. He neurotically counts off food items and supplies strewn around his bunker, as he has done a hundred times. A pretty cool hideout for a teenager, he has outfitted the shelter with many modern comforts, including a most important stack of porn magazines for when the internet goes down. His computer has several instant messages waiting from unknown cyber friends that regularly contribute to *Apocalypse Any Day Now*, a comic book style doomsday message board. All are eagerly watching Wolf's show to see if the meteor shower turns out to be a fateful night for modern civilization.

"If I lived as close as you I'd be there watching! Instead ur trapping urself in a dungeon. We r all gonna die. May as well have front row seats," one message from ENDITNOW says.

"I'm prepared, no, excited, to ride out the aftermath," he responds from his handle, Zombology15.

"Enjoy your canned beans. LOL," ENDITNOW retorts.

I will. Brandon turns and looks at his stack of canned beans; a four foot tall pyramid that graces one corner of his bunker like a temple offering to the legume and fart gods.

He's off from school. Christmas break. Unlike most of his peers, he'll willingly spend it locked in the reinforced shipping container buried under his parents' property; a remnant from the Cold War days. The idea is to give it a test run, to see what it's really like to survive in a bunker, to ration food and water. *Looks like this test run might turn out to be the real thing.*

Last week all the news channels could talk about was the so called Lazarid Cluster; a meteor shower that was recently detected and heading for Earth. After scientists discovered the meteor shower, it disappeared for three days and then later reappeared when using the new GOD, or Graduated Optical Depth, space imaging telescope. As such the scientists decided to name it after the biblical story where a man named Lazarus came back to life by the hand of God. The President and all his scientists kept reassuring the public that there was nothing to worry about. Brandon knew they were just trying to prevent panic, anarchy. He saw the websites; the ones popping up for a few hours and then disappearing, where scientists were claiming there would be a big impact.

Everyone knew the government was lying on some level. In their gut they knew it, but it was like no one cared. People simply stocked up on batteries, water, and canned food like they were bracing for a winter blitz that might never come. Even in his quiet suburban town, Brandon saw the shelves in the supermarket thin down and empty. *What a waste. That's only part of being prepared. An entire town can't stockpile in a week what they need to survive just by raiding the local supermarket.* He even posted the sentiment on the message board. *It's too late for them. They didn't prepare. All those supplies will be wasted.*

I don't have enough! Five months, maybe six. Swiping an occasional few cans of soup and boxes of crackers from his parents wouldn't cut it, so he got a job at the local comic book store. He made enough to pick up some essentials; large containers for storing water, MREs, batteries, and fuel for the generator in his parents' shed. *Not too bad for a kid. But others would be extremely well prepared; people from the internet.*

"If it ever gets too crazy out there, will you come try to find me?" asks Apocalypta, Brandon's long distance internet flirt from the message board.

"Hell yea. I have the directions to your farm written down in five different places," he responds with an added smiley face.

Like him, she is 15 years old. Only her parents have a secured compound in the mid-west. They live like the end has already come to pass. Brandon is jealous of how well prepared they are. Fully energy independent, a greenhouse protected from the elements, scores of weapons, and a fully sustainable food supply. They even have a security perimeter. Apocalypta feels like a prisoner in her own home, but after years of conditioning she's become accustomed to the lifestyle.

"I hate to say it, but I hope this thing really happens so that one day maybe we can finally meet," she writes. But before Brandon can return the sentiment, his bunker goes dark. A deep, sustained rumble shakes all around him. No lights, no internet, no nothing. Boxes of food fall from their shelves, his bean pyramid tumbles, and his stacks of comic books and porn magazines slide and flop to the ground. *Oh shit…*

He feels around, trying to make his way to the hatch. *God damn it. Why didn't I install a flip switch for the generator? Stupid asshole. I need to get up there and start it up before anything happens.* The generator itself is protected by cinderblock walls that he built around it, with a padlocked metal door on one side. *The shed might be blown to shit, but at least the generator will be safe.* He would also need to get his parents down there before the shit hits the fan. If a big enough meteor struck the earth close by, the whole house might be torn to shreds in just a few moments.

He gets closer to what he thinks is the ladder up, but in his haste he haphazardly steps on a can of food that tipped to its side. His legs kick up from underneath himself. *Those fucking beans!* He slams to the floor, cracking his head on another fallen can. He slips into unconsciousness, never hearing the banging and yelling from the hatch above, never hearing the cries of his parents.

CHAPTER 3

He knew something big was up when the power flicked and the whole place went old school for a good half hour. Emergency backups, manual overrides, keys instead of buzzer buttons, the whole nine. When everything powered back up, Marcus heard the guards whispering about running generators and the national power grid failing. But there was more electricity in the air when the power was out than when it was on. He could sense the tension, the calculation, the energy from his fellow inmates. *All it takes is a split second for a caged animal to find its way out.*

"How long those generators gonna last, mutha fucka?" Harley taunts the guards from three cells down, sparking a chain reaction of supportive screams and metallic banging throughout the entire cellblock. The prisoners are on edge, knowing they're restricted to their cells until further notice. Marcus sits quietly on his bed, refusing to join in the commotion. He doesn't mind the restriction so much. He likes being alone with his thoughts.

"Roll!" yells a guard from two floors down. "Stand up and face front!"

Where the fuck we gonna go? Marcus is more pissed about being disturbed than about being confined to his cell all day. He stands up and faces the bars of his cell, tuning out as the guard walks the row and calls out everyone's names, awaiting their responses.

"Better keep these doors fuckin' locked, mutha fucka! There's more of us than you, nigga!" Harley belts out again, rousing the others into a ruckus.

"William Harley Davis," says the guard. All falls quiet on the block.

"Fuck you, nigga!" Harley responds.

"Open 368!" the guard yells. The door pops open and the guard, along with two others, enter and beat Harley with their night sticks. Makeshift mirrors sparkle in the fluorescent overhead light along the row of bars in the cellblock, all trying to get a glimpse of the repercussions. Marcus stands still, resolute, unaffected.

When the beating is done, the guard continues his walk of the row. "Marcus Johnson." Marcus blinks from his haze of thought to see the capped guard standing before him, in front of his cell. He tips his head down and his eyes meet the guard's. It's Thompson. He and Marcus talk from time to time, and he keeps Marcus up to speed on sports. He's one of the nicer guards, but Marcus knows not to cross him like Harley just did. Flecks of sprayed blood speckle Thompson's face. *Harley must've gotten it pretty bad this time.*

"Here sir," he responds quietly from six and a half feet high.

"If blue keeps it up they'll be in the bowl this year," Thompson says, winning a grin from Marcus in response before continuing on.

At 285 pounds of solid bronze muscle, Marcus could have easily beaten the piss out of Thompson and the other scrawny white guards that put a beating on Harley. But he likes to think of himself as a reformed man, at least he wants to be. *It's tough to truly reform in a den of thieves and killers.* He knows his crimes earned him true damnation, something beyond the earthly punishments that mere man can dole out. He feels remorse. He truly does. *This prison is just a waiting room.* He often says so among the few people he socializes with. If he had it all to do again, he would have done things differently.

At 15, Marcus had already developed a customer base selling weed on the streets. It was small time, but it got the attention of some of the local dealers. He was a big dude, even at that age. The dealers saw him as an asset, a resource. Rather than make an example of him, if they even could, they rewarded him. He became an enforcer. A collector. A carrier. By 18, weed was long gone and he was on to more lucrative substances, and he had already killed. By his early 20s he was known by all the locals, and even a little bit beyond. Soon enough he was under police surveillance. But Marcus knew. One night he slipped away and stashed money, valuables, and even his truck in a rundown building outside the city that he bought with cash, using it like a storage unit. Then he paid a visit to the snitch and beat him to death. The police caught him after. That was the only crime they managed to pin on him, but it was enough to put him away for life.

He often wonders if everything is still there in the building, or if some bum stumbled upon it. It'd be like winning the lottery. He doesn't miss life on the outside so much, doesn't long to see anyone. But he does miss his freedom. *A man needs his space, his liberty*. Most of all he misses his truck; an '86 pick-up, jacked up on four foot high monster truck tires. Under the hood is a fully worked 350 cubic inch engine. The thing screamed, and Marcus was so feared on the outside that he could leave it unlocked on the mean streets and no one would dare touch it.

The rest of the night comes with a lot of hushed talk about what happened. Guesses mostly; a distant earthquake that knocked out power, a terrorist attack, a meteor, or even just a precautionary drill. Whatever it was, it whipped the population into a frenzy. *Something serious is about to go down. If there's riots, or worse, I'll stay in my cell. I wanna do my time in peace, with the Lord.* He knows he'll never see freedom again, but he also knows that his punishment is justified. He feels he's not fit for society if capable of such reckless disregard for life. *Reformed or not, there's no place for me out there.*

CHAPTER 4

By mid morning Sheryl gets an emergency call on her cell phone from Debbie that the winds shifted and a plume of nasty debris wafted over the west part of town. A grey dust cloud lingers there while their kids are out playing football. She can barely hear anything with all the interference on the line.

"What debris plume?" she asks as warning sirens start to reel up outside.

"Do you live under a rock?" Debbie replies, promptly hanging up.

"I don't have time for your attitude, bitch," she says to the dial tone.

When the sirens stop she calls her husband. Voicemail again. "Who the hell works on Christmas and can't answer the damn phone?" she asks herself aloud on the message she leaves. Between getting the kids ready, cleaning the dishes, sweeping up the dog hair, wrapping gifts, putting away the mess of toy crap the kids left in the den, and starting to prepare for Christmas dinner, she has no idea what's been going on outside the house or out in the real world. If she did, she forgot, or she tuned it out, or she was too busy to let it sink in.

The meteor thing? Her face contorts with incredulity. She tries to turn on the television to check the news but there's no power. Then she realizes that she might have put the kids in danger by letting them leave the house earlier. "Sure, go out and play," she told them when they asked, thankful to get them out of her hair for a few hours in the morning while she got everything ready. *I love my boys, but I hate Christmas break.*

She grabs the keys to the minivan and steps outside. She sees the dark mass of debris looming over the distant horizon at the end of her street. The neighbors are scattered, running all over the place. Jim and Nancy scurry into their house with water, food, and bags of groceries. Paul and his family are leaving their house, getting into an SUV packed full with belongings. The new guy next door is sealing and boarding up his windows and doors.

"You better get out of here, Sheryl!" Paul yells out as he rolls by slowly in front of her house. "Get your family and get out of here. That stuff is blowing this way!"

Sheryl speeds off in the minivan, ignoring stop signs and dodging frantic traffic at every turn. The congestion infuriates her. *Come on you fucks!* It's chaos, anarchy. The sirens blare again, and every kind of emergency vehicle races up and down Main Street in a panic. She crosses when it's safe, blowing the red light. She zooms to the football field, where she sees that the debris has passed. It has blown onward, to the outskirts of town, leaving behind a dusting of soot on the ground in its wake. But more is on the way, much more. She can see it coming.

"Get in!" she yells to her kids. Bobby Junior is ten, and Stephen just turned eight last Friday. They are everything to Sheryl. They give her the love and affection she needs, since her husband is never around. *He's married to his work more than me. Pathetic. I'm neglected, abandoned, and alone. But not when I'm with my boys. The boys love me...* And they're doubled over in a coughing bout. "Get in! There's more of that dust coming!" They catch their breath and jump into the back of the minivan. "You guys okay?" she asks. There's no reply. "BJ? Steve-O? Answer me. Are you guys okay?" Sheryl looks at them through the rearview mirror. They're exhausted.

"I can still taste it," BJ says, his eyes rolling back in his head. Stephen begins to cough.

Sheryl's eyes bounce back and forth between them in the rearview, ignoring the road as she drives. Sirens and screamingly loud emergency vehicles fill her ears again. Blood spurts out from Stephen's mouth. She turns her head to face him. "Steve-O, what's the matter?" Her voice shakes.

"Mom, look out!" BJ yells with everything left in him as they drive through the red light at the intersection of Main Street.

An ambulance screeches its wheels. Smoke and brake dust spit up from the wheel wells as it broadsides Sheryl's minivan at a high speed. Both vehicles flip and tumble, and they eventually slide to a scraping stop.

CHAPTER 5

The coughing subsided somewhat, but Wolf still tastes that lingering smell in the back of his throat. His chest feels burned and tender on the inside, and his lungs are labored in breathing. He leaves the crew at the motel and checks himself into the nearest emergency room, which is minimally staffed on Christmas Day and only partially powered up by emergency generators. *The staff recognizes me.* They whisper to each other with star-lit eyes, and all the nurses blush at his gruff handsomeness.

"I can see you, Mr. Camden," a stout, dark curly haired doctor says. "I'm Dr. Vogel." The two shake hands and walk down the hallway to a room. "My sons love your show, you know."

"Aye, thanks mate. I'll sign them some autographs before I leave, eh?" Wolf says, removing his shirt.

"That'd be great." Dr. Vogel listens to Wolf's breathing through the stethoscope, wincing in confusion. "Your breathing is normal, just slow," he says.

"I feel weak. I breathed in this smoke, or steam that came up from one of the small meteors. It had a strange smell, like burning plastic. I didn't get much of it in me, but it managed to keep me coughing for a few hours. I can still taste it in the back of my throat."

"Could be the smell from the heated meteorite, whatever substances are in it might mimic those plastic smells. The symptoms, the coughing, could just be some irritation from whatever you breathed in," Dr. Vogel says as he puts on a breather mask and some long rubber gloves.

"What's all that for?" Wolf asks. "Am I contagious?"

"Doubt it. It's just old habit. I used to do research at the CDC."

"Level with me, doc. I breathed in a bit of foreign substance and within half a day I feel like I've had emphysema for a decade," Wolf pleads. "I've had almost every kind of exotic bug there is out there. Whatever is happening to me is aggressive."

"I won't know anything until I run some tests, and some of the tests are going to take a while because I have to send them out to a lab, like for the blood work. I don't even know if these labs are up and running, given the meteor impact. Most likely what you've got is just some smoke inhalation, like what a firefighter might deal with," he says, muffled through the mask. "But better safe than sorry. We'll run the whole gamut. I'll draw some blood, you'll pee in a cup. But first, a throat culture."

Wolf opens wide. Dr. Vogel swabs the back of his throat and rubs the cotton tip around a pink Petrie dish. Next he draws some blood into a test tube, and then Wolf fills up a cup of urine in the bathroom. Finally he hands Wolf a wide glass jar. "I need you to cough into this for me. Try to get some of that garbage up from your lungs. I don't need wads of spit or anything, just some moisture that comes from deeper in the lung."

"Right," Wolf says. He does as he was instructed.

Dr. Vogel quickly seals the jar. "I'll be back in a bit. Sit tight," he says over his shoulder as he whisks out of the room with all of his samples.

Wolf's heart races from the forced coughing. He's in top shape for a 40 year old and is well known for running a marathon every month since his 20s. But expending that small amount of energy to cough makes him feel like he just ran wind sprints in his rugby drills. He puts his shirt back on, lies back, and tries to calm himself. *What the hell is happening to me? I wish we had more time to get further west last night, to my trusted doctors in LA.*

He had just crossed back over the police barricade when the big one hit. His crew stole him away in a speeding SUV outfitted with the latest weather chasing and sky mapping equipment. The roads were getting crowded when they made it to the air strip and their customized private jet. All the major airports in the northeast were already shut down, so anyone with a pilot's license was trying to get airborne and far away before the FAA grounded everything else. It was fortunate they didn't fly into one of the main airports when they came to film the meteors. They drove the truck right into the cargo hold of the jet and took off within minutes, ignoring the line of other small biplanes trying to lift off on the runway ahead of them.

They were only about 30 minutes out, heading west, when they were grounded. It was like 9/11 all over again; the sky was empty. The meteor shower kept raining down debris, and if even the smallest of rocks were to hit a plane in flight it could rip through the fuselage, change cabin pressure dramatically, and cause a crash. The nearest air strip with room for them to land was a small crop duster run, still just a few hours driving distance from the impact zone. There was barely enough room to come to a full stop. They rolled off the edge of the runway and into the tree line, damaging the landing gear and one of the wings, but all that mattered to Wolf was that they were on the other side of the metcor, upwind.

Dr. Vogel returns to Wolf's room. "The culture will take some time if there's anything to grow, but I did see something strange under the microscope when I swabbed the jar. This isn't the best place to study this kind of thing. Come with me," he says.

Wolf follows the doctor through a maze of hallways to another room. Wolf steps inside and Dr. Vogel closes the door behind him, locking it from the outside. *You've got to be joking.* Wolf pounds on the door. His icy, dagger-like blue eyes pierce Dr. Vogel through the small, cross-hatched window at face level on the door.

"I'm sorry," Dr. Vogel says. "Until I know more I'm going to have to contact the CDC and lock you down. There's plenty of food and water in the back there; I just brought it in."

Wolf ignores the doctor, and tries to ram the door with his shoulder, but he soon becomes tired, drawn out. IIe sits down in the corner to catch his breath. "Fucking crazy Americans," he utters between gasps. *Right mad wankers.*

CHAPTER 6

A headache wakes Brandon in the darkness. The back of his hair is wet. He touches it and knows right away. *It's blood.* He remembers falling. On his hands and knees he crawls to where he put the flashlight and batteries. Stupidly, they are each still in their plastic packaging. He manages to find and open them. With the push of a button there is light. It's eerily quiet in the shelter without his computer or electronics buzzing. He remembers he was about to go get his parents and bring them down. He runs over to the hatch, hurdling stacks of supplies, but when he gets to the top of the ladder he stops. *Fallout.*

Brandon fishes around for the AM/FM radio and loads some batteries into it when he finds it. He spins the knobs slowly. Static. He finds that the reception is better the closer he is to the walls, and as he climbs up the ladder toward the surface. Finally he hears something; a dissonant but familiar tone. The emergency broadcast system. He turns up the volume so that the eerie and ominous sound fills the bunker. Suddenly it stops. There is nothing, and the silence is so loud it's deafening. *Dead air. The world has ended.* He half smiles at the thought, but in the back of his head there is fear.

"THIS IS NOT A TEST." The voice booms and startles him. He lowers the volume. "This is a recording of the emergency broadcast system. All those east of Ohio and north of Washington DC are advised to shelter in place. All others should move as far south and west as possible. The debris plume resulting from the meteor impacts in the northeast is considered extremely hazardous. Those in the affected area should seal their windows and doors, remain inside and rely on air filtration systems whenever possible." The message repeats. He plays around with the knobs but he only finds the same message on all the other channels that have a signal, AM and FM alike. He shuts the radio.

It's dead silent in the bunker. Brandon wants to start up the generator and get his shelter powered up, but down there it's safe, and the air is filtered through vents. He convinces himself to try his luck topside. *It'll only be for a minute, and I have a gas mask incase the debris cloud is thick. If it isn't too hectic out there, I can try to get mom and dad too, and sack the house for supplies.* He struggles to open the hatch. There's something sitting on top, obstructing it, preventing it from opening. He pushes with all his might until something heavy rolls off from on top of the hatch. He shudders when he sees a lifeless arm tumble and flop to the grass on one side. *A body.* Once it rolls out of the way he quickly pops up from the bunker and shuts the hatch door. He looks down with a double take. There are two bodies; his parents. Grief sweeps over him in a rush. The excitement of the apocalypse turns to fear and sadness. He weeps in his white, elephant trunk style, Cold War era gas mask. He checks their pulses at the wrist. He can't feel anything. He looks around in a panic to see his house severely damaged. A wall is caved in, exposing the living room on one side. The roof has been pelted with debris, making holes into the attic. Sheets of shingles and siding have blown off, lying scattered across the grass, and a huge oak tree has fallen onto the cars, flattening them like pancakes. The shed is pretty banged up too, but it still stands. *The generator is safe.*

He drags his parents aside, near the edge of the woods adjacent to the property. He speaks a few solemn words under his breath, things he memorized in Sunday school. He wants to bury them, but he's afraid of lingering topside for too long. *I have to press on. I have to force myself to be strong, independent. It's the apocalypse. It's what I wanted, right?*

The air is still as he heads for the shed. An unearthly black dust covers much of the property. He takes an erratic zigzag pattern, avoiding the debris like it's hot lava. It's from the impact cloud, and he doesn't want to drag any of it back into the shelter. His years spent reading science fiction comic books make him extra cautious. This strange soot is poisonous, and he assumes the worst of all possible scenarios if he contacts it. He imagines his skin burning to the bone, or the debris dissolving his shoes or clothes, getting to his body and liquefying it into green ooze, or turning him into some bloodthirsty mutant. But his parents are physically intact, in one piece. He shakes everything from his thoughts. *This is what I've prepared for. I can do this.*

Brandon opens the lock to the generator with the combination he remembered. With a few draining tugs of the pull-start engine it rumbles to a rattling hum. He checks his fuel supply; he will have to ration it carefully, and attempt to get more if he plans to hole up at the bunker for an extended period of time. The closest gas station is about five miles away.

Eager to try to contact Apocalypta with his computer and electronics powered up, and frightened of the mysterious debris, he hurriedly turns back to the hatch. But he notices something on the way. The bodies; his parents are gone. He spins his head in all directions. His breathing frantically quickens with his heartbeat in tow. They are nowhere to be seen. *Were they still alive? No. I checked.* The panic consumes him. His overactive comic book imagination kicks in when he hears a light rustling in the woods behind him. Something moves among the trees within the lengthening early evening shadows. *Alien abduction? ... Zombies.*

Freaked out, he whips open the hatch, kicks off his sneakers, and scurries back down into the fully lit and buzzing shelter, hoping he didn't track in any toxic dust. *If they're alive they will knock.* He reassures himself again and again. He cries, thinking of his parents.

CHAPTER 7

Where am I? Sheryl wakes up in a hospital connected to machines by tubes and wires. A laboratory style gas mask covers her face. She feels pain in her shoulder, but she's surprised to see it in a sling. The last thing she remembers is Stephen coughing up blood. She pulls the wires and tubes off of herself, igniting a storm of alarming machine noises. She begins to peel the gas mask off her face, but then she remembers. *The dust.* A nurse rushes in, also wearing a gas mask.

"Leave that mask on, ma'am. The debris from the cloud is dangerous," the nurse warns. Sheryl leaves it on.

"Where are my sons? Are they alright?" she asks as the nurse pushes a few buttons to override the machines, stopping the noise.

A doctor enters the room and sits beside her bed. He too wears a mask. In fact Sheryl notices that the entire staff has masks on as they hurriedly pass by in the hallway. The hospital is buzzing with activity. *This can't be normal.*

"Where are my boys?" Sheryl asks with tears welling up in her eyes.

"I'm Dr. Levy. I fixed up your arm there. You had a dislocated shoulder."

"Answer me!" she yells.

"I'm sorry, Mrs. Bassonnet. They didn't make it. Stephen died in the crash, and Bobby passed shortly after due to complications from breathing the dust outside," he explains.

"Why am I alive? Why did you save me?" she asks.

"When the ambulance got to the accident you weren't breathing. They revived you on the way to the hospital and here you are," he says.

A storm of emotions churns inside Sheryl. *He answered how, not why. What reason is there to live without my boys?* She feels alone, guilty, angry, responsible. "Take me to see them."

"Mrs. Bassonnet, we can't," the nurse begins to explain.

"Now!" she insists. Dr. Levy nods at the nurse, giving the okay.

Sheryl's body aches with each step as they walk down the chaotic hallway that leads from the ER to the morgue.

"You're lucky to be alive," the nurse says.

"Am I?" Sheryl responds after a reflective pause.

"You didn't breathe the dust. People are slowly dying because of it."

"My life is nothing without my boys," Sheryl responds, almost angry.

"What about your husband?" the nurse asks. Sheryl doesn't respond. They come upon a pair of light blue swinging double doors labeled *morgue*. "This is it. Are you sure you want to do this?" the nurse asks.

"Yes," she says as she pushes the door open, revealing a cold, clinical room, brightly lit with buzzing fluorescent tubes overhead. The back wall is a grid of square metal doors for holding the dead in cold temperatures to prevent decay. Six stainless steel tables are lined up side by side in the center of the room; on each is a body covered in wispy hospital linen. The nurse pushes a smaller shelf-like wheeled table filled with crude looking medical tools to the side, out of their way.

"Stephen is here," the nurse says as she approaches one of the freezer doors. "His torso was badly wounded in the accident. He died quickly, painlessly." She opens the door and pulls Stephen out on the rolling metal slab fitted into the unit.

Sheryl whimpers when the nurse peels back the sheet that covers Stephen's face. He's been cleaned and stripped of his clothing. "My baby," she says as she moves her face close to his. *I want so badly to kiss his forehead one last time. This goddamn gas mask...* She yanks it off in frustration and plants a soft kiss on him, over the nurse's pleading objections and warnings.

Suddenly an alarm bell rings in the hallway. It blares violently, rapidly, like a fire drill in high school. Sheryl puts her mask back on. "Where is BJ?" she asks. There's yelling coming from down the hallway by the ER.

"We have to go now, Mrs. Bassonnet. I'm sorry. There's an emergency," the nurse says, taking Sheryl by the arm and moving her quickly out of the morgue.

"I need to say goodbye to my son!" Sheryl begs.

"Not now. We can't. I can't let you be here alone. We need to get you back to your room. You shouldn't even be up."

The smashing sound of broken glass just behind them shatters their argument as a maintenance worker breaks open the emergency fire kit in the hallway to reach for the axe inside. He rushes past them and out the nearby exit, by the ambulance port.

"What's going on?" Sheryl asks.

"It's been crazy here all day. We have to get you back to your bed, and I need to get to work, okay?" The nurse says with force.

Sheryl caves. "Okay."

They move back through the hall at a brisk pace. The alarm continues to ring, constant, piercing. Sheryl tries to ignore it along with her aches and pains. Doctors and nurses are rushing all around the ER in a frantic panic. They are overwhelmed, understaffed, and unprepared for what's happening.

"I checked her pulse twice just a minute ago! She was gone," one nurse argues with another just outside a curtained ER room.

"Well she's alive now," the other snaps back.

They hurry back to Sheryl's room and her nurse runs off after Sheryl is safely in her bed.

"What is Mr. Mortenson doing up?" Dr. Levy calls out in the hallway. "He needs to rest."

Sheryl gets up from her bed, confused. She peeks down the hall to see an old man shambling his way toward the nurse station in the middle of the run. Half naked, his ass hangs out of his hospital gown, which is in the process of falling off his body completely.

Dr. Levy trots over to him and takes him by the arm. "Mr. Mortenson, come back to your room. You shouldn't be up. Using all this energy to walk around will wipe you out because that dust is blocking the air from getting into your lungs." Mr. Mortenson groans at him, unreceptive. "Tina, I don't have time for this, I need to check on about twelve other patients right now," he complains to Sheryl's nurse. "I know we're understaffed but I need you to keep an eye on things. And he should at least have an oxygen intake." Dr. Levy tugs at Mr. Mortenson's arm, trying to lead him back to his room. He won't listen, and Dr. Levy becomes impatient with his patient. "Come on, let's go!"

In a flash of rage Mr. Mortenson growls, lunges, and bites Dr. Levy, tearing a chunk of stringy red flesh from his neck. Dr. Levy screams in pain and his knees buckle, dropping him to the cold faux tile floor. Blood pours and sprays out in all directions, coating the hallway. Dr. Levy begins to convulse violently, foaming at the mouth and vomiting. His pool of blood and bile smears as he twitches. Tina, Sheryl's nurse, runs over to him, putting pressure on his neck to try to stop the bleeding.

Mr. Mortenson turns and chomps at her, falls on top of her, and continues to devour her. She flails in pain and soon begins to seize like the doctor. One of the orderlies runs over and tries to restrain Mr. Mortenson, hooking his arms underneath Mr. Mortenson's arm pits, pulling him backward off of Tina. But the orderly slips in the blood, falling to the floor. Dr. Levy and Tina both slowly stop twitching. They're dead. The hall is full of chaos and panic, and more screams begin to rise up from down the hall by the morgue. The alarm continues to sound, and other patients begin to emerge from their rooms to see the horror.

Suddenly Dr. Levy sits up in death. His eyes are wide and crazy. Then Tina sits up, covered in blood from head to toe. They both race toward the orderly, tackling him back to the ground as he struggles to regain his footing on the blood slicked floor. The two ravage him, tearing him apart with their fingers and teeth. Mr. Mortenson, as if completely revived with energy, runs naked toward the other patients. His gown has slipped off.

32

Sheryl's heart races into a panic upon seeing the scene unfold before her eyes. She gasps aloud, and Dr. Levy's crazed eyes fix upon her between swallows of the orderly's flesh. He moves toward her. *Oh fuck, he saw me.* She swiftly slips her slender body back into her room and closes the door behind her. There's no lock. She jams it shut with a nearby chair, and pulls the hospital bed over with all her strength. She tries the phone on the bedside table but there's nothing on the other end, no dial tone. She gathers up her belongings, puts on her jeans, her sneakers, and struggles to get her shirt on, with only one arm through the sleeve. She digs around in her jacket pocket for her cell phone. There's no reception. *The meteors must have screwed up the signal.*

Suddenly there's a pounding at her door. *It's Dr. Levy. Tina too.* She hears the groans and growls of the dead outside in the hall, trying to get in. She ducks out of view from the door window and hides in the bathroom, locking herself in.

The pounding grows heavier and heavier, and soon the door to her room is broken down. She hears the alarm bells blaring louder. She puts her back against the wall and slides down to the floor. Tears and fog fill her gas mask. She prays that the lock on the bathroom door holds up.

33

CHAPTER 8

The Hillside apartment complex stirred with activity way too early in the morning, and it woke Willy Stanton from his slumber. He barely slept for anything longer than a nap after he came home from the war, even almost 40 years later. The nightmares still linger, though they've gotten much better in the last 20 years or so. But, little did he know, he slept clean through the meteor shower, all the while dreaming he and his platoon were under heavy artillery fire from the VC. He only found out about the meteors when the bus driver said "last bus for the day" as he boarded on his way to work, before the debris swept into town. He heard the sirens off in the distance. Apparently the town was under some sort of emergency, so he pressed the driver for more information. When he learned of the impact, he knew it would mean a hectic work day, but he had no idea just how bad it would get.

Willy had a television but he never watched it; he even stopped reading the papers too. It was all shit, and he couldn't bear to see it or read it. A lonely soul, he volunteered to work a double shift at the ER so that a couple of the other janitors could be home with their families for Christmas. He didn't have anyone in his life anymore. Even his Marine buddies had lost contact with him, moved on, or went AWOL.

After an hour or two into his first shift the hospital starts to look like the trauma tents at the edges of a battlefield. There are dozens of traffic accidents, severed limbs, and crushed bodies. But there's lots of seemingly spontaneous and violent sickness, too. He overhears strange talk about people biting one another out in the town, and victims coming in with flesh missing, like it had been torn off and eaten. Some of the nurses and orderlies are talking about how a cloud of debris from the meteor impacts had blown over town and started making people ill, and how the radio had a warning to avoid the northeast.

He doesn't think much of it until he sees the result for himself. From his office window he looks out across the ambulance bay. An ambulance pulls up, speeding and driving erratically, only coming to a stop after crashing into the cement walls that slope downward into the ground floor entryway, in the back of the ER. The ambulance spins 180 degrees after hitting the pier, and the rear doors fling open to reveal the horrors taking place inside. A patient is eating one of the EMTs alive, tearing at her neck and face with his teeth. Willy sees the cannibal rip her shirt open and bury his face into her breasts. *Is this some kinda sick rape? No. This is worse.* When the beast twists its neck to yank the flesh away, it nearly tears one of her breasts off her body. She screams in terror as he devours her. Blood spews from the driver's neck too, coating the ceiling of the ambulance cab with his red gravy. He begins violently convulsing in the front seat.

Willy darts out from his office into the hallway just beside the ambulance bay, smashes open an emergency glass fireman's box, and removes the axe from within. He scares the living shit out of a nurse and patient standing nearby, but he doesn't care. *The EMT needs my immediate help.* He runs outside, and the carnage begins to spill out of the ambulance and onto the drive ramp. The deranged, blood soaked patient looks up from his meal of meat and fixes a pair of piss yellow eyes on Willy. The sight of it takes him by surprise. His heart thumps out of his chest. Suddenly he feels a cold sweat come over him. Every hair on his body perks up on end from head to toe, and he freezes up. In his head the sound of machinegun fire fills his ears. Loud, but broken up and muffled orders from base command warn of incoming napalm. He shakes his head, trying to break it. He knows it's a flashback, a remnant of his PTSD. He looks at his walkie. *It is NOT base command. It's just frantic calls coming in telling him there's a bed pan spill on three, a broken window in triage, and a blood slick in the ER.* He starts to come out of it, but the machinegun fire rages on. He looks for the sound. Just ahead; the woman who was being eaten. Her leg twitches violently, and her foot taps the side of the gurney in the ambulance repeatedly, profusely. *It is NOT gunfire. It's just the rattling of metal*. He's brought himself back.

The cannibal lunges at him, but Willy steps aside and swings the axe up from his hip, burying it deep into the beast's stomach. The patient folds over at the waist and flips to the ground. Willy knows something is wrong when the animal immediately stands up and comes at him again. A second swing of the fire axe splits the cannibal's head in two. This stops him immediately.

After catching his breath Willy approaches the ambulance to check on the woman. Her ribcage is completely exposed; there is no skin covering her chest. Only blood. Her twitching comes to a stop but her eyes are wide and bloodshot. They glow amber like the patient's eyes, and a moment later she too attacks Willy, reaching for him with wretched bloodlust. He slams the rear ambulance door on her face and knocks her back, enclosing her inside. He circles around to the driver's side door to see the other EMT afflicted with the same condition. He backs away slowly. *They're filled with rage. No reason, no thinking, no speaking; only attacking, feeding.*

His walkie is rattling off like crazy. *There's too much to respond to*. He runs back inside to tell a doctor or nurse what he saw, but by then it's too late. The hospital is in complete mayhem. All sorts of alarms are blaring. A half naked old man is devouring his doctor down the hall in the ER. Nurses are complaining of patients biting them. People everywhere are being strapped down to beds, or coughing their lungs up with chunks of blood and pulp.

But when he passes the morgue an eerie feeling sweeps over him. The doors are left swinging open and shut, creaking and flapping with each pivot on their old hinges. Just out the corner of his eye he sees a white sheet rise up from the steel table in the center of the room. Someone has sat up in death. The sheet falls away slowly, slipping down from head to waist. The monster is facing Willy. He sees the gaping wound on her chest, from the left shoulder down across her breasts to her right pelvis. Her eyes are yellow, and they meet with Willy's. The creature moans and reaches her arms in Willy's direction; her legs dangle in the air, not yet off the table. Willy pushes his way past the swinging doors and buries his axe into her head. Blood and brain matter cast off in all directions, landing on some of the other bodies that lay on the cold metal slabs. He has awakened them. Another rises, then another, and another. Willy yanks the axe free from the dead woman's head and swings it back handed at the nearest one. The blunt side of the axe meets its temple and sends bits of shattered skull deep into what's left of its brain, killing it instantly. It flops back down to the table before the sheet can even fall away. He pivots and clubs the other two the same way.

Catching his breath from the battle is hard at his age, despite being in good shape. He leans against the nearest slab, partially sitting. He pulls a bit of sheet from the body laying on it and wipes some of the blood spray off his arms. A dead man's hand dangles off the edge of the table from under the sheet. Willy doesn't notice at first, but a moment later he feels a cold dead grasp on his thigh. The beast reaches its other arm up through the sheet toward Willy's face. Machinegun fire suddenly fills his ears again. Willy nearly jumps out of his skin. Incessant banging hammers on his ear drums, but he knows his mind is playing tricks on him. He presses his palms over his ears hard, trying to shut it out, as the man slowly sits up in death. *No. Not now. I need to keep my wits. There is no gunfire.* Slowly the gunshots morph back to a faint, muffled metallic rattle. He pulls his hands down from over his ears and searches for the sound. The ice boxes along the back wall. Several of their handles jiggle with clanging from the inside. The dead are trapped within. Willy blasts the rising dead man across the back of his head with all his might and nearly takes his head off. The beast stumbles and crashes to the cold tile floor, lifeless. Willy picks him up, shoves him back onto the slab, and tosses the sheet back over his body. The machinegun fire starts up again. Willy yanks the rattling ice box doors open one by one, destroying whatever is inside, until he hears no more warfare echoing through his ears.

But like the end of any battle, his nerves are shattered. His adrenaline pumps but his body is tired. His eyes want to close. He wants to sleep the nightmare away but his body won't let him rest.

The loud pangs of machinegun fire leave him with a ringing in his ear. He can even almost smell that gun powdery, hot metal scent of spent munitions tickling his nose. *There's no way I got them all, but at least they can't get out of those ice boxes.* Then even more chaotic sounds from the hallway and throughout the hospital creep into his head. Only Willy knows that those sounds are real. The hospital has erupted into a madhouse. In an instant the chaos overwhelms his senses. He quickly retreats into his office and locks himself inside.

A high pitched darting sound fills his head. Dissonant and prolonged, it's like an alarm clock that never stops. He covers his ears and shuts his eyes tight, pacing back and forth to keep the flashbacks from coming on again. But the ringing in his head is too much to handle. Pain shoots through his head strong and fast, needling its way over from his temples to behind his eyes. He knows if he opens his eyes again he'll be chest deep in some tepid river, holding a rifle over his head… or hunkered down in the thick of the jungle, covered with fire ants. He sits down and begins to rock back and forth on the floor, humming classical music to calm himself and drown out the sounds of death and madness coming from the hospital hallway.

CHAPTER 9

There are fewer guards than there should be, and rumors are flying about a quarantine and poisonous air on the outside. Marcus only had one meal, brought to him by a guy wearing a civil unrest style, police issue gas mask. Some of the other guards have masks too. *They might resort to tear gas.* His fellow inmates are riled up with rage, ready to riot at any moment. The guards were doling out beatings one by one, like they did to Harley, but that didn't work to subdue the masses. Shawn, the inmate next to him who spent a lot of time in the prison library, said the law requires that prisoners get outdoor time and three meals a day. Marcus hears him shouting about cruel and unusual punishment among all the other yelling. *But maybe it's dangerous outside, if the air is poisonous. Maybe that's why the guards have masks on. Maybe it's cruel to let us out.*

When the shift changes there are even less guards. Two of them argue over using a spare gas mask. The one that loses out ends up sitting watch by the levers that unlock the cells on Marcus' floor. He coughs violently into his hands every few minutes. *The rumors are true, then. The air outside is toxic.* Marcus tries to yell out to tell the others but his voice drowns in a sea of madness. He covers his mouth and nose with a t-shirt, tying it around the back of his head.

The guard continues to cough incessantly. He stands up, trying to call out for help to the other guards over the ruckus, but he's inaudible. The noise is so loud now that Marcus can't even hear himself think. The guard stumbles around, hacking and spitting up blood before finally keeling over onto the cell door levers. The weight of his body pulls several levers down as he flops to the floor.

Some cell doors open and the inmates immediately flood into the hall. They pull the other levers, opening up the rest, including Marcus' door. A few guards run up to try to fight the mob, but they're trampled and stomped as the prisoners rush them. There are gunshots; a shotgun and several pistols. Then Marcus hears the hiss of tear gas. *Poisonous air outside and inside*. The sound of fleeting thuds and grunts roll away under the fog of gas. The prisoners open more and more cells, leaving guards dead and bloodied in their wake. "There's more of us than you, nigga!" Harley's words echo in Marcus' ear.

Keys are swiped, doors are opened, and heads are cracked all over the place. The block empties as the mob moves on. But Marcus stays in his room until it grows quiet. *I told myself I'd stay in my cell, but I need to see what's going on.* When he finally steps out into the hallway he sees several guards and inmates lying on the ground. One guard bleeds out from a stab wound. Marcus can see through the guard's gas mask that it's Thompson. Marcus approaches him, putting his hand over the wound, but he knows it's too late. Thompson is dying. Marcus holds his breath and shields his eyes from the lingering tear gas down the hall.

"Take it. Take the mask," Thompson utters "Don't blow it this time," he adds before fading away. Marcus pulls the mask off his head and quickly slips it on. He looks around at the carnage. There is no guard left alive. He lingers in thought at Thompson's final words. "Don't blow it this time." *This is a second chance. Has God heard my prayers and pleadings for forgiveness? Is this a test?* Whatever it is, Marcus resolves to live the right way if he gets out alive. He knows the inmates will probably turn on him, and he'll need to fight. The gas mask will make him a target once they figure out that to go without one is a death sentence. *If I gotta defend myself, then so be it. Lord forgive me.* He pulls Thompson's night stick from his cold dead hands. His gun was missing.

Just then the lights cut out, and the block falls dark. It's daylight outside, but you would never know it when the lights go down in the cell blocks of a maximum security prison. He hears more gunshots. Rifles this time, likely from the tower. He creeps down the dim hall, following the trail of carnage that the riot left behind.

Marcus remembers some of the halls only vaguely, from when he was first processed and taken to his cell. He passes the lockdown, and moves cautiously as he gets close to the back end of the mob. He can see inmates using wet shirts to try to breathe. Some have fallen, slumped and coughing on the ground. Marcus kneels before one of the inmates that hacks uncontrollably, feeling obligated to care for someone in need. The young man sits cross legged, spraying pink droplets of blood onto the legs of his prison suit with each cough. Marcus puts a caring hand on his back as the young inmate starts to vomit. He tips over, gasping for air, dying. *There's nothing I can do.*

Daylight is ahead, but Marcus hears fighting. "Get 'em in the head!" someone yells.

Marcus steps out into the cold sunlight. But a cloud of gloom quickly turns an otherwise bright winter's day into something sinister and ominous. Through the dust he notices a dark fog rolling in from the southwest. His eyes quickly dart all over the place as he sees a most horrific sight; men eating each other. Biting and gnawing at flesh like rabid beasts. *Perhaps this Christmas gift of freedom is really a curse.*

"Yo Marcus!" Harley yells. Marcus can't pull his eyes from the mayhem. He stares in disbelief. "Marcus!" Marcus breaks his gaze and turns to see Harley standing a short distance away with a gas mask on his face and a shotgun in his hand. "Get over here, nigga. We need you. Help us kill these muh' fuckin' cannibals! Take your freedom back!"

Marcus lingers in thought. *Thompson has given me life, and the meteor has given me freedom while it gives others death. Freedom. Why? Is it a blessing or a curse? If this is what's out there, then perhaps I'm receiving that ultimate punishment I deserve. That punishment beyond what mere man can dole out. It's hell. Hell on Earth.*

He feels hands grab at his shoulders from behind. He turns to see the young inmate from the hall grasping at him. His jaw chatters like a wild dog chomping for food. Marcus backpedals toward Harley. Harley shoves the inmate backward and promptly blows his head off without hesitation. Bits of brain and blood coat the wall behind like a macabre abstract impressionist painting.

"That guy was dead a minute ago. Back in the hall," Marcus tells Harley in disbelief.

"They all comin' back, mutha fucka. Until you get 'em in the head," Harley explains. "You breathe the air, you die and turn into one. And if they bite you, you turn into one of them too, only faster. See?" Harley points to the ground nearby, where a guard twitches and convulses. Blood gushes from the bite wounds on his neck and arms, smearing onto the concrete as his body violently seizes. The shaking stops and his mouth foams up as he dies. A moment later he bursts back to life. Harley shoots him in the head, spraying the concrete with crimson death. "Then they eat people. Fuckin' zombies or some shit." Harley nods at Marcus' night stick. "Where you get that?"

"Thompson. Same with the mask," Marcus answers.

"Here's his gun too," Harley passes Marcus a pistol. "They're all gifts from me, then," he says with an evil grin. "Merry Christmas, brutha." Harley had exacted his vengeance for the beating Thompson gave him. It was Harley who killed Thompson. Marcus stirs with anger. He liked Thompson, and there is absolutely no remorse in Harley. *I think he enjoys this. He's tempting me. Is Harley a reflection of what I once was, beckoning me back to a life of evil? I may have been like that once, but no more. This is yet another test.*

"I vowed never to harm or kill a man again," Marcus says, unsure about whether he wants to keep the weapon.

"Well good, cause that ain't no man. That right there's a demon," Harley argues, pointing at the dead guard. "And if you hesitate and one of these muh' fuckas gets at me because of it, then I'll make damn sure I come back from the dead and kill yo' black ass myself." He glares at Marcus. "You rollin' with me now."

He speaks as if his word is Gospel, but maybe he's right; these things… they're not men. They're demons.

"Get those masks!" an inmate yells nearby, pointing at Marcus and Harley.

"Back the fuck up!" Harley points his gun with a warning, and a crew of masked inmates come to his and Marcus' defense.

It's just like I thought. The masks made us targets.

With his eyes fixed on the inmates, Harley points his gun to the side and blows away another cannibal.

"Come on, let's go. Let's get out of here," Marcus says. There's a clear path out through the main gates now that the tower riflemen have been overrun. With their guns raised and their eyes fixed on the inmates, Marcus, Harley and Harley's crew back their way out to freedom.

CHAPTER 10

Michael and Amy look out over the skyline from the window of their 16th floor apartment. Manhattan is eerily silent, empty. There are no lights flickering, no billboards running, no horns honking. The word from their neighbor Farrah is that the bridges and tunnels have been closed. It's a quarantine within a quarantine. There's no power, no heat, no water. Garbage is already piling up on the curbs of their neighborhood. But there's no one to clean it up, because no one is at work. The sanitation and power jobs don't pay enough to afford living in the city, so they are blocked out anyway, behind the closed off bridges and tunnels. The Mayor thought about trying to mandate some personnel show up to work, but he reconsidered after angry protests ensued. Anyone with sense is home attending to their families, trying to figure out how to survive without their normal comforts and conveniences.

Michael works in the city planner's office and even he wasn't going in. He doesn't make all that much money, working for the city, but Amy is in finance. That's how they could afford the apartment. She makes a ton, and works her ass off. But the markets are closed, and sitting at home bothers her. She needs to do something. She wants to work, but the economy has come to a grinding halt.

Even last week was really sluggish. Christmas was on the way, and the meteor news had everyone in a panic. Michael resisted at first, convinced nothing was going to happen, but on Amy's insistence they stocked up on some supplies before the stores ran out. Canned vegetables, bottled water, dry goods, and cat food for Minxie, their aging 11-year-old Maine Coon. They even filled the tub with water just in case. They already had gas masks as a precaution from a recent terrorist scare; some jihadist animals were caught with canisters of neurotoxin gas or something like that. So they ordered some black, Israeli style, clip and strap masks online. That purchase turned out to be a life saver, as they later heard on an emergency radio broadcast that the dust from the impact was poisonous. Since then there has been nothing; no word other than the bridges and tunnels being closed, which was just a rumor from Farrah.

They opened gifts in the dark with a flashlight just after the power went out late on Christmas Eve, when the big one hit. The iPads and Blu-rays they got for each other would be of no use to them, ever. On Christmas day they scrapped together a somewhat fresh meal for dinner, using whatever they had left in the fridge before it went bad.

They knew their vegan diet would have to change if anything went wrong. They wondered if they would get sick from the transition back to processed, high preservative, canned foods. It would not be a good transition to make with failed plumbing. But they stayed away from canned meat. Not even the apocalypse would keep them from eating healthy, they thought. Well, Michael thought. Amy missed having a nice, juicy, medium-rare steak once in a while. She especially missed her mother's traditional Chinese salted pork and stir fried beef dishes. Michael convinced her they should change the way they eat after reading the research on the Mayor's new food initiatives program. She was head strong with almost everything else in her life, but with Michael she was flexible. Deep down Amy thought it was a crock of shit to regulate salt, fats, and certain oils, but she supported her husband. She agreed to go along with him. That was almost a year ago.

But marrying a hippie did have its pluses. At least the spare bedroom was filled with edible greens. About six months ago they started doing some indoor gardening with a hydroponic kit they saw on an infomercial. It started out with herbs, then grew to include tomatoes, peppers, and lettuce greens. Good enough for a salad minus the dressing.

"We can last a while here," Michael says. With all the looting and rioting, they haven't gone back outside for fear of violence. It was good exercise while it lasted though, running up and down 16 flights of stairs.

"Look." Amy points out over their west-facing view. A wall of black dust creeps over the unlit grey skyline. They put their gas masks on and hold each other's hands as the debris lightly pelts the side of their building. The sound of fine sand blowing against glass fills their ears, and soot settles on the narrow ledges outside their window as the gust ceases. It happened many times throughout the day, but this was the biggest.

"A quarantine means they're leaving us to die. We need to get out of here," Amy says.

"I think we can ride it out," Michael responds.

"Who knows how long we'll be stuck here. They may never let us out of quarantine, if they even care that we're still alive," Amy argues.

"We can't get out anyway if the bridges and tunnels are all closed. It's not like we can hop on a subway or a train either," Michael says.

"Can't we at least try getting out? If we can get to my parents' house maybe we can regroup and then try to get further west, past the outer barricade," Amy suggests.

"Baby, they put quarantines in place for a reason. I'm sure they know what they're doing. I trust the government to make the right decision."

"Yeah that's the problem. They've condemned us to death and you're okay with it."

"We don't know that. Remember we saw military helicopters before? They might be doing rescue and recovery type things, or getting ready to."

"I don't like being stuck here. I don't want to stay. Can't we at least try to get out of the city?" she asks.

Michael reluctantly agrees after a few moments of thought. "Sure, but not tonight. Maybe some of this wind will die down by the morning." They lie down on their bed embraced in one another's arms. The sound of their breathing through masks provides them with a sort of eerie white noise that eventually numbs them to sleep.

#

A loud thud wakes them in the dawn. Amy bolts up with a gasp, dreaming she was shot and couldn't breathe. They hear a distant screaming in the hallway, and then all falls quiet except the continued sound of dust pelting the window. They get up from bed and peek out the peep hole in their door, but they see nothing except the fish-eyed opposite wall. They hear some gruff, muffled voices, and then another ear shattering thud. It's a gunshot, much closer in the hall than the one that woke them. They hear crashes through the walls, screaming. It's Farrah. Suddenly her screams are silenced with another shot. Michael's eyes widen in panic. He freezes in fear, his round blue eyes like balls of ice behind his mask.

"Let's go. We need to get out of here," Amy whispers while she slips a pair of sneakers on near the door. "Grab the bags." Michael stares past her, still in shock. "Go!"

Last week the news shows all suggested that people make "bug out" bags with enough food, water and basic supplies for 72 hours. They each packed one. And now they are about to abandon the comforts of their apartment to brave the dangerous streets with nothing but those bags.

Michael returns with them, and they both quietly slip them on their backs over their coats. Through the thin walls they can hear men rummaging around Farrah's apartment next door, looting for supplies. They grunt, cough, and give angered directions to one another. Michael grabs Minxie under his arm, and they slowly open the door to peek out into the hall. All is clear, but Farrah's door is wide open. They have to pass it to get to the stairwell at the end of the hall. They place their steps carefully. Amy nudges Michael on the arm and motions for him to quit breathing and making a racket. They hold their breath and sharpen their ears to the sounds within Farrah's apartment. Minxie squirms under Michael's arm. She wants to run loose, but Michael holds her tight with nervous fear. Glass breaks and heavy objects topple onto the floor within the apartment. Just as they are about to cross in front of the door, the sound of rummaging is right next to them, behind the wall that abuts the hallway. They're rifling through the kitchen for food. Michael and Amy freeze in their tracks, waiting. A moment later the sounds move; they're deeper in the back of the apartment. Michael and Amy dart in front and pass the doorway, moving at a quick pace to the end of the hall without daring to look behind.

"Hey!" one of the men yells out before coughing. He runs to the door, blindly firing a shot down the hall in their direction. "Hey!"

Amy and Michael run to the stairwell and fling the door open, starting their descent to hell. The man chases after them. He fires at them as they wind downward in a dizzying clockwise circle, half floor by half floor. Michael and Amy stay close to the walls, away from the inner shaft. They are at least a floor ahead. They can hear him coughing, labored in his breathing. He shoots again and again. Michael and Amy move as fast as they can. Minxie claws at Michael, whining and hissing, tearing at his skin, but he holds onto her.

"Just let 'em go." They hear the deep voice of another man echo from above, nearly drowned out by the clattering of their footsteps in the cavernous stairwell. After what feels like an eternity, Michael and Amy safely make it to the building lobby. There is no doorman anymore. There's not even a door. Their glassed, upscale, luxury building is wide open to whoever wants access.

"My back. It's wet. Have I been shot?" Michael asks, confused, craning his neck to look around his side. Panic starts to build up within him.

Amy checks him over. There's a hole in the side of his pack. She feels around but he's not hit. "They must've hit one of your water bottles."

They catch their breath for a moment, but they're still reeling with fear. Michael tries to ease his nerves by petting Minxie.

"We better keep moving," Amy says.
The windy winter morning awaits them outside.

CHAPTER 11

Is this what I wanted? Brandon's tears are still flowing. It might have been cool in comics, in movies, in games, but in reality it terrified him. *I'm one of those people.* There's always one in every apocalyptic story. The panicked, over-emotional and usually useless person who freezes up or gets everyone killed when the gravity of the apocalypse finally sets in. *But I didn't freeze. I boldly went out to turn the generator on. I'm only a kid, after all, and I just found out my parents are dead, or undead.* His confidence builds and the tears stop. *The trick is to stay focused, have a purpose. What is my purpose?*

Brandon has no luck getting online with the computer. The cell phone is useless too now. But the video game consoles work. He grabs a bag of chips, since the MREs taste like shit, and pops in his favorite zombie themed first person shooter. He's already finished the game before, but now he's playing on expert mode. He escapes to a fictional nightmare, convincing himself that he's training for the real one that awaits him above. Hours go by before his eyes start to blur. He finally pauses the game, taking a break.

He thinks back to before the impact, when news stories about bums getting high on bath salts had everyone joking about the zombie apocalypse. The drug made them so hot that they stripped their clothes off, and the aggressiveness made them try to eat each other's faces for some reason. It was fun to laugh about it back then, but for Brandon the real thing is much more frightening. *I need to get beyond the fear and into the excitement. I need to approach life like it's a game, otherwise I might not survive it. I need to suppress the fear. I need to become the guy that I always imagined I would be in the apocalypse. No more weak, scrawny nerd. No more pasty, awkward target of bullies. The meteors hit the reset button for me, and I have a new start.*

While pissing into an empty water bottle, Brandon realizes he pissed half the day away. He turns back to look at the video game screen, studying his array of weapons; a machete, a sniper rifle, a pistol, grenades, and of course a shotgun. *I need real weapons.* The only items he has with him in the bunker are a box cutter, a heavy flashlight, and a pair of foam nunchucks. *Weapons. That's my purpose.* He sorts through his books, looking for the survivalist ones, and then further narrowing the selection to those that discuss makeshift weaponry. But there's an easier way. His father had hunting gear in the upstairs closet, and there are the tools in the shed. *I need the can opener from the kitchen anyway, if I ever plan to get into those damned beans. I can grab some weapons, refill the generator with fuel and clear out mom and dad's cabinets.*

He suits up with his gas mask and slips on a pair of rubber boots. He pops open the hatch and closes it quickly behind him. The air is still, calm. The woods are silent. There is less dust around. *It must have been kicked up by the winds and blown somewhere else, but I still wouldn't dare take the mask off or go traipsing though the poisonous soot.* There's a clear path to his home. He enters the living room though a hole in the side of the house. He fills garbage bags with food from the pantry and grabs the remaining boxes of bottled water from the garage. He brings those down into the bunker first, and then heads back to the house. He goes upstairs to his father's closet and comes back down with a crossbow and a rifle. There are only a few boxes of bullets and a handful of arrows, but they'll do. He slings the equipment over his shoulder and heads for the shed, leaving the gear on a clear patch of grass next to the hatch.

He shuts the generator so he can refill it with fuel. There isn't much left in the gas cans afterward; maybe enough for a few days or even a week if he conserves power. He knows he'll have to head to town and refill if he plans to stay in the bunker for long.

As Brandon fills the generator with gas, his thoughts soon wander to his computer, and whether there will ever be internet service again. His mind quickly drifts to Apocalypta. He imagines what she might look like. A bit shorter than him. Dark hair in pigtails. Huge, bright green eyes. A short black and pink skirt with knee high fishnet nylons. Tits too big for her age, but on a slim, petite figure. *I've been looking at my porn magazines too much.* He adjusts the crotch of his pants. At that moment the fuel starts to overflow out of the generator's gas spout, sputtering out onto his hands and pants. He fumbles the gas can for a second, and then caps it. He tugs at the starter.

He's weak. Lanky. It takes a few yanks but the generator finally turns over and runs, and Brandon starts to look over the tools in the shed. A hammer. An axe. A shovel. A pick. A sledge. *These will do. Not the chainsaw though; too loud and messy, plus it requires fuel, and I need to ration my fuel.* He reaches up and pulls the tools down off their wall hooks one by one.

The rumbling of the generator drowns out the shuffling noise behind him. Only when the light shifts and changes to shadow does Brandon realize that someone is coming into the shed behind him. He grabs the sledge off the wall and spins to face the intruder in one clumsy motion. The sledge weighs almost as much as he does, rounding him a good half turn past his intended about face.

His father stands before him, wild eyed and bloodied. *He's been feeding.* A foul stench of body odor, shit, and old cheese lingers with him. Brandon can smell it, even through the gas mask, prompting a fleeting question that darts through his head: *Is the mask even working?* The thought passes faster than it came to him, and his arms go up, struggling to hold the sledge above his head. The handle is thicker than his frail, bony arms, but he manages to drop it down on his father's head as he lunges at Brandon with a hungry grunt. His father drops to the wood floor with a thud, but he keeps coming. Brandon lifts the sledge up and back down again, smashing it down at his father's head with nervous adrenaline. He misses, crunching the floor beside his father's ear. Brandon's father crawls at him, grabbing Brandon's leg below the knee and pulling it toward his mouth. His teeth drip with saliva. Once more Brandon heaves the sledgehammer over his head and brings it back down with rage. The fat of it meets the back of his father's head with a meaty thud. His father instantly flattens on the floor, and blood gobs out of his skull.

Brandon stares at his father in shock. He killed his first zombie, but he didn't like it one bit. *It wasn't like the video games, where seeing their brains explode out the back of their heads made me laugh.* But he was surprised at himself; he was able to detach. *I didn't pause because it was Dad.* He read enough cosmic dust zombie comics in his day to know it was no longer his father. He's seen enough horror movies to know that hesitation is what gets you eaten. It wasn't his father; it was a monster.

In a zombie situation, you almost have to try to enjoy killing them, because it'll be an everyday part of survival. If you can't do it, then you'll die. And you might as well enjoy what you have to do to make it through the day. Perhaps he would have enjoyed it if it was a stranger. But it was still messy and dangerous. He looks down at the sledge, covered in bits of brain. He grabs a rag and rubs the meat off of it. But it was too heavy, and it left him vulnerable with every swing. *I won't use this again. If there were two or three zombies, I would have been overtaken. The other weapons are lighter, faster.* He leaves the sledge and gathers the others.

He opens the hatch and begins to drop the tools down into the bunker when he sees her from the corner of his eye, near the edge of the woods. His mother. She races toward him, attracted by the noise of the generator and the metal weapons clanging on the floor of the shelter below. Brandon arms himself with his father's rifle. Aside from video games, he's never fired a gun before, but he's seen it done a million times. He fumbles the box of bullets, but manages to get one loaded in the chamber, pointy end forward. His mother has closed the distance though, and in seconds she's on him. Brandon backpedals blindly as he struggles to cock the old bolt action style rifle and take the safety off. But he keeps his eyes on his mother. Her soiled and wet muumuu clings to her lower half, where it seems she has pissed and shit herself, and worse. She's easily three or four times Brandon's weight, so Brandon can't let her get on top of him or else he'd be stuck. He feels the bolt click, locking the bullet into place. He swiftly lifts the gun up to her face, point blank, and fires. A red mist sprays out the back of her head and she collapses to the ground.

He knew it was a risk to try the rifle. *What good is life without having to overcome any challenges?* He felt like Lee Harvey Oswald, loading and getting off a shot in fractioned seconds. There was no anger in the kill. All those times he was mad at his mother for taking his comics away or banning him from the computer as punishment for stupid crap like not eating vegetables didn't even cross his mind. He didn't see the creature as his mother. *I think maybe I enjoyed that one. That's a good sign.* He forces a smile as he descends back into his hole, but not before grabbing a six pack of beer from his parents' fridge. *There's no age limit for drinking in the apocalypse.*

CHAPTER 12

The alarm is still raging but the sounds of panic are gone. Willy's symptoms have subsided. No more piercing headache, no more cold sweats, no more ringing in his ears. He steps out of his office into the eerie hallway leading to the ER. Despite the blaring alarm bell, he hears some commotion coming from the far end. But there are no sounds of words or talking; only an occasional grunt or low growls. Willy knows what happened. *The patients changed into those man eating beasts.* He begins to stalk up the hallway to strike them down one by one. Most of them are occupied with feasting on the dead, or strapped down to their beds, so they are easy prey. He makes sure he sees their glowing eyes before swinging, just to be safe. But all the blood and gore makes his mind wander again to the brutal memories of war. Memories like his brothers collecting the ears of enemies they killed in battle, like trophies, as a way to dehumanize them and cope with the mental anguish of war. Memories like having to quietly sink a blade into his dying friend's skull because his whimpers were too loud in the night and would give up their platoon's position to the enemy. Memories like cutting off the fingers of a captured village woman one by one, until she gave up the locations of her VC command's hidden bunkers. *That was different. These things are beasts, not men. But in war, any man can become a beast if they lose their sense of morals, their sense of duty, their sense of honor. God knows I did.*

When he gets to the end of the hall, there are three creatures rummaging around in one of the patient rooms. Two of them come out into the hallway when they hear his footsteps. He runs up and splits the first one's head open with his fire axe. The diseased corpse falls to the floor right there in the doorway to the patient room. He knew the man by sight but not by name. *One of the ER doctors.* But Willy now saw the man as an enemy, a beast, not a coworker.

Willy steps back, spins and buries his axe so deep into the head of the second one that it gets stuck in the base of her neck. *This one was a nurse.* He knew her by sight too. The third one comes out of the patient room and gets his hands on Willy as he tries to free the axe from the dead nurse's neck. It's a naked old man, at least 20 years Willy's senior. The same one he saw devouring a doctor earlier. *A patient.* His grip is abnormally strong for a frail old bag of bones. He yanks Willy's bicep close to his face and bites into his skin. Willy panics as he feels the warm, gummy mouth squeeze down. He shoves the old man off, frees his axe from the nurse's neck, and clubs the old man with the blunt side. A gaping hole opens on the old man's head, and he falls to the floor in death.

Shit! Willy examines his arm for any damage. He saw how people changed once they were bitten. He wipes the stringy, blood fouled saliva away to see that there is no harm done; there is no wound. Confused, he looks down at the old man to see an empty mouth, completely void of teeth. Willy looks upward with a sigh of relief. After taking a few steps back toward his office he sees a broken set of dentures lying next to the body of an orderly. This person he knew well. *It's John D'Avanti. The poor bastard.* But the old man's furious biting must have dislodged the dentures from his mouth, rendering him, for the most part, harmless.

After that, Willy steps outside to dispatch some more that are wandering around the outside of the hospital. There's so much blood covering his body he barely breathes in an attempt to avoid getting any of the filth into his mouth. He takes breaks, shutting himself away in his office every so often to wipe his face down with rags and catch his breath. It helps keep the flashbacks at bay as well.

During one break the power shuts down. The alarm stops, and everything is strangely silent. He goes back out to check on things. It's almost nightfall, so he treads carefully to avoid making noise.

Without the alarms blaring everything else becomes loud, every step. *The generators up on the roof must be out of fuel.* They're supposed to have a three day supply, but Willy remembers an outage a few weeks back that lasted half a day or more, so some of the fuel must have been used up and not replaced. He pokes around trying to get them to restart, making a racket of noise in the process, but it's no use. The generators hadn't been properly maintained or checked by the technicians. They burned through the oil too, and that seized the engines. Even if he had fuel they wouldn't start back up without some serious dismantling and labor.

On the way back down to his office he hears the distinct sounds of a struggle from out near the ambulance bay. *Could be those cannibals I locked away in the ambulance figured a way out.* But when he investigates he sees a man pulling and yanking at a woman's foot as she tries to shut herself inside a car. He gnaws at her sneaker, trying to bite through it. More zombies have drawn closer from around the outside of the hospital now, and they're running toward Willy. *The sound of my tinkering on the roof attracted them back to the building, and now they're out for my flesh.* He makes a run toward the car, axe in hand. It's his only way out. There are too many coming for him to fight them all off.

CHAPTER 13

Sheryl hears grunts, but not like the kind Mr. Mortenson made in his attack. These are the sounds of fighting; strikes and thuds. Then all becomes quiet, except for the constant sound of the fire alarm in the hallway. She sits still, waiting. She waits for hours, days, maybe more. It feels like forever. After quite a bit of time the lights begin to flicker, as if draining. When they go out, the silence grows. Machines whir down to a stop, the heat shuts off, the fire alarm finally stops. Her ears become sharp to the slightest of noises; a distant and slight rattling down the hall, a flapping of fabric closer by. Sheryl works up the courage to stand, pressing her ear to the door. The noises sound like patterns to her. Unliving, but not undead. She quietly opens the door. She tucks the wooden handle from the toilet plunger under her bad arm to use as a weapon. Peeking out into her room she sees a mess of toppled and splintered furniture throughout. Broken machines are scattered about the floor. Smudges and splatters of blood cover the walls. She sees a pair of legs on the ground, face down, connected to a body that lies partially outside the door frame and into the hall.

She squeezes her thin body out of the bathroom door, barely opening it so as not to squeak the hinges. She tip toes quietly toward the body straddling into the hallway, plunger handle in hand. She pokes at its shoes. There's no response. She moves to the side to see the rest of the body outside the door frame. A puddle of blood surrounds the head, and a nice sized chunk of skull is missing, as if hacked off. It looks like Dr. Levy, but his white smock is so drenched with blood that it has turned a deep burgundy. She prods him several times with the plunger handle. *Yup, he's dead.* She sticks her head out into the hallway.

Bodies are strewn about haphazardly and a cold ghostly wind fills the corridor, gently blowing the curtained partitions midway down the hall near the main section of the ER. *The flapping sound.* Her heart races and her adrenaline drowns her aches and pains. She shakes with fearful energy as she slowly begins to walk the hall. She passes Mr. Mortenson. She passes Tina the nurse, and the orderly too.

Up ahead the doors to the ambulance bay are wide open, just past the morgue at the far end of the corridor; they become her goal. A glaring sun beams in as it sets, or perhaps rises, from beyond. The bodies become silhouettes, darkened bumps on the ground. She has to partially shield her eyes from the blinding rays. The glare bounces up off the blood-reflective floor, filling the glass of her gas mask with white and turning the hall a macabre ruby shade of red. She can't escape it. The light fills the entire hall.

Sheryl slowly passes room after room. Some are filled with death. Windows are broken in several of them. *People must've jumped out to freedom. That might be the best idea.* Fearful of the hallway, she steals into an empty room with a broken window in hopes to climb out, but she sees the mayhem that was once inside the hospital is now outside. The picturesque field surrounding the hospital is dotted with gore. *Everyone who breathed in that debris must have gone to the hospital, died, and come back to attack people. I'm in the worst possible place for safety. I can't outrun them; I'm injured. I need to get to a car if I can. There must be something near the ambulance bay. There has to be. It's my only chance aside from hiding. If I can get away, maybe I can ride out the mayhem at home.*

She continues to walk the hallway. The sunlight becomes less obtrusive; it is setting. She's afraid to look at the grotesque bodies, ripped apart as if by wolves, but she must. With each one she passes, she waits quietly to see if they still stir. She passes the nurse's station and moves into the ER. The curtain partitions eerily flow up and back down with every gust of wind that whistles through the broken glass windows. *The flapping sound. It's nothing to fear. But does the breeze still carry the poisonous dust?* The flutter fills her ears, and visions of blood and horror fill her eyes. The fear grows in her. Her pulse quickens. She thinks she sees a man standing behind one of the curtains. She turns with a gasp, plunger handle at the ready. But as the curtain blows away it reveals an IV stand with a coat draped over it. Her frightened eyes have deceived her. *Stupid.*

But then there's a growl, a crash, and one of the other curtains comes rushing at her. Behind it is a bloodied man filled with rage. Sheryl backs away, swinging the handle frantically with all her might. She strikes him on the head and he falls forward, onto her. She winces in pain at the pressure on her bad arm. The hospital curtain blocks his mouth, but the faceless, unrelenting horror tries to eat her alive through it. She spins out of the way and lets him fall to the ground. She strikes his head over and over. The curtain covering him begins to soak through with blood as she incessantly smashes him. The curtain rips, and blood casts off in every direction as she flings her arm up and back down with each swing. She hears the crack of his skull and sees his brain spill out onto the floor, but she keeps pounding until he stops moving.

The handle drips with red sludge and brain matter when she's finished. Her gas mask is covered with filth, and clumps of her wavy brown hair have turned black with the wetness of death. Disgusted, she wipes herself down with another nearby curtain and catches her breath. But not for long. The sun has dipped below the horizon, and night approaches. *I need to get home before dark, otherwise things could get much more dangerous.*

She moves faster, trying to ignore the pain that floods her body again after the fight. She starts to hear the rattling sound growing louder. *It's coming from the morgue.* As she passes by the swinging double doors she tries to look inside, but it is too dark to see in the windowless room. In a fit of courage she pulls a door and props it open. All is silent but the rattling. The room is dim, lit only by the fading sunlight that creeps in from the ambulance bay. It barely reaches the back wall, which is still shrouded in darkness.

She sees bloodied bodies left on the stainless steel tables, covered in reddened hospital sheets. *Their heads are all smashed open, but will they still sit up in death and come at me?* She pokes one with the plunger handle. There's no response. *It must be safe. They're dead for good. Someone has been through the hospital, killing the undead.*

Blood pools on the floor beneath the corpses, slowly making its way into a drain in the center of the room. She looks to the back wall, and her eyes find the source of the rattling sound; the latch on one of the freezer boxes flickers as it catches the fleeting light with each shake. *It's the one next to Stephen. Someone is trying to get out from inside. It's BJ, I know it's BJ...*

The rattling suddenly stops. Emotions sweep over her like a hot flash as she is filled with thoughts and memories of playing with the boys, cleaning their scrapes from rough housing in the yard, and those first moments in the maternity ward where she gave birth to them. *That was just upstairs from where I'm standing. Things were happy then, and easy.* She's overwhelmed with grief, horror, and shock as the rattling of the latch starts again, pulling her back into reality. She resolves to put BJ out of his misery. *He's turned into one of those things, one of those zombies. Unnatural. Evil.* She clenches the plunger handle so tight that her pink fingertips turn white. She pushes into the darkness. Her own shadow blocks what she can see in front of her, but she makes her way toward the freezer. Like pulling off an old band-aid, she yanks the door open quickly and jumps back, out of the darkness.

BJ sits up from his slab and turns toward her. His eyes seem to glow in the dark like an animal's. The sparse light gives him a vague shape, making him a silhouette among shadows. He slowly steps forward into the light. She can see him now. He's naked. His jaw is twisted and crooked. One of his ankles drags behind as he moves forward. His arm is broken, as is Sheryl's will to do what she set out to do. *It won't be like killing the man in the hall. This is my son, one of the only things that bring me joy. I think I can still see the light of love in his eyes.* She's wrong. There is only hatred, hunger, and bloodlust.

"BJ?" She says with a quiet lunacy shaking through her voice. There's no response; nothing but a distant stare. "Come to mommy, BJ." *I must sound so stupid. I know what he is, but my heart hurts*. She cries in her mask, and it begins to fog. She hears a growl and a shuffle. BJ shambles toward her. Sheryl stumbles back in fear, dropping the plunger handle. She grabs for it blindly as the inside of her mask clouds up almost completely. Her hand grasps a cold metal rod. She gets her footing and pulls it over. It's heavy and connected to something else. The fog clears and she sees that she has hold of the small wheeled shelf containing medical tools.

BJ lunges at her. She yanks on the shelf and it rolls in front of her just before BJ can reach her with his cold grasp. The corner of the table meets with his delicate head. He falls lifeless to the blood-muddied tile floor, his frozen eggshell skull cracked like thin ice. She whimpers over his corpse for a moment. *Goodbye, my baby*. She places a gentle hand over his heart before leaving him.

In the last minutes of daylight, Sheryl hurriedly exits the hospital through the ambulance bay, leaving the plunger handle behind. She sees a nearby cop car with its lights flashing, parked with the door open. A man in uniform slumps at the wheel. She lightly shakes him a few times. When there's no response she flops him to the ground beside the car. She fiddles around looking for the car keys. *They're not in the ignition, not in the car. They must be in his pocket*. She looks over at the corpse and studies him. *He's not wearing a gas mask. He has no wounds, and there's no blood on him. He choked from the debris*. With apprehension in every step, Sheryl approaches him. *I have to move quickly before he comes back to life or wakes up*. Fear grips her.

She feels around his body for the keys, and finds them in his front pocket. She reaches in, glancing at his empty gun holster. As she pulls the keys out she hears him moan. His eyes burst open, glazed and clouded with white, but also bloodshot and slightly glowing yellow. He sits up sluggishly and Sheryl falls backward into the driver's seat with her legs out the door, facing him. He stands up and shambles toward her. He walks into the car door and it shuts on her legs, hurting her, trapping her there as he pushes forward, trying to claw at her face from above the door window. Sheryl starts the car. Her jeans rip as they scrape against the metal of the door jamb when she tries to yank her legs inside. When blood starts to flow from the cuts underneath, the beast begins to frenzy. He looks down and sees her legs, turning his attention from Sheryl's head to the meat sticks that dangle from the bottom of the car door. He reaches for them. For a split second the door is freed and she pulls her legs in a bit further, but he has hold of one of her ankles. She can feel his teeth gnawing at the rubber on her sneaker. His grip is tight like a vice. She yanks and yanks with everything she has left in her.

Then, in that moment, she hears footsteps quickly approaching on the asphalt, running toward her. She panics. *More zombies are coming to get me. They'll pry the door open and drag me out for dinner.* In a flash she sees an axe arc down from above. Blood sprays across the car windows and the cop falls to the ground, dead again. The maintenance man buried the fire axe into the zombie cop's head.

"Lemme in," he says, trying the door that Sheryl quickly closed and locked as soon as she had the chance. Sheryl looks him over as he circles around to the passenger door, checking for wounds or bites. He seems alright, but his clothes are soiled with a crimson stench. "Come on lady there's more of those things coming!" Sheryl lets him in and they speed off into the dusk.

CHAPTER 14

The hospital is quiet, seemingly empty. Wolf tried the cell phone for hours to no avail. His battery is almost dead anyway, so he sits on some medical supply boxes. He eats the pre-packaged pudding that Dr. Vogel left for him. He feels a bit stronger than before, so after finishing a container of vanilla and chocolate swirl, he starts kicking at the door again. *It's no use.* His lungs don't feel like they're burning anymore, but it still tires him out to exert that kind of energy. *But if Dr. Vogel were here, I think I'd be able to gin up the rage to beat the tar out of him.*

Wolf looks all around the room, sizing things up. The vent in the ceiling is too small to crawl into. There are linens, some scrubs, a mop bucket, cleaning supplies, and a broom. He grabs the broom and pulls the brush off, jamming the stick between the door and metal handle. He pries at it, trying to pop the handle, but the broom snaps. Frustrated, he jabs the end of the wood at the door window, but the reinforced glass won't crack. He throws the broom against the back wall in frustration. It makes a dent. His eyes widen at the sight of it. He puts his hand on it and feels around. *The other walls are solid, but the back is sheetrock. At some point the room must've been partitioned.* He musters his energy again and rams his shoulder into the back wall, caving in the drywall between two wooden studs. He uses his foot to hammer out the rest with a few more big bursts of energy, pushing through to the other room. It's dark, but there's a door ahead, and it's wide open. He reaches back in and swipes some scrubs. He puts them on, and slips out the door after peeking out into the hallway.

I blend in well enough, looking like an employee, but if anyone does a double take they'll recognize me. He quickly grabs a clip board hanging outside a nearby room and holds it at face level, pretending to read it as he passes by others in the hallway. He follows the exit signs and soon he's back out in the parking lot, undetected. It's night, so even easier to go unnoticed. He looks around suspiciously before getting into the truck.

He tosses ideas around his constantly calculating brain as he heads back to the motel and his crew. *We could fill up on gas and take turns driving nonstop until we reach the Pacific. We would need some supplies and food though. Then again if we had to I could help us all live off the wilderness for as long as it takes to ride out the effect of the meteors. We could also hijack a crop duster from a local farm and fly low, under any radar that might be working.*

Wolf fiddles with the radio as he thinks through his options. There's nothing except the emergency broadcast he heard on the way to the hospital. Poisoned air, and now he assumes there's a more strict quarantine, based on how Dr. Vogel locked him up.

Shelter in place, he thinks to himself as he hears the radio message loop. *That's a bloody death sentence. I was exposed to the dust, but I'm on the other side of the quarantine. I'm a danger to the entire system, to the world even. But that's only if the officials managed to contain everyone else. I doubt they did.*

Americans have a unique way about them; they don't like to be bossed. It was something that he, as a rugged Australian who grew up frequenting the wild outback with complete freedom, could identify with. It was part of why the American audience loved him so much. He was a rough rider. A cowboy. A self sufficient man of action.

He tries the CB radio and hears a clatter of voices so thick he can barely make out any coherent sentences. The channels normally designated to emergency and highway information are a mess. He flips through a few more channels and comes upon a less populated one. He listens in on the conversation. A man with a high pitched crackling mid-western accent is mid-way through a story.

"And then after a few minutes the sum' bitch gets back up! I mean I just watched him drop to the ground and stop breathing. I was already started to diggin' a hole, and was fixin' to give him a burial, proper like. And then he starts comin' at me, angry like. He didn't respond to nothin' I said. He was like one of them zombies from the old movies, you know? So I fired a warning shot in the air. That didn't stop him. Then I fired at his leg. Hit him just above the knee cap. I tell you what, that bastard kept comin' at me! I put the final bullet right between his eyes and that sure stopped him. Over."

Another man with a deep, raspy voice joins in. "I know they're saying that air over the east is poison. I guess it always has been. Didn't take no meteor to tell us those yanks were crazy." The men chuckle. "But you just proved them other rumors true. It makes you die. But then you come back, and when you come back you're bloodthirsty. A cannibal, like. Reckon you might be right when you call 'em zombies there, Spider. Heard about some meteor impacts overseas too. Over."

Wolf grabs the talk piece and presses the call button. *These kinds of folks are my bread and butter audience.* Mid-west US patriots, or so the ratings people tell him, are his biggest fans. *Maybe I can get some info from them.* "Breaker one six, breaker one six." He waits for a response.

"Cough Drop here. What's your handle?" asks the second man with the throaty voice.

"This is the Wolf," he replies.

"Spider here," says the first. "You ain't from 'round here, are you? Over."

"No sir. From Australia originally. Over."

"Australia? Wolf? You mean like the guy on TV?" Spider asks through a laugh.

"I *am* the guy on TV, mate. We made it just west of the impact before they put the barricade up and grounded the planes. Over."

"Well that's swell for you, but it ain't so swell for us," Cough Drop says.

"How so?" Wolf asks.

71

"If you think the military is bad, wait'll you see what the locals will do," says Spider. "Infected folk ain't s'posed to be west of the quarantine. People are already spreadin' this plague around, causin' panic. They don't care who y'are. They'll shoot ya dead if they see you sick. It's like survival of the fittest. Over."

"How are you still alive, Wolf? I saw the show. You were right there, breathing that stuff in," says Cough Drop. "Unless this is a punk kid messin' around. Over."

"I'm not messing with you. This is the real Wolf. I was coughing for hours after that bit. My lungs burned, I got real tired, and I couldn't do much of anything without feeling wiped out. I went to a doctor and the guy tried to lock me up in a room, probably because I was west of the quarantine. I broke out when I started feeling stronger. Whatever this dust is doing to people, it isn't working on me anymore. It's like I'm immune. Over." There's silence for several moments. "Breaker one six?" He calls out again. Still nothing.

"You better watch yourself out there," Cough Drop breaks the silence after a moment.

"Yeah man. The people love you, but it ain't like it used to be," Spider adds. "It's already like the wild west, good buddy. Amazing what happens when the shit hits the fan, eh? Suddenly us redneck folks are the wise ones again, bein' prepared with guns and all."

"You folks always were the wise ones, Spider," Wolf responds with a smile they can't see. "Thanks for the warning, fellas. Over."

"Godspeed, Wolf," Cough Drop adds.

He pulls up to the dark motel. Lots of people were on the road earlier, filling up the roadside motels. Many were escapees like him who made it past the impact zone before the big meteor hit. Wolf and his crew took the last vacant rooms when they arrived. He thought it would be buzzing with activity, but it's quiet. There's no power, but at least there are beds. He could use the rest.

He sees shadows moving behind the curtains in his darkened room. *The other guys must still be awake.* As he approaches the door he notices a foul yellow pool of vomit at his feet. *Looks like they found some beer. Nothing else to do but have a rage.* His crew was like that. A few of them were his old rugby mates, so they often went on binges during the down time between shows.

He opens the door and is greeted with a vile stench. It's like puke, piss and shit all mixed into one putrid potpourri. His arm comes up to his face to shield his nose, when Dale, his cameraman, grabs it and tries to bite it. Wolf instinctively shoves his palm into Dale's face, knocking him back into the room.

"Sorry mate," Wolf says. "What the hell are you doing in here, having a romp?" There's no reply. The moonlight creeps in from the doorway and he sees the shadow of a body on the floor. The 1970s era olive green carpeting underneath is wet and reddened with blood and entrails. "What the?"

Dale lunges at him, knocking him to the puke covered ground outside the door. Wolf manages to roll him over and get on top. He sees his eyes shine in the moonlight; an inhuman golden amber with no sign of a pupil. His mouth is foaming like a rabid dog, and he pulls at Wolf's ER scrubs, trying to get close for a chomp. Wolf clenches Dale's throat so tight his thumb and forefinger nearly touch behind Dale's wind pipe. The pain doesn't seem to faze Dale. With his other hand Wolf reaches down to his boot, where he always keeps a small utility knife. He swings it open with his teeth and holds the point to Dale's temple. "Don't make me do this buddy," he says, remembering Spider's story about how the only thing that stopped the infected was a blow to the head. He hopes the knife would do the same trick as the bullet. "Say something if you're still in there," he says, but Dale doesn't respond with words. He only growls, drools, and tries to bite and claw at Wolf's arm. Wolf closes his eyes and slowly pushes the knife into Dale's head.

"No don't do it!" Buzz, the sound tech, yells from the window of the next room. But it's too late. Dale has stopped moving. Buzz whips open the door and steps outside. "What did you do?"

"Did you see him, mate? He was trying to eat me alive!" Wolf yells, catching his breath from the scuffle.

"Yeah I saw. But it's Dale. It's Dale!" Buzz's eyes are wild, panicked.

"Come over here and look in the room. Come see what he did to James." Wolf points and Buzz peeks into the room to see the carnage. He's in shock. He steps out of the room confused, backing up into the parking lot.

"No. No this can't be happening! This is crazy! What are we going to do?" he says.

Wolf hadn't noticed at first, but many of the other motel rooms have their doors open. *It's so quiet because everyone else is dead.* "Look out!" Wolf yells. A zombie charges Buzz from the room right next to him and tackles him to the ground, ripping his neck open. All the yelling attracted the other ones from their rooms, and soon there's a swarm of five out in the parking lot, devouring Buzz.

Wolf grabs a 2x4 from a pickup parked beside his SUV and starts whacking them in the head with all his might. He coughs and breathes heavy, but it works. With a few swings he cracks their skulls open and kills them. One down, two down, three. *They're one-track minded. They don't pay me any attention when their meal is sitting there.* Wolf wheezes, his lungs too tired to swing anymore. He can hear Buzz gurgling in pain beneath the last two savages. He pushes himself to keep going and swings at one of them, knocking him off of Buzz. Buzz's intestines are out, lying on the pavement like tubes of sausage. Wolf brings the 2x4 down again, killing one. Buzz starts to twitch and convulse, and the last zombie stops eating him. It immediately turns to Wolf and lunges, but Wolf steps aside, and the demon's face meets the end of a rod of rebar that hangs off the back of the pickup truck, impaling itself through the eye and killing it instantly.

Buzz stops twitching and starts to vomit. Whatever's left of his digestive system pushes out of his bladder and remaining intestines. A purging. The smell is repulsive, and Wolf himself begins to retch. Suddenly Buzz stops moving, seemingly frozen in death. Wolf knows what's going to happen next. *Buzz is going to come back to life if he's not too far gone, and he's going to attack.* He shoves the dead zombie off the rebar in the pickup, flopping him to the ground. He rifles through the stuff in the truck bed, looking for a better weapon than a 2x4. He comes up with a crowbar. *This will have to do.*

He stands over Buzz, catching his breath and waiting for him to stir back to life. He hears the moans first, and then the growl. When Buzz gnashes his teeth, Wolf crushes his skull with the rounded end of the crowbar.

CHAPTER 15

Manhattan is in chaos. It's like something out of a bad 1980s movie that depicts the future. Anarchy. Lawlessness. Rampant crime. Looting. Old barrel fires from the night before rage on unattended. There are bodies strewn all over the place, and the winds continue to fill the streets with soot. People are kicking in doors, trying to escape the poisonous air. Others, like Michael and Amy, have their eyes and mouths covered and are on the move. The streets are eerily void of traffic. Even parked cars seem to be missing from the scene.

Michael complains about the water running all over his bag, chilling his skin in the cold. Minxie seems to be relaxed as they make their way toward the Holland tunnel. Amy stays alert to some masked looters across the street who break into storefront windows, stealing anything they can carry.

"What are they going to do with TVs and stereos?" Michael asks.

"Maybe bribe the guys at the bridges and tunnels to let them cross," she answers.

"Don't stare. I feel like if they see us watching they might attack," Michael warns. But as they avert their eyes they are met with the hollow end of a pistol.

"Don't fucking move or I'll blow your brains out," the man says through his sinister looking, dual filtered biohazard mask. "Take off your packs and toss them to the ground, next to me." They do as they're told. Michael places Minxie on the ground and she clings to his leg. "Now keep moving. Hands up! Turn around and you're dead." They walk past him, headed in the direction of the tunnel. They don't put their hands down until they round the corner at the next block. Michael quickly lifts Minxie back into his arms.

"The masks are all we need right now," Amy says, trying to reassure a dispirited Michael. "Once we get out of the city things will be different." He returns a depressed nod. He's too angry, scared, and bewildered to respond. The packs weren't much, but they meant something. They were a three day guarantee. They were light, food and warmth. They were life. They were hope.

As they get within five blocks of the tunnel, they see strings of automobiles jamming the streets in every direction. Everyone had the same idea; get out.

"The tunnel must be blocked," Michael says.

"Let's see for sure," a determined Amy responds.

Minxie begins to cough and hack in Michael's arms. He places her on the ground and kneels down beside her.

"What's wrong girl?" He lovingly pets Minxie behind her head. "I thought people were saying this stuff doesn't affect animals. I just saw some pigeons flying around doing fine a minute ago."

"Minxie's a fat, old, out of shape apartment cat. Maybe she can't take it like other animals can." Amy wanted a dog; a substantial dog, or nothing at all. People with pets in the city annoy her, but Michael had Minxie since his freshman year of college.

Minxie labors in her movement, and her legs weaken under her drooping belly. She pukes little puddles of yellow bile as she tries to get closer to Michael's boot. She lays on her side, huffing panicked, strained breaths in and out. She dies. Amy stands by with her hands on her hips as Michael softly weeps in his mask.

"We should probably keep moving," Amy says softly after a few moments.

"Don't you have a heart?" Michael asks, angry. "Just give me a minute, alright?"

"We don't have a minute. It's fucking insane out here!" There are gunshots and distant screams, and an increasing number of homeless looking vagrants wandering the streets.

Michael scoops Minxie up into his arms and carries her through the maze of empty parked cars over to a tree by the sidewalk. He gently places her on the small square patch of dead grass surrounding it. He pets her one last time, and then turns to Amy. "Okay let's go," he says sluggishly.

They see a small crowd of people near the tunnel entrance, and as they get close they hear yelling and chanting. It's a protest of some kind. Tanks and armed military humvees block the tunnel, and faceless soldiers wearing hooded gas masks and bulletproof suits stand ready to fire their weapons if anyone steps out of line. There are others with riot shields, and more still behind makeshift sand bag bunkers. Even up on the rooftops nearby there are MPs with assault rifles, looming over the scene.

"I guess we're stuck here." Michael says.

Just then one of the protesters hurls a flaming Molotov cocktail toward the barricade. It breaks against the ground near the men with riot shields. The fire is quickly extinguished, but the military volleys a can of tear gas into the crowd. Those who are already wearing gas masks are unaffected, but the ones without eye and mouth protection begin to flee or drop to the ground. The remaining protesters begin throwing rocks. They pry up the cobblestone bricks from the street and launch them at the MPs, but the MPs fire back at them with rubber bullets.

"We are authorized to use deadly force if necessary. I repeat: we are authorized to use deadly force," one of them warns through a megaphone. The protestors yell even louder, and start to surge at the barricade. There even seems to be some scuffle rousing up among the protesters. Infighting. Suddenly machinegun fire echoes off the buildings nearby, filling the quiet morning air with dread. The protesters scatter but several are left dead in the street. Others are zip-tied and thrown in the back of a military truck.

"Oh my God! This is no joke. What are we gonna do?" Amy asks as she and Michael run back the way they came.

"I have half a mind to go down there and protest! This is bullshit!" Michael complains.

"Are you nuts?" Amy glares at him through her mask.

"Let's just head back home. Maybe those looters left. If we can reclaim our apartment we can board it up and lock ourselves in, and be ready to defend ourselves better," Michael suggests.

Amy doesn't like the idea. She doesn't like the thought of being contained, but it's the only plan, and the streets are too dangerous to press on. "There has to be another way," she says.

"I can't think of anything," Michael responds.

"Didn't you help assess the tunnels for the city planner's office when they were studying the homeless, trying to get an accurate figure of the people living underground?" Amy asks. The sight of scores more shambling wrecks on the street gave her the idea. *I wonder; where are they all coming from?*

"Yeah. Yeah!" he says. "There was an old abandoned PATH tube just a few blocks from here. It was supposedly cleared out, and the way in was sealed up. If we can break through it, maybe we can get out."

"Will they know about it? Will they be guarding it?" Amy asks.

"If they checked the records it would say that the area was properly sealed off, so maybe not," Michael says. "It's worth a try while we're out, and it's close by." Michael points down the street when he sees Minxie in front of him. She walks in a zigzag without her characteristic feline poise. Her eyes are yellow, and she gnashes her teeth.

"What the fuck?" a startled Amy blurts out. Michael starts to walk toward the cat. "Don't. Stay away," Amy warns. Minxie hisses at them. All the hair on her back stands on end. It seems she is beginning to regain her wits, but her demeanor is angry. She stands still in the street, just a few strides away from them. Suddenly a rat crawls out from the sewer grate beside Minxie. She lunges at it without hesitation and begins to devour it alive. "Come on let's go!" Amy yells. Michael follows.

CHAPTER 16

Marcus looks up into the poisonous air. He's free, but trapped behind a mask. The prison walls fade into the horizon behind the group of inmates as they trek down a lonely highway on the west side of the Hudson. They keep cover in the woods along the roadside in case any authorities are on the hunt for them. The air is cold. Occasional blusters of dust pelt them as they walk, shivering. The debris from the meteor is settling, but it's no less dangerous to breathe. All it takes is one particle to kill you.

Marcus and Harley's band of escapees found that out the hard way when a few of the others took their masks off for a moment earlier. They coughed for a few hours afterward and then collapsed. And then they changed. There are twelve of them left now. Harley was eager to put the other three down. *I wonder if maybe they could've been cured. Maybe some doctor could find a fix for it in a lab or something. But it's too dangerous to risk keeping the risen with us, and what doctor would help a crew of convicts?* Marcus didn't like it, but he understood why Harley did what he did. *The dead have to stay dead.*

Everyone is getting hungry, so they cautiously veer off course to a rest stop. The signs leading up to it show all the icons of the big fast food chains. They get excited at the thought of burgers and fries, bragging about what they're going to order, not thinking about how they can pay for it with nothing in their pockets. They hope against reason, but soon realize that with the power out they aren't likely to get any food. They see several cars parked outside, but no one is in sight. The doors are open, and the lights are out. Inside it looks like a bomb went off. Chairs and tables are flipped and knocked over, cash registers are smashed on the floor and emptied, and there are bodies all over the place with bullet holes in their heads. Their dreams of a hot meal are dashed.

"Switch outta your clothes," Harley commands them.

They begin to undress the dead and exchange their prison jumpers for bloodied civilian clothes. *I guess it's a better look than convict orange.* Marcus finds a big guy whose clothes might fit him. He can smell the stench of death through his mask as he undresses him and eyes his marbled green skin underneath. The man lies in a pool of foul ooze that drips from every hole in his body as his insides turn into liquid. *I'll stick to the coat and boots. Everything else is nasty.*

"Got a gas burner out here. Camping equipment in a car. Propane," one of the other inmates calls out from near the door.

"Marcus, go grab us some burgers," Harley calls out.

Excited by the allure of fresh burgers, Marcus hops to it and heads back to the kitchen through the double doors beside the register. There is rancid meat, lettuce, onions and tomatoes all over the counters, and there are more bodies. He hears a light scuffling sound coming from back behind the fryers, near the freezers where he needs to go. He looks around for a weapon, hoping it's just a bunch of rats. There's only one bullet left in Thompson's gun, so he wants to save it, if even use it at all. He finds a thick metal grill scraper on the nearby counter and picks it up.

Marcus slowly creeps toward the back of the kitchen, careful to make each step in silence. The sounds grow louder; the sounds of someone eating. Ravenous. *It's one of them.* Through the cracks between the stoves and overhead steam cooking compartments, he sees the undead feasting on the dead. Suddenly his appetite escapes him. The monster is eating a dead employee right in front of the freezer door.

Marcus thinks back to all the reading he did in the prison chapel. He read the Bible cover to cover, over and over. He remembers Lazarus rising from the dead, and then Jesus. But the frightening parts were when the prophets spoke of the dead coming back to eat the living. One line he remembered from Jeremiah was "I will make them eat the flesh of their sons and daughters, and they will feast upon one another." There were more references in Revelation about the dead coming back to life and striking horror and fear in the living; the end times. *If this ain't the end of days, I don't know what is.*

He's a changed man, and he refuses to become one of these things. He says a prayer to himself, asking forgiveness for what he is about to do; he vows to kill every one of them he sees, to stop them from changing men into monsters. At the same time, he renews his vow to never again bring harm upon the living.

He swiftly approaches the zombie and jabs the metal grill scraper down with both hands, just below the back of its skull. After a few quick strikes the beast's head detaches from its body and tumbles aside, but its mouth still chews at the flesh dangling from its teeth. Horrified and disgusted, Marcus stomps on its face with the heel of his dead man's boots until it stops moving. A thick, goopy blood sludge covers the tiled floor in front of the freezer. *Thank you God, for keeping me safe.* He breathes a sigh of relief, and gets back to his mission, food.

With any luck some of the burgers are still cold and okay to eat. He grabs the biggest pack he can find; a 36 count box that's still cold to the touch. He even remembers the buns and some ketchup. He steps outside to cheers from the others, who sit waiting for him around a small portable grill fire. The burgers begin to cook. Marcus wraps himself in a large black blanket he finds in a nearby car to stay warm as the sun sets. It forms a hood over his gas mask.

Harley hops up into the cab of a large delivery truck and starts it up with the keys left in the ignition. He drives it over to where the rest of the group sits and turns it so the driver's side door is blocked from the wind by the rest of the truck. He crawls over the seat and into the back cab. "We can eat in here." His voice echoes from inside.

"You gonna be the first to try?" one of the inmates asks.

"Already got my mask off, wiseass," responds Harley.

When the burgers are done they all climb into the back of the truck and eat with jackets and shirts covering their heads to block the air even further. No one gets sick.

CHAPTER 17

Michael and Amy round the corner to see a mobbed street, filled with maskless people. They shamble and shuffle about aimlessly, in a daze.

"What's wrong with them? Are they sick?" Amy asks quietly.

"I guess so."

About halfway down the street a young man bursts out of a doorway and into the commotion. He runs full speed in Michael and Amy's direction, with a young woman trailing behind. "Hurry!" he shouts at her. The sick start to chase them. They quickly swarm around the girl and tackle her to the ground. The young man turns and tries to pull her out, but she's deep under a pile of the infected. Her hand reaches out for him. He yanks with all his might. But it's no use. She's buried. Her muffled cries gurgle to a stop. He gives one last tug and half of her arm rips loose. He falls backward and screams in shock as he looks upon the gnawed limb in his hand. Blood pours out from where her elbow used to be. Loose skin and flesh dangle as he shakes in fear. He tries to get up and run, but the crowd turns on him, burying him just like the young woman.

"Run. RUN!" Amy says.

"Where?" Michael asks, panicked.

Amy blurts out the closest location she knows. "Let's go to Madison's place."

Michael nods his head yes, and they turn around and run in the other direction. He always hated Madison. She and Amy were roommates in college all four years, so Michael had to get used to faking it around her. She was fat, loud, unhealthy, and from the

Bible belt. He always wondered why the hell Amy hung out with her. He assumed some "beauty is on the inside" bullshit, or that they went through some sort of "first friend away from home" bonding in that daunting freshman year at an Ivy League university, where it's all backstabbing and one-upping for the best grades. He thought he was rid of the blob until she landed a job in the city some years back. A few chaotic minutes later they're knocking on the front door of Madison's apartment building.

"This is fucking nuts. I told you we wouldn't be able to leave," Michael says.

"Well we didn't really have a choice, did we?" Amy huffs under her mask, trying to catch her breath. "We're still going to try for the PATH tunnel, right?"

Michael struggles to breathe as well. He takes a moment to answer. "If we can make it there in one piece."

The infected wander the street. They see Michael and Amy and start to run at them. Michael panics. He pounds on the door repeatedly. "Come on you fat fuck," he mumbles under his breath. "Open up, Madison!"

The door swings open and Madison tries to make them out through the gas masks. "Amy and Michael? Are you guys alright?" Her hearty voice booms even through her own mask. The flab on her arms swings and dangles as she props the door all the way open and hits the brick wall behind. "Come on in," she says.

"Hurry. Get in!" Michael says, pulling Amy inside.

"What's wrong?" Madison asks. Her head is turned away from the street as she looks at Michael.

"Look out!" he yells.

But before Madison can shut the door one of the infected rips a chunk out of her arm, just below the armpit, where the flab hangs the lowest. Amy kicks the beast back out into the street and they close the door. Madison brays like a goat, reeling with pain and marinating in the red gravy that pours from her arm. They walk back to her apartment door. Amy is covered in blood. Her fingers slip as she tries to squeeze Madison's wound shut. It squirts everywhere, hitting the missing cats and furniture-for-sale flyers on the cork board, coating the mailboxes and stairs, and slicking up the shitty linoleum vestibule floor. Michael opens the door to her small, crappy ground floor studio. It's the best she could afford in this neighborhood. Michael was always convinced that she moved there just to torment him. *Close enough to fling a chicken wing at*, he used to say.

Amy immediately wraps Madison's arm with towels and anything else absorbent that she can get her hands on. Madison finally stops her incessant moaning and instead breathes like a wildebeest, sucking in and out like she just ascended 15 flights of stairs. A look of pure disgust coats Michael's face under his mask. *Someone so out of shape, and trying to breathe through a mask. That'll do it. She's winded.*

"Her heart's beating mile a minute," Amy says. "She's burning up. Grab me something from the freezer, anything that's still cold. I have to try and cool her down."

Michael opens the freezer. It's nearly empty. All that's in there is a shrink-wrapped pack of hamburger meat, now half-frozen and squishy to the touch. He hands it to Amy, and she puts it on the back of Madison's neck.

"The towels are soaking through," Michael says, pointing.

"Grab me another?" Amy asks. She pulls back the blood soaked towels to reveal a blackened wound, festering with freshly formed pus.

Michael hands her a new towel, and pokes around Madison's fridge for some water. But there is none. It too is almost empty. There's just a can of high caffeine, high sugar energy drink and some condiments left on the door.

"The bleeding isn't stopping," Amy says.

Madison's eyes grow heavy behind the mask. They close, and she starts to twitch and convulse. Her fat ripples and jiggles on her neck, just below her mask. The folds and rolls in her body flap around, slapping skin against skin under her oversized pajamas. Her mouth foams up underneath her mask, filling it with liquid. The shaking is so violent Michael can feel it across the room; her tremendous body rattles the floor beneath. Then suddenly she seems to calm down, and a moment later her elephantine heart stops.

"Is she?" Michael can't believe it. "Just from a bite? She's dead? It's like she had a coronary or something."

"Oh my God. What are we going to do?" Amy asks, frantic.

"I don't think there's anything we *can* do. The whole city is shut down, in chaos. The phones are dead, and I have no signal on what little remains on my cell battery."

Then there's a long drawn out breath. Amy feels her leg soak with a warm liquid through her jeans. Madison is pissing herself. Amy jumps back with a start.

"What is it?" Michael asks. "Was that her breathing?"

Then there's a groan. Amy tries to rationalize it. "I don't know. I heard things about what bodies sometimes do after people die. They can groan, and expel liquids. All sorts of morbid crap happens in morgues."

Then Madison sits up. Her mask is foggy and foamed up inside. The eyes look like glowing lights. She stumbles to her feet, stomping and rattling the shitty parquet wood floor as she gets up.

"Well maybe she's not dead," Michael adds sarcastically. He raises his hands in the air as if presenting Madison to a crowd of game show viewers.

"Madison?" Amy says.

An instant later she blindly charges at Amy like a wild bull. Amy steps aside toward Michael, and Madison crashes through her flimsy bathroom door, splintering it into shards. Madison goes down hard, flopping chest first into the toilet and shattering the porcelain on her way through it. The stagnant, unflushed shit water pours out all over the floor, filling the room with stink. A stalagmite of toilet porcelain remains. Covered in shit and sheared off to a jagged point, it proudly stands tall where there once sat a majestic throne. Madison gets up again. She lunges at Amy and Michael. But her foot slips on a massive log of dump, and her body lurches backward into a fall. The back of her head lands right smack on the tip of the pointed porcelain monolith. The sheer force of her fall plunges it out the front of her gas mask, popping the glass eye piece. She lies motionless in a pool of her own excrement. The glass eye piece spins and wobbles to a slow stop on the tile floor. And all is silent.

88

#

"I can't believe someone so fat has nothing to eat in their apartment," Michael remarks as he rummages through Madison's cabinets.

"How can you say that? She just died," Amy says.

"I'm just saying. You think there'd be *something*. I guess she ate through it all in the last few days."

"Well, I mean look at her kitchen. It's nonexistent. A hot plate and a mini fridge? It's like college. She probably eats out a lot," Amy reasons.

"Yeah. Fish sandwiches and furburgers at Café Dyke," Michael mumbles inaudibly. "This is a waste. She doesn't have anything we can use to recreate our packs."

"So then let's just try to relax. We can leave first thing in the morning," Amy suggests.

"Okay. Hopefully there'll be less of those animals out there if we get an early start."

CHAPTER 18

All is vacant, calm, and pitch black in the night. Sheryl drives down the winding road from the hospital back to town. An occasional buzzing sound comes through the police radio, but there are no voices. There's no life on the other end.

"What's your name?" she asks.

"Willy," he says.

"I'm Sheryl."

"I live over in the Hillside apartment complex in the west part of town. I ain't got no kin or nothing, and the buses ain't running. Do you think you could…"

"No. I'm not taking you there," she cuts him off. She knows where it is. The woman her husband had an affair with some years ago lives there. A girl, more like it. A secretary in his office, no more than twenty years old, but trash. Sheryl immediately begins to judge Willy, despite him saving her life. She associates anyone from that place with her husband's fling, with pain. She wouldn't even let the boys go there to play with friends from school.

"I say somethin' wrong?" Willy asks, confused.

Sheryl glares at him. "No."

He's older than she thought at first glance. Mid 60s. Weathered, white skin crinkles his brow. His bright emerald eyes burn into her mind. He's fit, and actually quite handsome for a Hillsider, and for an older man.

Sheryl softens. "I have to get home and see if my husband is okay, but I'll drop you off first," she says.

But really she doesn't care about her husband. She hasn't cared about him since she learned of the affair. That's why he was so "focused on work." When she found out he said he would end it. She always wondered if he actually did.

"You know you should cover your mouth with something. Otherwise you might turn into one of them," she says to Willy.

He eyeballs her up and down, noticing the bandaged arm first. He pulls out a small blade from his pants pocket. Sheryl grips the wheel tight in fear. "Thanks," he says as he begins to unbutton and remove his custodial uniform shirt, revealing a white wife beater beneath. His eyes never come off her. Hers bounce between his, the road, and the blade. She's a spitting image of what his daughter would look like today if she were still alive. Sure, she's attractive, but all he sees is his daughter, especially around the eyes. Half obscured by her mask, they're transformed in Willy's mind to be exactly the eyes of his little girl.

"Keep your eyes on the road. I'm not gonna hurt you," he says. He finally unlocks his gaze from her and fixes it instead on the back of his removed shirt, where he begins to cut a length of unsoiled fabric, untouched by blood and gore. Sheryl's heart sinks back down from her throat to her chest, and she loosens her grip on the wheel. Willy ties the strip of shirt around his head, covering his nose and mouth in front. He returns the blade to his pants pocket.

Sheryl pulls off the road and into town. A few more turns and they're at Hillside. "Which building is it?" Sheryl asks as they approach the darkened complex. She slows down along the fencing that lines the buildings, coming to a stop.

"Hold on. Keep driving," Willy warns. They come from everywhere, out of the thick darkness, swarming the car. Before Willy can even finish speaking there's one pounding on the hood of the car, crawling its way up and trying to claw at them through the windshield. Then another on the driver side window, and another. Sheryl flips on the high beams, fumbling at first to find them in the unfamiliar car. They're surrounded. The beasts' yellow eyes glow in the night like animals.

"Hang on!" Sheryl yells as she floors the gas pedal. There are clunks, thuds, snaps and bumps as she mows over the diseased cannibals, crushing them under the car. The one on the windshield hangs on with unearthly strength. She yanks the wheel to the right, finally shaking it off. She starts to turn around, flattening more of them with the rear end of the police cruiser as she circles in reverse. She puts the car in drive and heads back the way she came at top speed. She can see them running, chasing the car in the red glow of tail lights through the rearview mirror.

"I guess you can't go home just yet," Sheryl says. A sort of smile ekes out as she considers the fate of the home wrecker that lives there. "You can stay with me until then. It's the least I can do."

The roads on the other side of town, across Main Street, are eerily empty. Save for a few bodies slumped on curbs and lawns, it's a ghost town. She meanders her way around abandoned cars and carnage until finally arriving at her house. Her husband's car isn't there. Still. He had no idea what happened to her, to the kids. *Is he even alive? Should I even care?* Sheryl begins to cry, hanging her head down and pressing it against the steering wheel. Her emotions have finally caught up to her. Everything from the accident until she parked the police car in her driveway had been one big surreal blur. The horrors, the sorrow… it was too much to hold it together.

"What is it?" Willy asks.

"My sons. I lost my two boys. One of them…" She can't say it, but Willy knows.

"Turned?" he asks, completing her thought. She nods and sobs, confirming it. "Let's get you inside and cleaned up."

"You had no mask on for a while. You think it's safe to breathe?" she asks.

"Better wait 'til we get inside. Maybe I was lucky. I was only outside a little while. I holed up in my office mostly, 'til things got quiet. I tried gettin' a bunch of 'em at first, all around the hospital. But the whole place was overrun. We were lucky to get out," he says.

"That dust isn't blowing around anymore," she says.

"Better just wait. Probably should try to head west too, past the impact. The winds are blowin' right at us. If we get past there it might be safe to breathe," Willy suggests.

"Good idea."

They go inside and everything is as Sheryl left it. The turkey is still out, only now starting to stink with rot. The gifts are still half wrapped. The sight of them saddens her, knowing BJ and Stephen will never play with them. Dog hair still coats the couch. Just then Rocky, her German Shepherd, comes running out to greet them.

"Rocky!" She almost feels joy upon seeing him. She hugs him, and hears his stomach groan with hunger. "You must be starving boy," she says, grabbing a bag of dry food from the pantry and filling his dish. "I'm surprised you didn't have at the turkey!" She tries the sink for his water, but the pipes groan and shudder. Nothing comes out.

"Pumps," says Willy. "Water needs pumps. Pumps need electricity. We ain't got none, nowhere. Whole grid's out, and I guess the generators are all down too. No wells or towers neither that I know of."

Sheryl opens the fridge and empties a bottle of spring water into Rocky's water dish. He laps it up and then devours the dry food beside it.

"Looks like it might be safe. The dog is fine," Sheryl says as she removes her mask. Willy does the same. Sheryl passes him a bottle of water. She takes one and starts to clean herself over the sink. A rusty pink-orange liquid washes down the drain as the crusted blood lifts from her skin.

"Better conserve these after we clean up," Willy says about the bottled water.

Sheryl nods in agreement. *He reminds me of dad before he died, only a bit younger.* She finds herself agreeing to his advice without question like a daughter. Perhaps she needed that comfort. *If only dad were really here with me.* For so long she needed no one but herself. She loved only her children. She grew stony without her dad, since her husband eventually stopped caring as well. But she missed the times when she called on her father for help, or knew he was there for her if anything went wrong. She wanted that comfort now, and, without knowing it, Willy was filling that void. "Want something to eat?" she asks him.

They split a can of meat ravioli with some sliced white bread that hasn't gone moldy yet. Willy looks over her pantry and dry goods with approval. "We'll pack it all in the car, as much as we can. Especially the water. You have any guns or weapons?"

"Yeah. My husband keeps a pistol somewhere in his closet," she says.

"Good. If we can ever get into my place I have a rifle and a shotgun," he says. Sheryl nods but she doesn't want to go back there, back into danger. She doesn't even fully know if she wants to bring Willy with her when she leaves. *I guess I owe him the favor, and the companionship can't hurt now. Otherwise what point is there to go on living? The boys are gone, and my husband abandoned me. Why live in this nightmare?* She starts to think crazy thoughts; that perhaps Willy is her father's spirit somehow, looking out for her now when she needs him most.

She wonders how they'll all fit in a packed car if they find her husband, or if he returns home. She still tells herself that she must find him, but she doesn't know why. In her gut she knows he was somewhere in that mob of monsters at Hillside, probably with his pants down or half naked, having turned into a zombie during a Christmas morning tryst. *That bastard.*

After they finish eating Willy puts his makeshift mask back on, pulls the car into the garage, and starts packing the trunk and back seat with supplies and food. Sheryl roots around her husband's closet for his pistol with Rocky right beside her, wagging his tail with his ears perked up like it's some kind of game. She knows her husband keeps the gun well hidden so the boys can't find it. She pops open shoe boxes, and pokes behind his shelves. Nothing. But up on top, behind some unopened packaged shirts, she sees a small box. She takes it down. It has a combination lock, and she doesn't know the numbers. She brings it to the kitchen.

"Locked," she says.

Willy examines the box. It's nothing complicated. He sees that it's weak. The lock is useless. He takes the hammer and a screwdriver from his tool belt and begins to lightly chisel between the box and the lid, popping it off its hinges and opening it from the back. Sheryl marvels at him. *That's something dad would've done.*

95

Inside is a gun wrapped in newspaper and a few boxes of bullets. But underneath there's an envelope. Sheryl snatches it from Willy's fingers. She knows what it is before she even opens it. But she has to. She has to see with her own eyes. Pictures of her husband and the girl from Hillside, doing everything, in every way, sexually. Recent too. The date from the digital camera they used to take them was printed on the bottom right corner of each. Some were as recent as last week. *He never stopped seeing her.* And there are two other girls in the pictures too.

"Fucking scumbag!" She yells. She tells herself that she isn't going looking for him. *He can fend for himself and rot in this hell for all I care.* Willy doesn't pry, but she involves him anyway. "Why did you save me?" she asks.

"You wouldn't have done the same for someone in danger?" he asks in response.

"Maybe I'd be better off dead. Did you ever think of that? What do I have to live for?"

"Don't throw your life away. Trust me when I tell you I've been down that road. It ain't worth traveling. Life's one of the few gifts we get."

"Feels more like a curse now."

"Maybe. But you have to press on. This may be the beginning of the end, but how you act now matters more than ever. It's no feat to be a good person during good times. The challenge is to be a good person even in bad times."

Dad used to say something similar. Willy walks away and continues packing the car. After Sheryl cools down he shows her how to use the gun without actually firing it. She eventually thanks him for saving her, almost calling him "dad" in the process. She takes Willy's advice. How she acts now matters more than ever. She convinces herself. *I need to find him even though he doesn't deserve it. It's the right thing to do.*

CHAPTER 19

Marcus wanders alone through the woods heading south. In anguish, he wonders if he could have done more to prevent what happened. Regret fills him, but what he needed to do would've required him to break his vow to not harm the living. He curses himself as he walks.

They burned down the empty highway at breakneck speed in the delivery truck. Whenever they came upon an abandoned vehicle they siphoned off any gas they could. They were down to fumes when they happened upon a group of travelers at a rest stop on the other side of the highway.

"Hang on!" Harley yelled as they bounded across the grass between the south and north arteries, aiming the truck right at their family friendly sport utility wagon. He screeched to a stop just inches from them. As if understood by all, Harley and his gang jumped out of the truck, brandishing weapons and yelling. "Get the fuck out of the car! Get your ass on the ground!" Marcus was confused and in shock. But part of him was excited, he admitted that much to himself. The lure of his old ways tore at him, trying to claw him back into that familiar comfort zone of taking, hurting, killing. The easy way through life. The adrenaline coursed through his veins, pumping hate through his body. It found familiar pathways to trigger old memories; what to say, how to act, how to crazy-up his eyes to instill the most fear. It all came rushing back. But he resisted.

"Get the fuck out of the car! Get your ass on the ground!" Harley and his men commanded.

One of the travelers didn't listen. A young kid, maybe 19. "Leave us alone!" he yelled back, defiant. He was the oldest male among what must have been his mother, a younger sister, and a still younger brother; they all looked alike. The eldest kid was their protector, and Harley wanted what he was protecting. The car. The gas. Whatever it was, it didn't even matter. Without hesitation Harley pistol whipped him, and when he didn't go down Harley put a bullet in his chest. Just like that. No thought. No pause. His mother ran to him as he dropped to his knees, holding him in her arms one last time.

"I said get on the ground!" The younger kids listened through their tears, but mom was still clinging to her oldest son as he faded into the afterlife. Harley wouldn't tolerate insolence. He pressed the gun to her temple and squeezed the trigger, coating her dead son and the rear fender of their car with brains. They tied the young boy up and shoved him in the truck, and they took the girl off the highway into the woods one at a time. Marcus could only imagine what they did to her. She couldn't have been much older than 16.

When Harley finally calmed himself down from the rampage, Marcus told him he was leaving and would go his separate way. Despite not really wanting to, Marcus shook Harley's hand in return when he extended it.

The young girl's tear streaked face and the panicked horror in her screams haunt him as he walks. *Is that how others saw me, how she saw Harley then? What kind of monster was I in the eyes of my victims? Worse than the zombies. Have I even truly reformed? No. I should have saved her!* The dread she felt at the hands of Harley's marauders was worse than any zombie could instill in someone. Marcus constantly reassesses his vows, his code. But this is his second chance. This is his test. If he fails now, this world will seem like a day at the beach compared to the hell he imagines; the real hell awaiting him after this one. *Being on the outside is just like being on the inside; trouble has a way of seeking you out. You have to work hard to get away from it.*

Up ahead there's a clearing. A farm. He sees a barn near the edge of the woods. It's half painted; a fresh coat of white partially covers a flaked and weathered apple red. He creeps inside to find the remaining unopened buckets of white paint. An old 1950s era pickup truck rots on the earthen floor in the middle of the barn, rusting and fading with time. On the walls hang all manner of farming tools. The one that strikes him is the scythe. He takes it in his hand and strokes the blade softly with his fingers. *It's still sharp.* When he turns he catches a glimpse of himself reflected in the old pickup window, hooded in black and carrying a scythe. He pries open a can of paint and starts to outline the crude shape of a skull on his mask, using the reflection in the pickup window as a mirror. The spots that have too much paint begin to drip down, creating an even more ominous, melted look to the design.

His vows begin to trouble him again. *What about when the living harm the living? I must strike fear into their hearts to stop them.* He sees it as his mission, his duty; the reason God gave him a second chance at life. He would become a reaper; an angel of death to the undead. And if possible he would strike fear into the soulless hearts of the demons that yet live. *Perhaps fear will cause them to stay their sinful hands upon the very sight of me.*

With much of the day left ahead of him, he continues walking on. Following the dirt road out from the farm he eventually comes upon a small town. Empty. He sees a church on the main stretch of town and enters. He seeks guidance from God on his new vow, his mission. "Is this your plan?" he asks aloud, wondering if happening upon a church is a sign that he is on the right path.

A deep voice echoes off the pews and stained glass windows. "Behold, the angel of death." Marcus stops dead in his tracks and raises his weapon, looking all around for the source. A weathered priest lurks in the shadows behind the altar. He emerges with a rifle over his shoulder. "What is it you seek?" he asks.

"Guidance." Marcus lowers his scythe.

"Guidance comes from God. All a priest can do is help people to see it," the priest says.

"Why would God do this to his people?" Marcus asks.

"Maybe God isn't doing anything. Maybe God is just letting it happen," the priest suggests.

"God is all powerful. He can stop it if he wants."

"Sure. But it wouldn't be unfair if he didn't. We're all sinful beings. He could leave us to die but he gives us a chance at forgiveness." The priest's eye catches the prison uniform under Marcus' hooded cape and jacket. "Even you."

"That's what I'm trying to figure out. Why? And what am I supposed to do? What's my purpose?" Marcus asks.

"The why is love, grace. The purpose is for you to find."

"I think I'm supposed to kill these things, these demons. But when I see men still harming each other in the face of this evil instead of coming together, I wonder if I'm already condemned to hell. I vowed never to harm another person, but I don't know if I can hold true to it anymore. But you. You're a priest. Priests are supposed to be peaceful. So what's a priest doing with a gun?"

"To effectively shepherd those through the valley of the shadow of death, we must have the means to strike down the evil that might block the path. I'm merely protecting my flock, even if it means killing them when they return from death."

"This is a ghost town. What flock is there?"

"There are some that still live, hiding. I killed the rest. Some were turned, and some weren't."

"You're a priest murderer then."

"Not all killing is murder. Jesus told his disciples: 'If you don't have a sword, sell your cloak and buy one.' Even he, who turned the other cheek, warned that self defense is necessary at times. You took up a scythe to arm yourself, but only to reap the dead? You vowed to protect the living and do them no harm, but now you see that maybe some of those yet living pose an equal threat to peace. Perhaps the living can be worse than these cannibals. You see, this condition affects the living as well as the dead. Soulless, and driven by nothing but survival, man will abandon all notions of morality, humanity, and consequence in favor of anarchy. With lawlessness comes godlessness. With no eternal consequences for our actions, man becomes beast. We become ravenous, soulless, just like the undead. Only we arrive there through reason, through choice, through a Darwinian survival mentality. I don't know which demon is worse; the risen or those yet living."

"So you're telling me it's okay to kill people?"

100

"You must do what you believe is right, son. I have not struck down the good, only the bad. I feel no remorse or regret in it, just as God feels no remorse or regret in denying evil's entry into his kingdom. Earth is still the kingdom of man, and we remaining kings must protect our castles until we are called to our final home by God. Being a man of God does not mean you cannot defend others, protect yourself, or uproot evil. No. And perhaps now, more than ever, being a man of God even commands those actions. Do not bind yourself to protect these animals at all cost. Nurture those that yet have good in them, and dispatch the ones who are too far gone for saving. Do it not with hate, but rather with prayer, even love. Just as a rancher puts down a horse that is injured beyond repair, or as one puts down a rabid dog."

"But the rancher owns the horse. It's different. Putting a man down is not the same. In society that is killing."

"Ahh but you are no man, and this is no society. You are an angel. The angel of death, loosed from its shackles. A reaper, freed from its cage and set upon this lawless wasteland, this hellish end-of-days, by God himself." The priest's eyes are wide with fury.

Marcus begins to question the old priest's sanity, but he understands his point. *My vows are flawed. They have no room for righteous justice. Even governments have death penalties and take the lives of men when they're guilty of the worst crimes.* That was a fate he might have met under different circumstances for the crimes he committed. Marcus sits down in thought.

"Tell me what choice you've made that haunts you." The priest seems to read Marcus like a book as he sits beside him in the pew. Marcus tells him of the incident on the road, how he wanted to help but was afraid of what might happen if he killed again, if he committed the same mortal sins that condemned him. "God is justice but he is also compassion," the priest says. "He understands your torment. Perhaps he wanted you to act, for God is righteous in his retribution too. These are difficult choices, and they are for you alone to make. Pray. Pray for guidance, and if the time comes again for such decisions, perhaps God will make your path clearer." Marcus prays with the priest in silence for several moments. They rise together. "Go down to the last house on the left. Eat. Change your clothing. Erase your past. Cleanse and renew yourself. Peel away the old man and become the new man. All that matters now and what is yet to come. Your second chance is here. Seize it," the priest tells him. "And as for the Lord's command to sell your cloak and buy a sword, since you already have a scythe, you should keep your cloak. You have a dreadful look with it. The angel of death." The old priest chuckles as they walk together toward the church doors.

"Some angel, huh? A fallen angel. Or more like a demon. Just like them out there."

"My son, the angels were the most frightening creatures in the Bible. When people saw them they fainted in awe and fear. I'd much rather face a demon than an angel any day."

"Can I take one of them with me?" Marcus asks, pointing to a Bible sitting in the pew closest to the doors. The old priest nods his head yes.

CHAPTER 20

Sheryl wakes thinking it was all a bad dream, and that her boys are alive. When her senses return she becomes angry. Her body aches. The early morning sun creeps in through her bedroom window, shining right into her eyes. "Fuck!" she yells, frustrated that her dream of normalcy was not reality. Then the sadness sets in. As she gets dressed she reminds herself that she must press on. She walks into the kitchen for some water. Willy lightly sleeps on the armchair in the living room. He stirs awake when Sheryl closes the pantry door.

They finish packing the car, and Sheryl, Willy and Rocky hop inside, setting out to determine the fate of Sheryl's husband and make another attempt at Willy's apartment. Their first stop is her husband's office, but the parking lot is empty. Same thing at the gym, so back to Hillside they must go, as Sheryl sees that as the only other place her husband could be. Their first stop will be Willy's apartment, to get his guns.

Hillside is clearer in the day. The cannibals must have dispersed through the town in search of more people to eat. But there are still a few lingering on the grounds, watching the car as it drives along the fence.

"Turn into the far lot, and get as close to the rear entrance as you can," Willy says. "I'm real close to that door, on the first floor. As long as the hallway isn't swarmed I can be in and out in under a minute." But Willy wonders if he can. He fears another episode, another flashback. Things can go bad quickly if he opens that door and suddenly he is on a tunnel clearing mission back in the war. He takes a few deep, calming breaths to prepare himself.

Sheryl pulls into the far lot and lines up the passenger side door with the rear entrance. Willy pops out and shuts the car door quietly. Sheryl immediately locks it. Willy keys himself into the building, disappearing inside. Sheryl looks at her watch, counting off the seconds in her head.

11… 12… 13…

Her eyes keep moving. Her neck cranes as she looks all around. *Are they coming?* The sound of the car door doesn't seem to have grabbed their attention.

25… 26… 27…

There are two on the grass near the side of the building, one by the street, and a hunched group feeding near the edge of the woods. But others that saw them drive up are starting to wander over.

43… 44…45…

Sheryl hears a thick muffled gunshot from inside the building. Every hair on her body stands on end. A murder of crows takes to the sky in response, shattering the crisp silence of the morning. Sheryl didn't even notice them picking at the bodies that lay all over the ground. Her eyes follow them as they fly up into the air. But moments later some of them seize. Their wings stop flapping, and they fall from the sky in mid-flight, crashing back to the ground in death. Rocky begins to bark wildly, and Sheryl struggles to silence him.

52… 53… 54… Am I counting too fast?

The zombies turn their attention, and they start to run toward the building. She counts six of them, all running in the direction of the gunshot, the direction of the rear entrance to Willy's building, the direction of Rocky's barking, the direction of the car.

59… 60… 61… Shit! It's more than a minute now. Sheryl begins to panic. She tries to keep counting in her head, thinking it will calm her, but she just keeps repeating *61* over and over. Her mind races and her eyes dart back and forth between the door and the coming dead.

Another heavy gunshot follows. Startled, she nearly lifts out of her seat. She gasps when Willy kicks open the door and emerges from within with a shotgun on his hip. He steps over a corpse and stands beside the car. Within seconds the zombies are upon them.

He unloads shot after shot over the hood of the car as they approach him, pumping empty buckshot shells into the air after each blast. He reaches for the car door but it's locked. Sheryl fumbles in releasing the mechanism, as one zombie has its face pressed to the driver side window, smearing it with fleshy bits of stink.

"Open up!" Willy's muddled shout fills Sheryl's ears between the thuds of shotgun fire. She pops the lock, but Willy circles around to the last beast on her side of the car and blasts it before getting back in. Blood and brain coat the driver's side window.

"There's more coming," he says as he flops a rifle into the back seat and starts stuffing more shells into his short barreled, pump action shotgun. "Inside and outside. People who turned inside got stuck in there. I guess they don't know how to open doors. I heard 'em through the walls, scratchin' around in the apartments on either side of mine. Then there were some in the hallways."

"Let's just get out of here," Sheryl says.

"No. I'll help you find your husband. Remember what we talked about. If ya don't look for him you'll always have regret eatin' away at yer insides."

"Regret is better than the dead though," Sheryl responds. Willy just glares at her, and Sheryl simply nods her head in response.

"Which buildin' is his mistress in?" he asks.

"The first."

As Sheryl pulls out of Willy's lot she sees more zombies running toward them. It's like they kicked a hornet's nest and released a deadly fury of blood lust. She mows a few down with the car. The fleshy slaps they make as they collide with the front end of the car make her cringe as if by instinct. But she fights it, and drives over them like speed bumps. When they turn into the other lot they see more of them. The first floor windows to most of the apartments have been broken. The undead climb in and out, feeding on whatever bodies aren't moving.

Sheryl circles around the rows of cars in the lot. Her husband never knew that she knew where his mistress lived, so if he was here the car would be in plain sight. And it was.

"There," she points to the new red mid-life crisis. "That's his car. He must be inside. Believe it or not I've been checking every one of these dead bastards to see if one is him. Unless he's wandered off, he must be up in her apartment. It's 3G." She continues to circle the lot, occasionally crunching a zombie under her wheels if they get too close.

"This might get ugly," Willy says. His building wasn't as overrun as this one. There are at least 15 by the main door, and a handful at each of the side and rear entrances. "The G units are toward the back. Mine is a G. Small one bedroom. That's it right there." He points up to the third floor. The windows are draped with dark curtains. One of the windows is open just a crack. "Okay here's the plan. We do like we did before, only this time you got to come with me. Keep the car doors closed but unlocked. Rocky stays in the car. Pray that he doesn't bark again, otherwise we'll have a swarm waitin' for us when we leave. Shut the engine so the noise don't attract 'em, but leave the keys in the ignition for a fast getaway. Ain't no one stupid enough to come 'round here now but us, so don't worry nuthin' about someone stealing it. When we get inside, you close the door behind us. When we get into the stairwell, you close the door behind us. In fact, we go through any doors, you close them behind us. Got it?" Sheryl nods. "My key can get us in the building, but if the apartment is locked we're gonna have to shoot our way in. That's gonna attract 'em to us. So we gotta be quick, in and out. Your gun loaded?"

She checks. "Yes."

"Full clip?"

She checks. "Yes."

"Extra ammo in your pocket?"

She checks. "Yes."

"Safety off?"

She checks. "Yes."

"If we get up there and they changed, you gonna be ready to pull the trigger if I can't for some reason?" She gives a cold nod in the affirmative. Willy studies her. *Part of her wants to shoot 'em, whether undead or alive. Her fear is only matched by her anger right now.* "Alright then. When you're ready, pull up like we did last time. But ram some more with the car so they can't move too fast with broken legs and all. And remember; if you shoot, get 'em in the head."

To Sheryl it feels like there are so many instructions. Lots of things to think about, to remember; how to load and use the gun, the keys in the car, the door closing, the head shots. It seems simple enough but she's nervous, scared. She circles the lot several more times, running down cannibal after cannibal, immobilizing them.

"Yeah that's good, that's good," Willy says, boosting her confidence. When the lot is basically motionless, they pull up to the rear entrance door and leap out of the car. Willy's key is in the apartment door quickly and they enter. Sheryl closes the door behind them, quietly. But she accidentally took the car keys with her, through routine and habit. *Shit! I was supposed to leave them in the ignition.* She curses herself for the mistake, for not following Willy's instructions.

Willy takes a sharp turn and they go through another door and into the foggy windowed stairwell. The daylight from outside illuminates the metal stairs, creating a shiny white surface. Their footsteps echo, as does the click of the door when Sheryl closes it behind them. Willy puts a finger to his lips motioning to Sheryl for silence. He listens intently to the sounds. With his shotgun in one hand, Willy reaches backward to silence the hook and strap on the rifle he has slung over his shoulder that rattles with each step.

There's a faint grumbling from above, inside the stairwell. The building has five floors, but the sound could be from any one of them. They slowly ascend the stairs, step by step, guns drawn and aiming upward to the landing ahead. They reach the landing, turn, and quietly ascend to the second floor landing. The sounds grow louder, but they continue up. Another landing, another turn, another landing. They're on the third floor. The noise sounds like it's right on top of them; a fleshy chomping sound, coming from on the stairs leading to the fourth floor. Willy peeks through the glass window on the door into the third floor hallway. The coast is clear. He slowly turns the door handle until it clicks. Then suddenly the chomping sound stops. It's dead silent in the stairwell. Willy has the door open. He motions for Sheryl to pass through into the hall but she's frozen with fear, her eyes fixed on the stairway, her gun drawn, her breath quivering, and sweat beading on her forehead despite the cold. Willy nudges her and she breaks her gaze, following him through the door. She closes it behind her as quiet as she can. They move on.

The hall is dim. Their eyes play tricks on them, and they think they see the faint glowing eyes of the undead ahead of them, at the end of the hallway. With no electricity and no windows, the only light available is behind them, creeping through the stairwell door. It flickers as shadows pass behind it, breaking the rays of light. The beast that lurks within the stairwell stirs. Willy guides them as they quietly creep to the third door on the right. The buzzer reads 3G, just below the peep hole. He turns the doorknob slowly until it clicks open. *Lucky it was unlocked.* He cautiously opens the door and they both go inside.

A gentle breeze blows through the dark apartment from an open window somewhere, but not from the living room. Light barely gets in from the heavily curtained windows there. A small pile of clothing sits at the foot of the couch, and a trail of undergarments leads back toward the bedroom. Sheryl sees her husband's shirt among them. She holds back the anger, the frustration. After all it's just what she suspected.

Willy sweeps the living room, looking behind the couch, and Sheryl peeks over the countertops to check the kitchen. They turn toward the other rooms, where light trickles in from an open door at the end of the hall. Willy creeps up to the bathroom door and puts his ear up against it. He hears nothing, so they move toward the bedroom. The cold, gentle breeze blusters down the hallway toward them. The light ahead shifts and moves. Sheryl wonders if it's them, or if it's just the bedroom curtains blowing with the wind. Willy moves forward. They step quietly on the carpeted floor. When they reach the door Willy peeks his head around to see inside. He turns back to Sheryl with a finger over the mouth area of his mask, signaling quiet.

Then, in a heartbeat, he turns into the room and swings the butt of his shotgun around, using it like a club. Sheryl follows him into the room where she hears the meaty thwack of Willy's gun crack the back of a head. A girl falls to the ground. Sheryl knows she's one of them; she can see it in her eyes. But it doesn't matter anyway, even if she's still a human. What Sheryl does is more out of hatred than survival or self defense. Without hesitation she begins to kick her over and over. In the body, in the head. The girl growls and squirms, trying to grab and claw at anything she can. Sheryl tries to remain quiet but the anger is overwhelming. She stomps on her head, furiously grunting with each blow until finally there is no movement beneath her heel. When she lifts her foot a string of bloody goo stretches up, connecting the bottom of her sneaker to the mess of brain matter under it.

Then they hear pounding from outside the room, from the bathroom. Someone or something *is* inside, and is now trying to get out. Sheryl wonders if it might be her husband, still alive inside, hiding from his mistress. But the door isn't locked; it locks from the inside and opens inward. She knows he's turned.

"We can leave him," she says to Willy. He shakes his head no. He knows she needs closure. She needs to face him head on and confront him.

"We have to be quick about it. The rest of 'em are gonna come at us," he says, motioning to the gun in his hand. Sheryl nods.

Willy fires the shotgun at waist level, pumps it to reload, and blasts off another shot before kicking the door in with his boot. The door is riddled with buckshot holes and nearly falls apart after he kicks it. Sheryl's naked husband stumbles back and falls into the tub, taking down the shower curtain, a piece of crappy wall art, and some scented potpourri jars with him. A gaping chasm in his stomach pours blood, and his dick is completely missing, as if bitten off. Sheryl steps in and points his own pistol at him. She squeezes the trigger and hears a whiz past her ear. She missed, and the bullet hit the tub, ricocheted off the tile and nearly ended her own life.

He scrambles to get up but Sheryl kicks him back into the tub. She steps closer and fires another round. This time it hits right between his yellowed, bloodshot eyes. She stands above his corpse, looking down at the blood as it pours from his head and begins to spiral down into the drain. She belts out a maniacal laugh that makes the hair on Willy's neck stand on end.

"We gotta go," he says to her calmly.

Suddenly tears begin to fill Sheryl's eyes. Thoughts of all they had been through fill her head with confusion. She stares at her dead husband, but as soon as the first tear cools her cheek in the winter breeze she balls the fist of her bad arm in anger. "Why'd you have to do it!" she yells at her dead husband. Willy steps back out of the bathroom. "Why'd you have to fuck it all up!" She growls and screams with rage as she fires shot after shot into her husband, emptying the entire magazine of bullets into his dead body.

Willy waits to speak until she calms down, and even then he's hesitant. *I've seen this kind of emotional break before, on the battlefield. Hell, even I've felt it.* "Reload," he says plainly.

Sheryl does as he says. The process takes some special positioning and leaning, since her bad arm isn't at full capacity yet. *The soreness must mean it's on the mend,* she thinks. She hears noises through the walls all around them, even above and below. The grunts and growls grow louder from outside the apartment. Just then Sheryl realizes, but it's too late: *I forgot to close the apartment door behind us. They're inside.*

Willy runs out into the living room, firing at the undead as they enter the dark apartment. Sheryl follows him, waiting for a lull in the swarm to close the apartment door. But she's grabbed from the side as one of them gets past Willy. She instinctively shoves the grotesque beast away and it topples over the couch. She pulls her gun to eye level and fires a poorly aimed shot into the darkness that grazes the zombie's shoulder, knocking it back into the entertainment center. The flat screen television shatters and falls to the floor, and the cannibal takes down the rest of the shelving that surrounds it. Sheryl fires again and hits the zombie in the neck. A stream of dark liquid sprays all over the room, coating everything with a layer of blood. The zombie keeps coming.

Suddenly Willy turns, pumps, and fires across the room at the beast, taking its head off and splattering it onto the curtains. Stray buckshot shatters the window behind. Willy kicks the door shut and spins the dead bolt into place, locking out the rest of the corpses.

The wind blows the brainy curtains around, letting light into the living room. It illuminates the dark crimson blood to a bright ruby red. Sheryl's senses are numbed with adrenaline, but after the deafening ring of gunfire fades from her ears, she can hear Rocky furiously barking in the car outside.

CHAPTER 21

"They can't patrol every inch of ground," Amy says.

"Sure they can. They can use those predator drone things. They already use them on the border, don't they? And who knows where else." Michael asks.

"We need to find food and water. Something." Amy looks around at the storefronts. "The grocery store is close, but it is probably overrun with looters and emptied by now."

"There's a mom and pop pharmacy. Not one of those chains. Let's try there." Michael points to the small store. It's locked, but the windows are already broken from previous looters. Amazed at what's left, they grab some water, medicine, lighters, batteries, a flashlight, and dry foods, shoving everything into a few plastic shopping bags from behind the counter. They even grab extra bags from beside the empty register. Amy feels around underneath the counter for something. *These kinds of places always have a weapon back here for protection.* Her fingers find a metal baseball bat. She takes it with her.

The old PATH entrance is boarded up with blue painted plywood and padlocks, but it isn't secure enough to keep anyone out if they wanted to get in. There are no guards around, not even on the rooftops where they saw some military snipers just a few blocks away. Michael begins to jab his heel at the wood near the bottom. It's weak and rotted from older water damage. The board begins to flake apart with more and more blows. Amy alternates with swings of her bat, and soon there's a hole big enough for them both to crawl through.

"Shit!" Amy shouts once she gets through. The stairway down into the old PATH station has barred gates, closed and padlocked at the bottom. Michael tries to squeeze between the two gates, but the chain between them doesn't allow enough space for him to fit through.

"The lock is rusty," he says. "Try to break it with the bat."

Amy slams the bat down over and over, smashing the lock with everything she has. The chain rattles noisily, echoing through the tiled corridor. She hits the chain, the gate itself, and the lock again. Nothing. Michael examines the links closely, looking for a weak one, or one that has more rust than the others. They're all strong. But the lock is slightly bent. Amy sees it too. She quickly pulls a few lighters from her bag. She sets one on top of the lock and cracks it with the bat, covering the lock with lighter fluid. She ignites it with a second lighter and keeps the flame hot underneath it. Michael joins her with another.

"Keep it going as long as you can," she instructs him. "Maybe something inside will get weak and pop open if we heat it up enough and hit it some more."

After several minutes of finger burning agony they pull their calloused thumbs away and begin to hit the lock again and again with the bat. The metal is bending more, but still locked in place. They go at it with the lighters again, this time emptying two in the process, leaving them with only one in their bag. The lock is glowing hot as Amy beats it again with the bat. After a few dozen swings the lock finally pops, hissing with steam as it hits a puddle on the tiled floor beside them. Michael unravels the chain from the gates and they pass through into the darkness.

Amy puts some batteries into the flashlight and they begin their walk. They make an uneasy jump down into the subway tracks against all their better judgment. Dirty, muddy, wet, and foul. Every step requires looking down. You never know what you are stepping on when you're in the subway tunnels. Once their socks soak with sludge, they decide to tie some bags around their feet so they stay dry, but soon it doesn't matter. The water is too deep. They climb out of the tracks and onto the narrow ledge on the side of the tunnel. By the time they're about halfway through the tunnel, the tracks are submerged in waist high shit water.

"The subways are all getting flooded. I read once that in just two days without power the subways will start to flood. I guess it was pretty accurate," Michael comments. "I hope the other end is clear. What if we get all the way through and it's closed up better than before?"

"Let's have some faith," she says.

They begin to walk slightly uphill in the tunnel, and the water collecting in the tracks is not nearly as deep as before. They're past the halfway point.

"Hey what's that up there?" Amy asks.

"What?"

"A light. Flickering up ahead, like a fire," she explains.

"Yeah I see it. Maybe it's a bum or something," Michael says.

As they get closer they can tell it's across the other side of the track from them. A campfire of some kind, set in a nook along the tunnel wall. Amy turns off the flashlight, cautious of what might be lingering ahead. Soon they hear the gnawing, the profuse eating. One vagrant hunches over another, tearing at his stomach with both hands, biting and ripping at the intestines between his teeth. Amy's face contorts with disgust, and Michael's jaw drops open in shock.

"If we're quiet we can get by without him knowing," Amy whispers against Michael's ear. He nods in agreement, and they begin to creep forward. But the pungent odor of the homeless mixed with death assaults their noses through the masks. They hold their breath. In the dancing campfire light, Michael sees the tube-like strings of guts being stretched, snapped, and shoved into the bum's mouth. He gasps and coughs in his mask, about to fill it with sick. The zombie lifts its bloody face from its meal and turns to face them, its eyes glowing yellow in the blaze. It walks toward them, shambling directly through the fire. Its tattered pants catch flame, and soon its entire body ignites. Michael and Amy break into a sprint past it, staying on the narrow tunnel ledge beside the tracks. The cannibal runs toward them, setting the entire tunnel aglow with fiery horror. The light lurches in all directions, and shadows shift as it chases them up the tracks. It's gaining on them, and soon it's just steps behind.

Without warning Amy turns and swings her bat at the beast, cracking its kneecap. It tumbles to the ground but still comes at them, broken leg and all. It feels no pain. It knows nothing but bloodlust. It struggles to get to its feet again, limping in the process. Amy swings again, this time making a meaty connection with its neck. Michael looks around for something to swing as a weapon, but the tracks have nothing to offer him. When he turns around he sees the homeless cannibal's head tipped sideways with its spine sticking out the skin on its neck. Yet it still stands. It still walks toward them. The flaming beast still reaches out in death for a taste of their flesh. Amy lifts the bat over her head again and slams it down tomahawk style, landing a skull shattering blow to the risen corpse's head. It falls to the ground in death, but Amy swings at its head again for good measure, casting a thin string of blood and brain into the air.

CHAPTER 22

It wasn't long after Wolf escaped that Dr. Vogel learned he was gone. He asked Betty, one of the night shift nurses, to check in on Wolf and keep him company while he toyed with Wolf's samples in the lab. Betty was thrilled. She was a fan, and single, and hot. She prettied herself up beforehand. Put on a fresh coat of makeup, tied the skirt of her uniform a bit higher, let her hair down, and grabbed the push-up bra from her locker to make her tits sit up tall. But when she saw the broken wall through the maintenance room window, she panicked. She ran to Dr. Vogel in the lab to give him the news.

Dr. Vogel tried calling the CDC but the phones were dead. The satellites were damaged by meteor debris, so the cell phones were useless too. And he knew the generators would run out of fuel soon enough, because no one was coming to check on them. *I'm on borrowed time*, he thought. *I don't have any clue as to what kind of illness I'm dealing with, but I know it can't be good. I can't even send Wolf's fluids out for further tests or get in contact with the labs.*

He was at a loss until he heard the emergency radio broadcast. *Poisonous air. There would have to be a military presence at the quarantine border. There was one in Rwanda with the Ebola scare, and another more recently in western China, when the ox flu broke out. An airborne disease is just too risky to do anything less, especially if it's on the magnitude that requires an emergency broadcast. If there's one thing I can count on, it's that the CDC will act according to protocols once they knew how the disease is transferred. Wolf is a liability if he's a carrier.*

The first thing Dr. Vogel did was drive to the police station to report the incident. But the police started questioning him about locking a man up against his will. It didn't help that the cops were all fans of Extreme Naturalist. *They don't understand,* he thought. *If the quarantine was otherwise successful, then Wolf could cause an isolated and contained epidemic to spread into a nationwide or global pandemic.* As a former CDC immunologist, Dr. Vogel felt like that was on him; it was his responsibility to keep Wolf under wraps. But he had gone about it the wrong way. When he saw the hole in the maintenance closet wall where Wolf had escaped, Dr. Vogel immediately knew he handled Wolf all wrong. *Wolf is an uncontainable man. I should have known. Locking him down against his will was the dumbest thing I could've done. I should have communicated more with him.* He blamed it on his lack of experience. The years he spent squirreled away in the CDC labs prior to practicing medicine ruined any chances of developing a good bedside manner. But he knew he had to do more. The police didn't seem to understand how serious this was. They just radioed the rest of their guys to be on the lookout for Wolf.

So Dr. Vogel decided he would drive east to the quarantine zone with the bizarre, unearthly samples. They had already multiplied on the Petrie dish, and when he looked at them under the microscope the structure was like nothing he had ever seen in a life form. They were almost crystalline. Studying them any further would require the full capabilities of the CDC; a lab with equipment far surpassing that of his bare-bones hospital. *Once I'm at the barricade, I'll try to convince one of the military personnel to give me an air lift down to the CDC, since all the airports are shut down.* He needed something faster than just driving down the traffic-snarled roadways that snaked up and down the east coast in this panic. *It's a long shot, but it's my duty to try.*

His wife Joanna wasn't too happy with the decision. She was always apprehensive about his lab work job, knowing he was constantly surrounded by deadly viruses. On top of that he often had to travel to remote and dangerous places to fabricate and administer vaccines. For 11 years they had a home front just outside of Atlanta to be close to his job at the CDC. When he told her that he wanted to switch to medicine, Joanna was ecstatic. They moved back to her home town to be closer to her parents, and the kids were growing up fast. When he explained what happened, and why he was leaving, Joanna became upset, and the kids were scared. He explained that what he had in his possession could be something vitally important. He kissed them, and told them to wear their gas masks and stay indoors if the plume shifted with the winds. So off he went, driving toward the sun as it rose in the east.

Not too much further now until I reach the Pennsylvania border. There he imagines he'll start seeing some government personnel on the roads, possibly some barricades, check points and warning signs. Despite knowing all the CDC protocols, he wasn't exactly sure how this kind of quarantine would work in the US, so heavily populated. *The roads are vital to food supply, fuel, and everything else that society depends on every day. It's not like rural western China, where the risk of spread was much less serious. Here, there's massive influx to and from regions on a daily and hourly basis, especially the northeast. It's not like the jungles of Rwanda either, where the outbreak was isolated to a remote tribe.*

The highway is jammed in the opposite direction. Everyone is heading the same way; away. But Dr. Vogel is going toward the plume. He can almost make it out; a dispersing and fading dark grey mass hovers up ahead in the distance. He hasn't seen any other cars on his side of the road for quite some time. Across the highway horns blare, lights flash, and there are accidents everywhere. Soon the cars begin to cross the median and start driving on his side of the road. He sticks to the right lane to be safe, but more and more are coming, and it's getting too dangerous. They're speeding.

Dr. Vogel has to pull over in frustration when the road becomes too crowded. He slowly creeps along the shoulder at about ten miles per hour. But he hears the dragging sound of rubber on the road, a deep, prolonged horn blare, the shattering of glass, and the crunch of steel. A massive pileup is happening. He watches it as if in slow motion. An 18-wheeler jackknifes and a dozen cars get tangled in its wake one by one as it topples onto its side. But that isn't all. Three more cars screech to a smash, then six more behind it. Soon enough the crash ensnares upwards of 25 cars behind the truck. People are trying to drive around it but there's no more road to drive on. Even the grassy area between the highway arteries is filled with cars.

Dr. Vogel hears people screaming in pain. He has a medical kit in his trunk. He grips the wheel in contemplation. *The samples. I have to get those samples to the CDC, but I can't just ignore those people out there. My real duty now, my sworn oath, is that of a doctor, not a scientist.* He stops, pops the trunk, puts on his clongated, grey, rubber WWI style chemical warfare mask, and gets out to retrieve his kit. He runs out between the parked cars sitting on the highway and makes his way over to the nearest pile of twisted metal. A man is nearly cut in half and hanging out a broken windshield. Blood trickles down from his severed abdomen, finding a convenient home within the cracks of glass as it drips down. He moans in agony, and his eyes roll back into his head. *Too far gone. I can't help the man.*

He hears coughing coming from open windows as he passes between cars. Most of the cars in the accident are just dented up, or have blow outs, but ahead there's a woman sitting on the asphalt, propped against her car door and bleeding profusely from her arm. It looks bad. Dr. Vogel kneels beside her and opens his medical kit. He soaks up blood from the wound with a towel first to see how serious it is. A deep, ragged rip exposes muscle and bone from her armpit all the way down to her elbow joint. *She must have dragged across something in the accident.*

"It's gonna be okay. You'll be alright," he says to her, but it's a lie.

"My husband…" she mumbles. "Where is he?"

Dr. Vogel looks around for him. He isn't in the car. But he sees a hole in their shattered windshield, and then a mangled body a few yards in front of the car. "We'll find him after we get this bleeding to stop," he says. But he knows he can't do it. He looks around to see if there's anyone else that needs his help.

"I'm a med student. I can help," a young man says between coughs as he approaches.

Dr. Vogel looks up at him. He can't be more than 20 years old; probably just started. "Are you infected?"

"What do you mean infected?" the kid asks.

"How long have you been coughing?" Dr. Vogel asks, but a split second later he hears some screaming from behind him. A woman shrieks in terror, running from a man.

"Hey. HEY!" Dr. Vogel yells at the man.

The man turns. His eyes, golden and bloodshot, fix first on Dr. Vogel, and then on the woman with the cut arm. He runs at them, wild and rabid. Dr. Vogel and the medical student back away. Suddenly the wild man is upon the woman, biting and gnawing at the cut on her arm like it's a turkey leg at a renaissance fair. Blood smears across his face as he buries it into her. She can't even scream in pain. She's lost too much blood already. In seconds, it seems, the arm is shed of its meat. The ravenous man then starts to rip open her stomach.

"What the hell is going on?" Dr. Vogel turns and asks the kid. But he is on the ground, twitching and convulsing. A white foam trickles from his mouth. Dr. Vogel attempts to stabilize him, straightening out his body and preventing his head from bashing against the asphalt. But a few moments later the kid stops his fit. He lies motionless. Dr. Vogel checks his pulse. *He's dead.* Panicked and distraught, Dr. Vogel stands up, wiping the sweat that began to build on his brow above the mask. He hears a groan and a grunt. He looks down as the kid sits up in death. The kid's eyes are the color of the urine that begins to soak his pants. Dr. Vogel stumbles backward in shock. The hood of a nearby car breaks his fall and he slides off the front end to the ground, all the while his eyes fixed upon the living dead standing before him. *The creature eating the injured woman had the same look in its eyes. This debris, this disease, is killing people, but making people come back from the dead afterwards.*

Dr. Vogel runs with all his energy back toward his car. The kid begins to chase him, gaining on Dr. Vogel, two strides to one. The beast tackles Dr. Vogel to the ground and both tumble to a stop. There's more screaming coming from within the cars. Dr. Vogel can see the bloodbath spraying across the windshields, both inside and out of the frozen traffic. One boy gets out of a car when his mother tries to grab him, running between Dr. Vogel and the deranged medical student. The student turns his attention to the boy instead and chases him down, sinking his teeth into the boy's face. Dr. Vogel watches with shock and disgust as the medical student feasts upon the child. But a moment later the boy begins to twitch and convulse just as the student had earlier. The student stands up and stops his chomping, looking around for someone else to eat. The cannibal turns and sees Dr. Vogel again, and begins to run toward him.

Dr. Vogel makes it to his car and gets back inside, locking the door behind him. He turns the ignition just as the zombie medical student rams his head into the car window, giving it a healthy crack from bottom to top without shattering it. He growls like an animal, scratching at the window and trying to get in. Dr. Vogel cranes his neck to see what has become of the boy whose face was just devoured. He's back on his feet, and the same crazed look fills his remaining eye. The other is still clenched between the teeth of the medical student as he rams his face into Dr. Vogel's driver's side window.

Dr. Vogel slams his foot on the gas and veers onto the grass along the edge of the woods. His car spits up dirt and gravel. He leans left as hard as he can, as if his weight might keep his car from rolling on the steep decline beside the road. A few tense minutes later and he's beyond most of the wreckage. He gets back onto the highway, but the road ahead is still a minefield of oncoming traffic. There's even more mayhem in his rearview mirror. Men, women, and children attack each other, eat each other. The dead rise to feast on the living. But he keeps his eyes focused on the dangerous road as cars continue to speed by him in the other direction. His heart pounds out of his chest.

I have to get these samples to the CDC. Maybe we can find a cure. Wolf. Wolf didn't die. Maybe the samples are more valuable than I imagine! Wolf could be immune! He shakes his head, arguing with himself. *No. He might've turned into one of those monsters too. And to hell with the quarantine. They've broken through and I've got to let someone know! I've got to tell them at the barricade!*

He lays on his horn and tries to weave around the crazed drivers, but there are too many now to keep his speed up. He slows and tries to pull over to the side of the road again, but no one gives him any space. He's forced to come to a stop in the center lane as cars whiz by all around him. He waits for his opening, hoping he can jump out between traffic. Then he sees a truck coming right for him in the center lane. *It's now or never.* He floors the gas and veers right to avoid the truck, but the right lane isn't empty. He closes his eyes as he crosses over.

He hears the smash before he feels anything; a loud crunch of thin metal and the shattering of windows. Then he feels the air bag and the tight tugging of his seat belt. *This isn't too bad.* The thought flashes through his mind as the car spins out, but it flees as soon as his body lurches around the inside of the car. With no control whatsoever he slams into the ceiling of the car, then the door frame, then the ceiling again. The sounds grow louder from every direction, like being in the bowels of a giant mechanical monster. He's pelted with bits of glass over and over. After what feels like an eternity the thrashing finally stops, and he finds himself smothered in a claustrophobic panic.

CHAPTER 23

Wolf didn't get very far before he had to pull off the road. The traffic was jammed up on both sides of the highway, despite being west of the quarantine. There were countless accidents, sick people wandering along the roadside, and bodies all over the place. *So much for the quarantine.* He parked the SUV along the edge of the woods, behind some brush that would keep it relatively hidden. There were so many abandoned cars on the road that he wasn't concerned about anyone messing with it anyway. But he disconnected the CB radio and took the car battery with him. He grabbed a big bag of survival gear from the back, and headed deep into the woods.

My best chance at surviving this is to set up a home front that I can defend if necessary, just until the mess blows over. Once I hear some news of progress on the CB, I can emerge back into civilization. He was far enough from the road to avoid trouble, but close enough to scavenge for supplies from abandoned vehicles if needed. He found a small stream for water, no deeper than a few inches. He spent some time finding a good, thick branched, sturdy tree for sleeping and using as a lookout. Then he began to set traps for squirrels and field mice. He hoped he'd see a deer, but he had no luck. He had a bow with him; one he made on an earlier episode of Extreme Naturalist about primitive hunter gatherer societies. But he would need to make arrows for it.

After catching a rabbit in one of his crude traps, he starts a small fire the old fashioned way with dry wood, fibrous tinder, constant friction, and patience. He skins and roasts the creature, slowly turning the spit stick that he skewered up its ass and all the way out its mouth. Soon the raw, purple, muscular flesh crisps into a savory brown meat, and he begins to pull his dinner off the bone. *Wish I had some salt.*

The day turns to dusk, and Wolf huddles by the fire to keep warm. He connects the CB radio to the car battery and rigs a makeshift antenna to his lookout tree. He tries all the channels, hoping to hear the twang of Spider's voice or the gruff of Cough Drop's, but there's nothing. Not even on the crowded traffic and emergency channels. They're all silent.

There's always tomorrow, he says to himself after he climbs his tree and straps himself into the thick branches. It's what he always said in his shows before turning in for sleep. It told viewers that no matter how bad it gets, tomorrow is always hopeful. The new day offers new chances at survival, new ways to cope. But remembering the events at the motel makes him think there's no hope. *Perhaps I'm the hope. I walked out of a crater unscathed by the poisonous air. Maybe I'm immune to the debris. But what if I'm bitten?*

Leaves rustle and twigs break under the weight of someone or something traipsing through the woods. The fire fizzles out, and a silver wisp of smoke rises up from it, tickling his nose with the fresh scent of pine sap and bark. The shuffling becomes louder as it draws near. *Maybe it's a bear, attracted to the campfire and the smell of blood on the rabbit skin that I buried.* He listens intently as the steps get closer. *No. Not a bear. Too light footed to be a bear. It sounds like a person.* Then he sees it. A bloodied walking corpse. Jawless, it is doomed for hell within hell. It's tongue dangles in the air, shriveled, grey, dry and useless. *How can it eat without the ability to bite and gnaw?* Wolf watches as it passes beneath the tree, smelling the stench of piss and shit that hangs in the air with it. He nearly vomits from the putrid stench. *It's a good thing I have a strong stomach.* As a survivalist he has to eat everything from slugs to spiders on the show, teaching viewers how to survive even when there seems to be no food available. Insects, he often says, are packed with protein. Protein is energy, and energy is life. Insects; nature's most abundant fuel.

The zombie lingers near the camp. *It smells something. The rabbit skin.* Within moments it finds the loose patch of dirt where Wolf buried it. After a few swipes at the ground the monster unearths it and immediately shoves it down into its throat. No chewing, no gnawing; it simply places the bloodied flesh into its stomach, reaching forearm-deep into what's left of its mouth. Finally it meanders off.

#

In the morning Wolf climbs down and sets up a makeshift perimeter to alert himself of the wandering dead. Nothing complicated, just a set of strings and twine tied around trees in a wide circle with unnatural objects dangling from them that would make distinct noises if rattled. An empty soda can with a rock inside, car keys, some harness hooks, etc. He tries the CB radio again. Still nothing, so he starts to comb the ground for some good sturdy branches. He gathers a bunch and begins to sharpen the tips into crude spears. He lines them up along the perimeter of his camp, near the twine trip wires. He puts one up in the tree for easy access while he sleeps, and he keeps a few near the base of the tree for when he has a campfire burning.

Next he looks for two specific types of rock. A nipper and a chipper. The nipper is for banging away pieces and shards of the chipper. The chipper, once shaped properly, can be used as a cutting blade, a hand axe, or, if made smaller, an arrowhead. He makes good progress. But these tasks take up most of his day, and the sun begins to set before he realizes he hasn't eaten. Without any traps set, he resorts to some grubs that he unearths under a moist and rotting log; a rare find in the winter months for sure. He washes them down with some cold, fresh stream water. *Maybe I'll fashion a net for fishing and some arrows for hunting. Maybe I can catch a wild turkey or a pheasant. They're slow enough, and the meat will be tasty in a stew. Their feathers will make good arrow flights as well.*

"There's always tomorrow," he says aloud with more hopeful thoughts. But just then he hears the unmistakable clatter of pebbles in a tin can. One of his alarms has been tripped. Then another, from behind; the jingle of car keys pierces the air like a knife. He placed the old soup can on the opposite end as the keys, so he's about to be surrounded. *I set up camp too close to the road.* He grabs the nearest spear leaning against his lookout tree. No time to climb, or to think about the location of his camp. He can hear their tracks closing in. He tucks the spear under his right arm and steadies it in front of himself with his left hand. He sees one of them, shuffling its way toward him through the trees against the setting sunlight beyond; a grim silhouette. He circles around to get the fading sunlight out of his eyes. But the cannibal sees Wolf and starts to charge. With another spear nearby, Wolf launches the one in his hand at the creature, burying the tip into its chest and knocking it backward to the ground. Wolf grabs the other spear and runs up to the fallen zombie. With one big thrust he splits the demon's head in two, jamming the spear down through the zombies' skull and into the ground below. He quickly rips it out and holds it back at up the ready, listening with razored ears and watching with daggered eyes for the rustling of the other creature. He waits, hoping the shifting light of the woods and the dried crunching of fallen leaves will give up the beast's location. But there's no sound. There's nothing but the quiet thumping in his chest and the shaky, whistling, foggy breaths that pass softly in and out his icy nostrils.

CHAPTER 24

With the burning body of the dead homeless zombie fading into the darkness behind them, Michael and Amy press on through the PATH tunnel. They nervously hold their flashlights as they walk, creating shaky circles of light with each rattle of their hands.

"I never thought we'd be so excited to see New Jersey," Michael quietly jokes, trying to lighten the mood. Amy smiles but doesn't allow a laugh. She's worried that more cannibals may be lurking in the shadows.

"I guess this dust not only kills you, but it makes you come back as a zombie," she says.

"Do you think it's like airborne rabies or something?" Michael wonders. "Minxie and Madison had the same look in their eyes as the bum."

"I don't know. Whatever it is, I don't want to catch it."

Up ahead their flashlights reflect off the grey wall tiles of a station platform. They climb up. Yellow caution tape has been stretched across the entrances and exits, and signs are hung that read "station closed."

"We're locked in here from this side?" Michael asks with frustration.

"No. This station has transfers to other PATH lines, so they wouldn't shut the entrances just because this one tunnel is closed. There." Amy points. "There's light up ahead."

Sunlight pours down from a stairwell that leads up to street level. They shut their flashlights and jog towards it. They've made it through.

Trash blusters all around the ghostly streets; loose papers and plastic bags circle up into miniature whirlwinds as the poisonous breeze blows through Jersey City. Unfamiliar with the area, Amy begins to walk away from the grey, lifeless New York City skyline across the river. Her plan is to head west into the setting sun. Amy's parents live in a little town in Pennsylvania. *If we can make it to their house, maybe we'll rest for a while before trying to cross the quarantine to safety.*

"We've got to find the interstate," she says. "Once we're on it I can get us to my parents' house. I just don't know how to get to it from here."

"Won't the roads be crowded with traffic?" Michael asks.

"Yeah but we'll be walking."

"Walking to Pennsylvania?" Michael asks with shock.

"It's the best option we have right now. It's not like we can rent a car, and we don't know how to steal one."

"Maybe we can find bicycles," Michael suggests sarcastically.

Just then Amy hears a gurgled growl from behind them, around the street corner. She pulls Michael into a nearby storefront vestibule and motions for him to be quiet. She peeks around to see the beast shambling across the street, wandering around in search of flesh.

"Lots of people stayed inside when the winds came, but this place is so densely populated that the streets could be swarming with infected people," she whispers. "This is not a good place to be."

"It's a good thing we got out of Manhattan then. I guess any place is better than there in terms of people per square foot," Michael replies.

"We need to get to the highway, or find a map or something," Amy urges.

Michael peeks out of the vestibule for a look. The street is clear. "Let's keep heading the way we were going. We have to see a sign eventually. I know it's close."

But as soon as they step out onto the sidewalk more infected emerge from around the corner. Panicked, Michael and Amy begin to run. The monsters see them and start to chase. Three, seven, and soon dozens. A horde of death trails them as they blindly run through the streets, looking for an open building to hide in, looking for anything that could save them. They make random turns in an attempt to lose the undead mob, but the swarm still follows them. A morbid choir of grunts and growls sings a dissonant and horrific tune that hangs in the air behind them. They strain to breathe in their masks. The restricted air and feeling of confinement tires them out faster than they expect, but they keep pushing, running for their lives. They want so badly to rip them off and breathe full, lung-filling breaths, but they can't. They run for what feels like hours. The daylight turns to dusk, and death is on their heels. The horde begins to gain on them.

"They don't get tired. They just keep coming!" Michael says between tired breaths.

They reach the outskirts of town, where old garages and warehouse buildings are seemingly left abandoned and in disrepair, but the windows and doors are all boarded up or locked to keep vagrants out. Amy runs up to an old garage and pounds her fists against the corrugated metal door, then does the same to the door of a nearby warehouse, trying to break in. But each attempt allows the swarm to draw closer.

"Help us! Somebody please help us!" Amy yells over and over, draining herself in the process.

"Look!" Michael yells, pointing ahead. "A sign for the highway!" He looks back over his shoulder at the mass of death that follows them. "We'll never make it."

Amy sees the sign ahead in the fading daylight; the icon for the interstate with an elbowed arrow pointing to the right. They can see the prize, but it's just out of reach. They're so close, but so far. *If we can't find shelter from the zombies to catch our breath, we'll be dead in moments, whether it's on the highway or not. What good is being on the highway if there are dozens of cannibals just a few strides behind?*

The zombies are a hundred feet away. Michael and Amy have already given up but they don't even know it yet.

Fifty feet. Amy continues to kick and smash on doors. Tears fill her eyes for the first time since she was a little girl.

Forty feet. Michael stands with his hands on his knees, exhausted.

Thirty feet. "Somebody! Anybody! Help us! Please God!" Amy yells it over and over.

Twenty feet. Amy drops her bloodied hands. She doesn't even raise the bat up to defend herself. What good is it? Michael holds her in his arms.

Ten feet. The beasts close in. An unrelenting hunger drives them against all other impulses.

"I love you," they both say as they embrace one last time. The grunts of the undead are so loud that they don't hear the door open behind them. They shut their eyes and hug each other tight, letting the chorus of grotesque horror fill their ears. A moment later they're pulled down to the ground and dragged backward. They hear the swift flash of a blade, a few thuds and gurgles, and then the heavy slam of a metal door. The groans of the undead become muffled and distant. They open their eyes to see Death looming over them.

CHAPTER 25

Marcus did as the old priest suggested. He washed up, changed his clothes, and rested at the empty house in town. In the morning he ate some canned food and then set out on his path. He considered stealing a car to drive back down to his stash of things, but he decided against it. *It's still stealing. Even though the owners are probably dead, and the whole world's a mess, I want to avoid the road, to avoid people, to avoid the corrupt humanity that fights one another just to survive. Steal a car and get onto the lawless road? I'd be asking for trouble.*

So he walks between roads, where he is alone with his thoughts. The trees shield much of the icy breeze, but it still chills him to the bone. The woods are quiet, peaceful. But they soon run scarce as he gets closer to the metropolitan area. Eventually Marcus needs to use the streets. He doesn't want to trespass on peoples' property, and when he's off the road, in the woods, he doesn't exactly know where he is anyway.

He stays on roads closest to the Hudson, but there are cars parked on the highways, abandoned. The road is in complete gridlock. Some cars have people inside, dead. Others were left with their doors wide open, their lights on, and their keys in the ignition. There's blood everywhere. The streets are stained with it. Scraps of corpses are scattered like road kill along the asphalt; a long bone with bits of flesh and clothing still clinging to it, a severed hand, a gnawed arm. And pigeons. There are hundreds of them. Some pick at the remains of the dead. Others are frozen in death, their heads splattered on the asphalt like they simply fell from the sky. *This is some biblical shit.*

Some of the demons still linger nearby, scavenging on the remains of the fallen. Fearless, Marcus cuts down each one that he sees as he walks along the grotesque roadway, leaving heaps of bodies in his wake. He even goes out of his way to open the doors to cars if they're stuck inside in order to rid the world of the scourge.

Mobs of the dead seem to congregate on the road. They shuffle between parked cars, they ravage corpses, and they train their glowing eyes on Marcus. He hacks away at them as they swarm. Focused, determined, he's every bit as unrelenting as they are. But soon they are too many, and Marcus has to run. He breaks into a full sprint when he sees his exit off the highway, but the beasts are closing the gap. Marcus is getting tired, and the zombies seem to come from everywhere. A pile-up of cars is stretched across the ramp. Marcus leaps up onto the car roofs, out of reach from the amassing dead. Their ragged arms reach up for him, but they are unable to follow past the car jam. He looks down upon them in disgust. Their eyes are sunken into their skulls. Blood and spittle hang from their jaws, and pieces of rotting meat cling to them, frozen to the remains of their skin and clothing. *When there's no room left in hell, the dead will walk the Earth.* Marcus turns off the dead highway, and soon gets to where he needs to be.

He enters the outer edge of town in the fleeting daylight and roams the streets looking for the building where he stashed all his stuff. At the time it was a dump, but a sturdy dump. He bought it outright with cash. A small warehouse in an old part of town that was rarely used by anyone other than bums and druggers. *They couldn't have done much damage. The place was locked up tight before I was arrested. But if someone got in, then my stuff might be gone. Most of it don't matter anyway. It's just cash, tools, and some personal shit… and the prize: my truck.*

The truck was the first real thing Marcus ever purchased. At sixteen he saved up enough cash from selling weed to buy it, and he continued to work on it over the years, adding the 350 engine, beefing up the tires and suspension, customizing the paint job. He parked it in a corner of the warehouse, covered it in a tarp, and stacked wood shipping pallets and skids all around it. *If someone got in, they wouldn't even know it was there in the rubble.*

When he found out the police had surveillance on him, he would often go out of the state to do his business, thinking that the New York cops' jurisdiction might prevent them from following him. He worried they would seize his money and his truck if they could connect it to his drug trade, so he started to hide everything in the event he was ever caught. He thought he was invincible back then. Untouchable. He was wrong. It turned out the cops teamed up with the feds, so state borders didn't matter. His world came crashing down fast, but the truck and the money were never found.

The front door is reinforced with steel and has a good dead bolt, and the garage part has a corrugated metal roll-down door with a trustworthy lock. The walls are concrete blocks. *The only thing that worries me is the roof.* There were leaks in a few spots before he was put away. But by now it might be the only way in. The warehouse keys are somewhere back in jail, along with his wallet and other small possessions that he had on him at the time of lockup. The truck keys should be inside the warehouse, right where he left them.

With his scythe slung across his back, Marcus walks around to the rear of the warehouse and leaps to grab the bottom rung on the metal ladder that leads to the roof. He climbs up, and sure enough where there was once a leak is now a gaping hole. It's large enough for him to squeeze through. Lucky for him, though, it sits just above the small lofted area inside the warehouse, so he won't have to drop 15 feet to the cold cement floor.

Everything looks just how he left it. Across the warehouse he can see the tarp still in place behind the wooden shipping skids. He climbs down from the loft and opens the top drawer of the desk in the glass-enclosed office area. His keys are still there. He spins around to the closet, opens the door, and up on the top shelf is a gym bag. He pulls it down and zips it open. *It's all still here. All my cash. My blood money.* Marcus shakes his head in despair. *I wish it wasn't. I wish some unfortunate soul stumbled across it while looking for a place to sleep and made a better life for himself. But what use is money now anyway? The world's all going to shit.*

Suddenly he hears a rattling sound coming from the garage door, and muffled screams; a woman calling out for help. *Likely being attacked by someone like Harley. Is this it? Is this my test? Does God want me to kill again, to kill another living human being?* He hears pounding on the door now, and more pleading for help. "Please God help us!" *She's pleading for God's help. I can't ignore her.* He runs to the door with his blade in his hand and flings it open.

CHAPTER 26

"What the fuck are you?" a shocked Amy blurts out.

Michael's voice shakes in fear as he looks up at Marcus. "Are we dead?"

Blood drips off of Marcus' blade. His heavy breathing through the mask makes him sound like an epic sci-fi space villain. "No, you ain't dead."

"Jesus Christ! Imagine the luck we have? Someone just happens to be in the one building we're in front of just before they got to us!" Michael exclaims as he and Amy get to their feet.

"Jesus Christ is right. But it wasn't luck. It was providence." Marcus says.

"Huh?" Michael responds.

"There's luck, and then there's fate," Marcus explains. "You were meant to find this building, and I was meant to be here to receive you."

"Is it part of fate to have a swarm of zombies around the building as well?" Michael asks with sarcasm.

"God will provide a path out when the time is right. I'm being tested," Marcus says.

Michael's eyes widen with condescending disbelief. There's even a bit of laughter behind them. He presses Marcus further upon hearing the dreaded G-word. "Tested?"

"He's testing me. Makin' sure I'm worth keeping alive," Marcus says.

Michael rolls his eyes through his mask.

"Thank you," Amy says. "You saved our lives." She glares at Michael as she says this. She's heard Michael argue over religion before, and many of Amy's friends were turned off by it, even if they weren't super religious themselves. He was often abrasive toward people of faith. He blamed them for wars, and slowing what he called progress. Marcus certainly seemed to be a believer, so she had to nip that in the bud before it even started.

"Come on in. Make yourselves at home. I was just about to light a fire to keep warm." Marcus walks back into the warehouse and begins to arrange some crumpled papers and break apart the wood from a skid.

"Make ourselves at home? This place is a fucking dump," Michael whispers to Amy.

"Shh." Amy quiets him. "Are you kidding me right now? It's better than being dead."

"I don't trust this guy. He's dressed like the Grim Reaper for God's sake."

"Well I do. And you don't believe in God or the Grim Reaper, so what do you care how he's dressed?" Amy asks.

"I don't like the idea of being trapped inside here with a religious nutter."

"Okay. Well let's see… so far he's saved our lives, opened up his… home... to us, and is making a fire to keep us warm. He doesn't seem too nuts to me."

"Yeah well you didn't grow up in New York City like I did," Michael whispers. "I inherently distrust people."

"Grab some wood and stuff. Let's at least help him make the fire," Amy suggests. "We still have a lighter, right?" Michael checks his bag and nods his head yes. "Is this your place, or are you just hiding out like us?" Amy asks Marcus.

"It's my place. I haven't been here in a while. Bought it before I went away…" Marcus catches himself. He doesn't want to bring up prison. *These two are already frightened of me; I can tell.* "I'm Marcus by the way." He extends his hand with a hidden smile behind the mask.

"Amy." She shakes it. "This is my husband Michael."

"Hey. I have a lighter if you need." Michael passes it to Marcus instead of shaking his hand, avoiding eye contact in the process. Easy to do with masks on. Marcus thanks him and flicks the lighter upon the papers beneath the wood. Soon the old warehouse glows with golden warmth, and smoke billows out the hole in the roof, wafting out into the poisonous air above.

They can hear the beasts moaning and clawing at the door and garage gate outside, no doubt still hungry for flesh, still thirsty with the scent of Amy's bloodied knuckles in their dead noses.

"Can they get in?" Michael asks.

"Not unless they learn to jump ten feet, climb a ladder, and find the hole in the roof."

"Or pick a lock," Amy says with a grin behind her mask.

Marcus chuckles. His deep voice booms and echoes off the cavernous walls. "It's all concrete block. We should be good."

Michael peeks into his and Amy's bags, looking over what they have.

"Got anything to eat or drink in there?" Marcus asks. "I've been walking a long way."

"Not all that much…" Michael starts, but Amy rips one of the bags away from his fingers and flings it over to Marcus.

"Take whatever you want," she says.

Marcus rifles through the bag, seeing things he hasn't seen in ages. "Swinkles? Oh man. I haven't had these in years. You mind?"

"Knock yourself out," Amy says. "But is it safe to take the mask off?"

"I'm gonna go in my truck," he says.

Michael perks his head up. "Truck?"

"Back there, under the tarp. I'm gonna head out west when it's clear if y'all want a lift," he offers.

"West. That's where we're going. To my parents' house, and then hopefully past the quarantine," Amy says.

"What quarantine?" Marcus asks.

"They blockaded everyone east of Ohio and North of DC. You didn't hear?" Michael asks. "We're lucky we got out of the city. They blocked that off too."

"No. Haven't really heard anything too reliable." Marcus doesn't care to explain why his knowledge is limited. Marcus lets the silence linger for a moment. "I'm gonna go eat this in the truck and take a nap. Again, make yourselves at home." He walks back into the area behind the skids and removes the tarp from the truck. Underneath is a black pickup truck with a custom paint job of glowing green skulls and orange flames. It's the kind of truck a mid-west teenager would kill for; a monster truck, with four foot high wheels and a blower poking out the top of the hood. It may as well be the legendary Bone Yard Crusher. Marcus has to leap up just to reach the step bar.

Michael and Amy huddle by the fire.

"Were you seriously going to say no to him and not give him something to eat?" Amy asks angrily.

"We only have a little bit. We have to make it last until we reach your parent's house," he explains.

"Yeah but he saved our lives." She huffs at him. It's been a long time since she spoke up to him like this. They used to argue a lot back when they first got together, but things cooled out when Amy stopped giving a shit about the multitude of quirks that bothered her. She began to choose her battles. But now, given all that's happened, she's letting them fly.

"Come on. Let's eat something," Michael says. "Why'd you grab Swinkles anyway? We don't eat that stuff."

"I don't have an appetite," she replies, staring off into the flames.

"You have to. We'll need the energy tomorrow if we're planning to walk out of here."

"You don't want to get a ride with him?" Amy asks with incredulity.

"I told you I don't trust him."

"Unbelievable," Amy says under her breath. "Well, I'm going with him. You were the one complaining about having to walk to Pennsylvania before. Now we have a ride and you want to walk?"

"Okay. I'm going to go eat in the office thing," Michael says with an attitude. "You can sit out here and cool off by the fire if you don't want to eat."

Michael walks back into the enclosed office area, closes the door behind him, and plops down on the swivel chair behind the desk. He starts popping open drawers and poking around a bit before unwrapping a granola bar. He slides chunks of it under his mask quickly and chomps away. He scopes out the room as he chews, noticing the closet on the wall. He opens the door and sees Marcus' gym bag. He pulls it down and unzips it, and his eyes widen with shock.

Holy fuck! The bills are haphazardly stacked, bundled with decaying, dry-rotted rubber bands. Twenties, fifties and hundreds. Michael grabs a few stacks and stuffs them into his coat. He shoves some into his semi-transparent plastic shopping bag too, but is careful to hide them among the other items inside. He finishes his granola bar and tiptoes back over to Amy, who is dozing by the fire.

"Amy. You gotta see this," he whispers loudly to wake her.

"What?" She's annoyed.

"You wanna talk about trusting this guy? He has a gym bag full of cash back there."

After a moment of thought she answers. "So what? That's his business. I don't want to know and I don't care." Admittedly, she *does* think it's a bit odd to have a stash like that, but part of her just wants to defy Michael at this point.

"There's gotta be like at least a few hundred thousand, maybe millions, I don't know. It's suspicious. I told you I don't trust him."

"Yeah well there's worse things to worry about right now than criminals," she says, motioning to the outside. The moans are still audible; it's like they're waiting.

"Maybe we should just grab some and get out of here," he suggests.

"What do we need money for? We have plenty."

"Not cash. Ours is in banks. We can't even get at our money right now."

"My money," she corrects him. She never thought of their money as hers, even though she makes 90% of it. But now Michael is getting on her nerves. "What good is money now anyway? Supplies are what we need. Shelter, which we have. Food, water. I can care less about a stack of money."

"This is all going to get better, just like everything else. The Department of Health and Human Services will work with the

CDC to help find and distribute a cure, and the government will make everything right again. We can come out of it with enough money to pay off all our debts."

Amy laughs at the idea. "We already have enough money to pay down our debts. Trust me. I am the finance person here."

"Yeah well I know how to deal with these kinds of shady people. I know he's planning something and I don't want to wait around until it's too late. You have to make the first move. That's how you do it. You fuck him before he fucks you," Michael says.

"Yeah? You want me to help you? To fuck him for money?" Amy asks with heavy sarcasm. "Let me go back to sleep." She ignores him for the rest of the night.

#

In the morning, Michael and Amy wake to the sound of Marcus trying to get the truck engine to start. He quietly moved the skids out of the way earlier, popped his baby in neutral, and rolled the beast out from behind the barricade. It cranks, but it won't turn over. It hasn't been started in a while. Marcus unhooks the stereo equipment from a separate car battery and swaps that one out for the one under the hood. After some good old fashioned tinkering, and of course some cursing and hollering, it finally roars back to life. A puff of black smoke shoots out the side pipes and the whole warehouse starts to vibrate with testosterone. Marcus revs the engine and the thing screams so loud Michael thinks it might shatter the concrete walls. The radio even works off what little power remains in the swapped battery. For a few moments, the chugging guitar riffs of a familiar heavy metal band echo off the walls of the warehouse before Marcus cuts the engine.

"Wooooooo!" Marcus cheers. "Still purrs like a tiger baby."

Amy has a grin from ear to ear under her mask, and Michael is in complete shock at the spectacle before him. It truly is an amazing machine.

A small fire dwindles on the cement floor. Marcus tended to it throughout the night. He napped comfortably but hasn't been much of a heavy sleeper since he went away to prison. After recovering from his startling awakening, Michael notices that there are stacks of money in the fire. The empty gym bag sits deflated a few feet away. It's all gone.

"Why would you do that?" he asks Marcus, pointing to the money in the fire.

"What, the money? Ahh man you don't want that. That's blood money. Besides, my secrecy is more valuable than a bunch of useless green paper right now. Those wood skids? That tarp? I ain't burning that stuff. If I ever need to hide my truck again, I'm coming back here. No one is the wiser when it's hidden back there." Marcus points. "Besides I can use the gym bag to carry things with real value. Food, water, weapons to protect myself from the demons…"

"Demons?" Michael presses him. "They're people. They're just sick."

"Sick people don't come back from the dead to eat other people. Zombies do that. Demons. Devil's spawn." Marcus curls a sinister grin on his face. Michael can see it in his eyes.

"So you're on a mission from God to kill demons and save people?" Michael asks sarcastically. Part of him wonders if Marcus is high or something. His outlandish giddiness discomforts Michael.

"Maybe so," Marcus answers, overwhelmed with excitement that his truck is in working order, and unwilling to argue religion at the moment. He changes the subject. "Hey we can get out of here. The demons have been exorcized," he says with a snarky twang to his voice.

"They're gone?" Amy asks with hope in her voice. She trots over to the door and presses her ear against it.

"None within eye shot. I was up on the roof a little while ago. They musta been distracted away," he answers. "You see? God provided the pathway out."

"Well what are we waiting for?" Amy asks.

"Your man," Marcus says, pointing at Michael.

"We can be at my parents' in a matter of hours," Amy adds.

Michael reluctantly agrees. "Fine. Let's go."

"Alright hop in!" Marcus says as he swipes the gym bag off the floor. He tosses it in the truck bed with some tools and supplies. He secures everything down with bungee cords. He clips the lock on the outside of the garage with a pair of bolt cutters, yanks open the roll gate, and gets into the driver's seat. The engine growls to a start, and heavy metal once again fills the air.

As soon as they approach the highway entrance ramp Michael begins to scoff at Marcus. Cars are parked, abandoned and jammed in nearly every square inch of asphalt leading onto the interstate. Dead bodies cover what little pavement can be seen, rotted, mangled and torn from limb to limb. Looking out from the truck's high vantage point, there's gridlock frozen in both directions as far as the eye can see.

"This is some path that the Lord doth provide." Michael remarks.

"Shh," Amy elbows him. She wishes she could turn her face to look out the window in anger, but she's stuck sitting bitch between Michael and Marcus, with her knees aimed toward Michael so Marcus has enough room to shift.

Marcus ignores Michael's intolerance. Instead he eyeballs the sleek bodied American sports car that's spun around in front of him, and the pimped-out, low-riding rice rocket just beside it. Both cars are extremely low to the ground, and sitting at the rear of the traffic snarl. Marcus backs the truck up a few car lengths and revs the engine with a sinister grin, peering at Michael.

"What are you doing?" Michael asks.

"Put your seatbelts on. It's gonna be a bumpy ride." Marcus laughs as he cranks up the metal.

He drops the truck into gear and it screams and thunders its way to the two cars at the back of the traffic jam. Its four foot tires hit the front end of the sports car like a ramp, and it barrels up the hood of the sports car with ease, using the door panels of the import beside it to guide it upward and keep from toppling over. They soar through the air for a moment and then slam down onto the roofs of the cars ahead of them. They crunch underneath the beastly truck as Marcus moves forward on top of all the traffic.

There is constant up and down – trunk, roof, hood, trunk, roof, hood… The thuds, the shattering of glass, the screeching of metal, and the blaring riffs of the greatest heavy metal band that ever lived combine into a hellish harmony. It all begins to give Michael motion sickness. His stomach turns with each gut wrenching lurch the truck makes. He closes his eyes tight and clenches the muscles in his abdomen to keep from vomiting in his mask.

Amy sees the queasy look on Michael's face and allows a smile. *This ought to keep him quiet and respectful for a while.* He would get a sour stomach just from certain subway lines, not to mention boats and airplanes. "This path works for me!" she hollers over the crunching cars and blasting music, holding onto the dash like it's a handlebar on a rollercoaster.

CHAPTER 27

Puke was everywhere. It was on his favorite comics and porn mags; it gunked up his game controllers and his keyboard, and it was all over his clothes. Brandon woke up to the smell of it, mixing with the scent of the warm skunked beer bottles that sat beside his head on the cold metal floor. It was almost enough to make him hurl again. His head pounded and throbbed with a pain that felt like his brain was split in two and dangling out a gaping hole in his head. For the first time in his life he was hung over.

The barfing was uncontrollable at times. The whole bunker was spinning and he was a terrible shot in his video games. He didn't remember to shut anything off when he fell asleep either. The bulbs were baking his skin, making him sweat profusely even in the winter underground. The agony seemed to last for days. He gobbled down some aspirin and burned through several bottles of water, both on himself and in cleaning up the mess he made. He was angry at how much supply he wasted on the episode. *I'll never drink again!*

The power cuts out. Low on gas, Brandon knows it's time to venture out into the zombie apocalypse to refuel. *It's a five mile hike in each direction through a bloody battlefield of cannibals. But I'm prepared for it. Shit, I'm excited for it!* With the hangover fading into memory, and the loose bowels finally working their way out of his system, he packs up his fastest, lightest and best weapons for the mission. The rifle, which can sling over his shoulder; a small hatchet, whose handle slips nicely through the wide belt loop on his jeans; and a gas can in each hand. *The way back will be difficult.* His arms are weak, and carrying a full gas container in each hand means he'll have to stop to rest often, and stay extra alert, since his weapons won't be at the ready. *A few more gallons of fuel isn't much, but I can make several trips if needed, and start a stockpile in here or the shed.*

With his mask on and his courage up, Brandon emerges from his bomb shelter. He quickly closes the hatch and drags some loose branches and tree debris over it to hide the entrance. It's quiet, and the bloated bodies of his parents still rot away in death where they fell. He pays them no mind, or at least he tries. *Those aren't your parents. Don't look. Don't even glance.* But he has to. Crows are plucking away at their eyes and stomachs, feasting on them like vultures. Their skin has turned an eerie shade of marbled greenish white, freezing them in decomposition. As Brandon's stomach begins to flutter with sorrow, and tears begin to well up in his eyes, he turns the other way. *Fuck it. I'm on my own. I don't need anyone.*

Brandon realizes quickly that this won't be like his zombie games, where the characters always start out in some heavily populated urban area, with things exploding and swarms of undead looming around each tight street corner. In a way it depresses him. He looks forward to the thrill of watching brains explode out the back of zombies' heads. But he's in the rural and suburban sprawl of Pennsylvania. If he's lucky he'll see one or two Zs on his gas trip, unless, of course, he goes to the mall. In the movies the mall is always jammed with zombies. But the closest mall is 15 miles at least, and probably wasn't even busy when the outbreak started on Christmas. Brandon will have to seek them out in the neighborhoods if he wants to see any action. *I'll have to hunt them, but only on the way to the station. Not on the way back when I'm loaded with gas.*

As he walks through his neighborhood he can't help but think back to video footage he saw of tornado damage. Some homes are perfectly okay, while others are completely shredded to shit. The scenery looks like all of his post apocalyptic games. All that's missing are the monsters. He keeps a sharp eye out for them.

At one house he sees some dead folks roaming around in a sunroom through the windows. The home is completely intact.

148

There's no damage like at his house and others. But the front door is wide open, leading into the sunroom porch. He starts throwing rocks toward it to draw the zombies' attention, hoping they'll shamble out into the daylight where he can watch their brains exit the back of their heads. *It's no fun if you can't see it.* A few throws later a man emerges from the open doorway. Brandon, sprawled out on the asphalt, looks like a corpse himself, only he has his eye trained down the barrel of his father's rifle, propping it up on an empty gas can to keep it steady. He squeezes the trigger and misses. The bullet whizzes past the man and shatters the windows behind. An undead woman comes out of the glassed porch then. They both wander around, confused, but after Brandon's second missed shot, they begin to follow the sound of the gun. They're walking right toward him. Brandon's third shot hits the man's knee and drops him to the driveway pavement. The fourth is a headshot, but since he's already on the ground, there's no flying brain. *One down.*

The woman begins to walk faster toward Brandon, realizing he is food. He fires and hits her shoulder, knocking her backward. She regains her footing and keeps coming. Another shot hits the neck. Blood gushes everywhere, and a string of crimson whips into the air. Brandon quickly adjusts and lets the final shot fly. *Right between the eyes.* Her brains spray out the back of her head so far that some of it lands on the doorstep, sailing all the way up from the bottom of the driveway.

"Yes!" he cheers. Brandon laughs hysterically in victory, but he knows it was a poor showing. *Seven rounds for two zombies. My aim needs to improve.* Real life is not like the video games. The gun has kickback instead of just vibrating like a game controller. His shoulder hurts because of it. He can't zoom in when using his gun sights either, like in the video games, so his glasses are necessary. And reloading doesn't happen with the push of a button. It takes time, concentration, two hands. *I need to work on my speed.*

Brandon heads up to the front door and enters the sunroom. His missed shots left shards of broken window all over the floor. The door leading to the inside of the house is closed and locked. But a window beside it is shattered as well, and now left wide open. His bullets went clear through the sunroom and into the actual home. *The two zombies must've wandered in, trying to get into the house.* He hears commotion inside the house. He realizes there may be people alive inside.

"Hello?" he shouts. He hears nothing in response. "Anyone in there?" He hears words he can't understand. *Another language. Not the grunts of a corpse.* He reaches into the window opening and unlocks the front door. He steps inside. He hears thuds and footsteps coming from upstairs. Then the sound of a woman coughing, and more unknown words coming from a man. He can't understand what they mean, but he sure knows they sound frantic. "Hello?" he says again as he approaches the bottom stair.

Suddenly a man with a gas mask turns the corner from the top of the stairs and charges at him with a handgun raised in the air. Brandon turns and runs for the door as the bullets fly past his head. He runs back down the driveway, grabs his gas cans and keeps on going. He hears more gunshots from behind. He runs in a zigzag pattern to avoid getting hit. He turns and fires back wildly, without even really aiming. He fumbles with his gas cans and rifle, but he keeps running. Then he hears screaming. *I hit him?* He turns to see the man keeled over on the ground in pain.

"Oh shit. Oh shit," he says, realizing he just killed a real person. *But was it? It's a man behind a mask. An enemy who shot at me first. And there was coughing too. They were infected. Did my misfired shots break the windows and cause the poisonous air to get in? Did I cause the coughing? Did they think I was breaking in to attack them? Maybe they didn't understand my words, like I couldn't understand theirs. It was all a misunderstanding. It was an accident.* In a video game he would lose points, or lose the information and items that the uninfected would provide for him. This is the real world though. There are consequences here, like punishment and jail time. He runs, and runs, and runs.

But would there be jail? Will I get caught? He looks around. *I'm in a ghost town. There are no rules. There is no law, only survival.* The wave of guilt suddenly washes away as fast as it came upon him. *I can do whatever the fuck I want! The world has bigger problems now*. He slows to a jog, then a trot, then a walk. He shakes the incident from his mind. *Back to the task at hand. Back to getting gas for the generator.*

CHAPTER 28

Willy draws the curtains back from the window, bathing the rest of the grotesque room with light. Sheryl peeks out the window. Two cannibals are at the car, scratching at the windows to get at Rocky. His barking is incessant.

"There's more coming," Willy says, looking off across the parking lot. Several zombies slowly make their way toward the car from all around. "And you need target practice. Since we're stuck here, you may as well start shooting."

Sheryl takes aim at one near the car. Even with a pistol it's difficult to shoot with a bad arm, but setting up like this is easier than before, when the zombies were streaming into the room to attack them.

"Not them ones. We got to get those close range. Don't want to shoot out our car windows," Willy instructs.

Sheryl turns toward the others. All is silent but Rocky's barking and the scratching at the apartment door from the evil that lingers in the hall. Sheryl tunes it all out, like she used to tune out the boys' fighting while she was trying to pay bills or cook dinner. Her heart sinks a little at the thought, but she exhales an even breath and squeezes the trigger. She blinks at the noise and kick of the gun, but she hits her target. The shot to the zombie's upper back spins it around. Now she can see its bloodied, ravenous face. She squeezes off another shot and hits it in the eye.

"Good shooting," Willy congratulates her. He takes the rifle down from across his back and puts the shotgun down. Sheryl watches him, confused. "Shotgun is like a spray of small pellets.

Not too good over long distances." Sheryl gives him an understanding nod. "Rifle is for hunting at a distance."

Willy uses the butt of the gun to knock out the remaining shards of glass left clinging to the window. He takes a knee and balances the rifle on the sill. He aims and fires. A distant beast drops in death. Willy spins and fires another shot. Another bull's eye. Then a third.

"You're like a sniper," Sheryl compliments.

"Used to be a sharp shooter. Was in the military. Marines." He pulls his sleeve back to show his tattoo as proof. "Keep practicing. You needa become one yourself."

Sheryl takes aim again and fires, this time at a more distant creature, hitting its kneecap and dropping it to the ground. Willy notices her face contorted in frustration.

"It's alright. If he can't stand he can't walk, and if he can't walk he can't get to us. Right now that's just as good as a headshot. Just need to clear a path to the car," Willy says between shots, reassuring Sheryl with confidence-boosting compliments.

They each reload and continue their target practice. When the zombies are too far for Sheryl to hit with her pistol, Willy shows her how to use the rifle. After a while, when the lot is somewhat clear except for the two zombies by the car, he instructs her to look for some rope. But there is none. Willy joins her in the search. He quickly decides to tie a bunch of sheets together as a substitute. He looks around the floor near the windows for something sturdy, something anchored down. He starts to pull the covers off the baseboard heaters, exposing the pipes that carry the hot water through the apartment. He threads the sheets around them and ties a tight knot, giving it a few tugs to test for strength.

"That'll do," he says. "Check around for supplies and such. Can never have too much."

Together they pack some dried goods and bottled fluids into a suitcase they find in one of the closets. Sheryl raids the medicine cabinet for some basics as well. There she notices the herpes medication prescribed to the bitch that stole her husband. *Good thing I stopped fucking him after he started fucking you*, she thinks to herself as she closes the mirrored door. The sight of her own masked face staring back startles her, and she gasps. At times she forgets she's even wearing it.

Willy lowers the suitcase down with the opposite end of the tied sheets, and he begins to climb down. The two remaining zombies by the car suddenly switch their attention from Rocky to him.

"Lookout!" Sheryl warns him.

"I'll hang here. When they get away from the car you shoot 'em," Willy says.

"What if I miss?"

"Don't," Willy says after a pause. He looks all around as he dangles. The shotgun and rifle slung across his back begin to slide and spin on their strap. He finds footing on the outer windowsill of the second floor apartment.

Sheryl fires and kills the first one, but the second one is nearly at the building already. The cannibal positions itself directly beneath Willy, and Sheryl can't get a line of sight on it. Willy is in the way. She runs over from the living room to the bedroom window and opens it wider. There's a better angle from there. She can see the zombie grabbing for Willy's shoe. She takes aim and fires; a clean headshot.

Willy climbs down the rest of the way and carries the suitcase of supplies to the car as Sheryl starts to make her way down the sheets. Her good hand is shaking with nerves, and her injured arm is useless, so she places her feet on the second floor windowsill where Willy did, breathing heavily and trying to steady her panic. Willy is beneath her now, keeping one eye on her and the other on the parking lot. A few of the wounded zombies with broken, twisted limbs that Sheryl mowed over with the car drag themselves over. Willy can see the hunger in their faces.

"Keep comin' now. You can do it. This is the easy part," Willy coaches her.

Just then there is a slam on the window in front of Sheryl. The entire pane of glass rattles and shakes. She screams at the sight of the zombie behind it, scratching and clawing at the window in a feverish attempt to eat her. The fog of its putrid breath on the thin glass obscures the horrific vision. Sheryl's face is only inches from the beast but the sudden start makes her lose her footing. She slips off the sill. Her grip was already loosened on the sheets while she was catching her breath. She grabs for the makeshift rope but it's too late. She falls backwards, away from the building, with her eyes fixed on the demon above. But an instant later she feels the bony, weathered, yet muscled embrace of Willy's arms as she falls into them. He caught her like a child.

He slowly places her feet down on the pavement. She doesn't have to thank him. He already knows she's grateful. Sheryl hands Willy the keys and they hurry to the car. Rocky greets them with excited whimpers and slimy licks. They drive off.

#

After burning west at top speed for a while, an array of lights start flashing on the police cruiser's dashboard. The engine is hot, and fuel is low. The signs on the highway say the next gas station is 11 miles away. The car sounds like death, but they press on, their eyes glued to the odometer. Willy is sure they can make it. A few mile markers later and they see the pull off up ahead.

"Think we can even fill up there? Everything is electronic. How do you get gas out when there's no power?" Sheryl asks. Willy isn't concerned.

CHAPTER 29

The road leading to the highway is filled with parked cars. Brandon tries them all but the doors are locked. One or two even have the unholy creatures trapped inside. The unfortunate souls turned into zombies while driving. Brandon can hear them groaning as he passes. He's half tempted to blow one of them away and take the car for a joyride. *Why not? I just killed a man and got away with it. There's no law, or at least in time there won't be any.* But he's half afraid, too. He never drove anything except the cars in video games where you get points for crashing, causing multi-vehicle pile-ups, and mowing down pedestrians. *It can't be that hard.* But he doesn't try.

He cautiously passes shopping centers and chain restaurants. Most were closed when the impact hit, so no one was out shopping. But afterward people must have gone out for supplies, thinking they could hunker down and survive this mess. There are stray zombies up ahead at some of the stores. He sees them. He walks quietly and slowly, crouching behind cars and hedges along the side of the road. His eyes scan the scene slowly until they come upon a naked woman. Then his gaze is locked. *Damn, she's hot! I'd hit that.* The glazed yellow look in her eyes is almost lost behind the long ratty blonde hair that dangles down in front of her face and falls upon her tits. *I don't care if she's a zombie. I'd still hit that. But what about the smell?* Never mind the blood and gore that smatters her skin. Brandon can see streams of piss running down her thighs and shit stains at the bottom of her ass. His face contorts in disgust. *I wonder if I'd catch the zombie disease from banging her. If not, I'd definitely hit that. Just have to tie her down, cover her mouth, and clean her up a little.*

He forces himself to turn his attention back to the road, despite the raging boner in his pants. He eyes Dickie's Outdoor Sports Shop and is almost tempted to go in for some supplies, but he worries about zombies lurking in the shadows within. *No lights inside a large building with no windows and lots of clothing racks and aisles to hide zombies. There may not be much left on the shelves, but whatever is there would be mine for the taking.* He had no problems with looting in an emergency like this. But he passes on the idea. *Too risky.*

Soon he reaches the highway, and the gas station is in sight. *Less than a mile to go.* But ahead in the distance he can hear a lone car approaching. Then he sees it; a police officer. He ducks back and slinks off into the woods along the road, peeking out behind some trees to see what's happening. *The last thing I need is a cop asking me why I have a gun.* Wild thoughts of rationality overtake him. *Maybe they already know about the man I shot. Maybe he or the coughing woman upstairs struggled to a phone and somehow called the police. Maybe they gave a description and they're looking for me. Maybe the world isn't ending. Maybe there's still law and order, and this is all trumped up in my mind. Maybe I'm going crazy.*

He stays clear of the dry leaves as he quietly continues to move closer and closer. The car pulls into the gas station and parks beside one of the pumps. Smoke rises up from the hood. Brandon can hear the bell ding twice as the front and back wheels cross over the strips of tubing that lay across the pump docks. The engine shuts. Brandon moves closer and closer, but no one comes out of the car. He flattens himself on the ground and props his gun up on a gas can. He looks down the barrel at the scene before him. Nothing moves. *Is the cop waiting for full service? Waiting for some young, greasy haired foreigner to pump his gas?*

Then suddenly a ruckus comes from within the convenience store, near the cash registers. Brandon hears glass breaking and things falling. *Maybe someone is looting. Did the cop hear it? Maybe his radio is on and he was talking, maybe he was talking to his partner, or maybe the sound wasn't loud enough to hear from inside the car*. But the sound of commotion cuts short as quickly as it began. Then the car engine starts again, and it rolls up to the next pump. The bell chimes again as they pass another set of rubber strips on the pavement. Immediately, the noises begin again from inside the store.

Then Brandon sees it. It presses its face against the windows on the inside of the store, between banners for cigarettes and motor oil. Blood smears across the glass as it moves toward the sound of the running engine. The driver's side door opens and an older man steps out with a shotgun and a rag tied across his face. *A bandit? No. What am I thinking? This isn't the old west. It's a makeshift breathing mask.* The man wearing it walks right up to the store window, lifts his gun to his shoulder, and blasts the risen creature in the face. The glass shatters and falls all around the dead zombie, piercing the air with mayhem. *That's no cop. That's a survivor. It's already become lawless. The guy stole a police car. The end is here!*

A moment later a woman steps out of the passenger side door wearing a cheap hospital-issued gas mask. Her arm is in a sling, but she has a slim, sexy body. *Nice... A MILF.* She walks toward the store, poking her head through the broken window to check for more cannibals. An instant later one of them comes running from the service garage in a mechanic's jumpsuit. Brandon instinctively fires a round at it. *Bull's eye.* The headshot causes a fine crimson mist to fill the air around the beast before it flops to the ground. The man and woman stop in their tracks. Their heads turn to follow the sound of Brandon's rifle. He stands up and walks over to greet them. *I'm getting good at this whole sniper thing.*

CHAPTER 30

"Thank you," Sheryl says to Brandon as he struts over to them.

"No problem," he says. "I came looking for gas."

"Us too," says Willy, who kneels beside a small manhole cover on the ground. He pries at it with his fingers but it's stuck. He wanders off in search of a crowbar.

"The pumps aren't working, so we're going to have to fish it out of the tanks underground," Sheryl explains. "I'm Sheryl and that's Willy. What's your name? And aren't you a little young to have a gun and be out here on your own?"

"Brandon Jessup. Lost my parents, so I'm on my own whether I like it or not." He was starting to like it. No rules, no bed time, no homework. Only jerking off, playing video games, and killing zombies.

Sheryl hears his name and immediately puts the initials together in her head. "Do friends call you BJ? I have... had a son named BJ. Bobby Junior. He was ten."

"You should be glad he didn't make it to high school then," Brandon coldly responds. "Only the bullies call me BJ. Blow job, cock sucker, pasty fag, and whatever else."

Willy returns with a crowbar and some other items that he plans to take with him in the car. He opens the trunk and tosses them inside. Rocky greets him with a paw to the back windshield.

"You got a dog?" Brandon lights up with a smile behind his mask, showing a flicker of his dwindling untainted, innocent youth. There isn't much left remaining.

Sheryl instantly responds like a mom would. "Come on let's take him out. He can use a little exercise. He's been stuck in the car all day. His name's Rocky."

"Leave your gas cans, son. I'll fill 'em for ya," Willy offers.

"How come he didn't turn?" Brandon asks as he pets Rocky.

"I'm not sure. I haven't seen any animals turn yet. Maybe they're immune," Sheryl answers. "Just saw some birds drop from the sky after eating a body, that's all."

Sheryl and Brandon take turns tossing a stick back and forth between them, playing fetch with Rocky. Willy pries up the manhole cover to reveal a five inch wide pipe leading down into the storage tank beneath the gas pumps. He rigs up an empty plastic bottle to a length of string and lowers it into the abyss. Once he feels it fill up with liquid, he slowly pulls it back up from the pipe. He smells it just to be sure. It's gasoline. He begins to fill the gas cans with fuel, one 20 ounce bottle at a time. Once they're filled, he cuts down a hose from the pump. He inserts the nozzle into the police car gas tank, and pours the gas into the back end of the cut hose, using it like a funnel to get the gas into the car.

Sheryl and Brandon see how painstaking the process is, and they decide to help, each making their own gas fishing rig with string and bottles. Eventually the car and Brandon's two gas cans are topped off.

"Think you guys can give me a lift back home? I'm just past town, about five minutes from here by car," Brandon asks.

"Sure, hop in," Sheryl answers before Willy can even think it over. Her eyes were lit up like a Christmas tree. She saw both her sons in Brandon. She tried to. BJ, older, more self reliant, and Stephen, meek and sweet. She wanted to take care of Brandon, to be his mother. But Brandon seemed a bit disconnected, detached from reality. In the little time Sheryl spent with him, she could tell something was off. *Too many video games and not enough real socializing*, she thought. *It's all too common these days… Well, maybe that will change now that there's no electricity. But there are all sorts of new problems involved with social interactions now.*

"I've got a bunker with video games and food and stuff, but I guess you guys are all stocked up," Brandon says as he eyes the car full of supplies.

So much for my theory about video games becoming a thing of the past, Sheryl thinks.

"What's your plan? Everyone has to have a plan otherwise they're doomed," Brandon asks.

"West," Willy replies. "Past the impact, where it's safe to breathe."

"That's what I want to do too. Just trying to figure out how to do it. I have a lot of stuff, food, supplies... not sure how I can bring it all with me. But there's a place I know where people have been surviving for a long time all on their own. They don't rely on anyone or anything. Totally self contained, remote."

Brandon goes on about the compound and Willy eyeballs him in the rearview mirror as he speaks. *That's just the kind of place I'd like to set up. Someplace safe. It'd be good for Sheryl. Somewhere she can rebuild her life. Maybe runnin' into this Brandon kid is a blessing. Sheryl can fill the holes missing in Brandon's life, and Brandon can replace BJ and Stephen in Sheryl's life.* He hopes, but he knows no one can ever really replace someone that was lost. He knows that first hand from losing his daughter to drugs, and losing his wife to... well, to the war. She left him soon after he came back from Vietnam. They had a daughter and things were going well at first, but soon the nightmares were creeping into reality. The horrors of war were always with him. Some nights he would wake up in the middle of strangling his wife or hitting her, without any clue as to why or how. He came back from war, but so did all the death, all the evil. He came back from the war, but the war came back with him, as they say. Like a plague it stayed with him, infected him. The veterans' mental health programs helped a little bit, more so recently, but by then it was way too late. His wife left him, and his daughter went with her. Some years back he learned that his daughter had gone off to Hollywood to be a star. She got hooked on drugs and overdosed in a swimming pool at some big shot director's house in the hills during a party. Since then Willy has

163

been numb, other than the occasional flashbacks. But now things are changing again. Killing a zombie, to him, is becoming just like fixing a pipe at the hospital, or mopping up blood in the ER. Routine. Normal.

"She said I can bring whoever I want. Maybe you guys can drive and we can go together, you know? I don't know how to drive." Brandon finishes rambling about his apocalyptic paradise.

Sheryl looks over at Willy with questioning eyes, as if asking "Can we keep him, Daddy? Please?" Willy nods his head yes. He already sees they're a good match. They're each what is needed for the other to cope. *What do I need? Maybe just to be needed again.*

"We'll take you," Sheryl says.

"I'll teach you to drive. It ain't so hard. They let old people like me do it, so a youngin' like you'd have no problem," Willy says, receiving a laugh from Brandon and a smile from Sheryl afterward. *One big, happy, fucked up, post-apocalyptic family.*

They pull into Brandon's driveway. Willy can smell the gasoline that leaked out from the crushed cars in his driveway. He looks around to see the damage the house and surrounding area sustained from the impact. "You're lucky you survived," Willy says.

"Not lucky. Ready," Brandon responds. "Back there is the bunker." Brandon leads them to his hole. They walk past his mother's rotting, stinking corpse along the way.

"What happened here?" Willy asks.

"Oh that's just my mom. Don't worry. She's really dead now," he says nonchalantly.

A queer look fills Sheryl's face as her eyes meet Willy's. She's sure of it. *There has to be some mental break with this kid. I can fix that.*

Brandon clears the brush covering the shelter, pops the hatch, and takes them down. He quickly covers his porn mags with a blanket, but the pungent scent of puke still permeates the air. "I was gonna make several trips for gas for the generator, but seeing how difficult it is just for one can to get filled, I think I need a new way to power my bunker."

"Well if you mean to leave for your friend's compound, then save your gas for the car," Willy says.

"Or for their generators," Brandon adds.

"Well I can help the people there build a wood-fired generator, or convert it from gas power to wood if they haven't already."

"And I used to be a school teacher once upon a time, before I had kids. If there's need for that kind of thing, I can help," Sheryl adds.

"Last thing I want to do is go back to school," Brandon jokes.

"Education'll help with survival," Willy says. "You sure they'll have us? Let us live there?"

"Yeah. She gave me the address and I have directions to get there."

"Alright then. We'll leave first thing tomorrow morning," Willy says. "How far is it?"

CHAPTER 31

Dr. Vogel hears more accidents on the road, followed by grotesque sounds of the dead eating the living. He wriggles himself loose from his seatbelt. He deflates the air bag to get a better look out the windshield, but there's no windshield, and the engine hood is completely flipped up in its place. One of the glass eye pieces in his gas mask is cracked, but not broken through. The window beside him, however, is completely shattered, and the roof of the car is nearly sandwiched down onto his head. The driver's side door is stuck shut from the point of impact, and there's no way he can fit out the window there. He's not sure he wants to either. The sounds grow louder; grunts, groans, gnawing, slobbering, heavy breathing.

One of the beasts eyes him and gets close to the car, reaching out for his flesh. Dr. Vogel quickly squirms his way over the console and into the passenger's seat, where there's more room and the window is still intact. The mindless zombie reaches for him through the driver's side window, but he's too far. *Just out of reach, you bastard.* After several moments there's finally a distraction, pulling the undead cannibal's attention away from the car.

Dr. Vogel examines himself for injuries. He's shocked. He barely has anything worse than minor cuts and bruises, though his left ribs feel extremely tender. *A fracture at most. Nothing life threatening.* His biological samples are still in their case, also undamaged. *I was lucky.*

Out the window he sees the insanity that has taken over the road. He thought he was clear of it, but more and more accidents jammed the entire highway as far as he can see to the east. The sick were driving, then seizing, and then dying, causing accidents. *The dead can't drive.* Anyone still alive outside on foot is getting mauled by the infected and crazed monsters. He waits. Several zombies press their face to the passenger side window, but Dr. Vogel sits still and quiet, out of reach and safe in his destroyed car. He waits, and waits, and waits.

Eventually things grow quiet, as the infected follow runners from accidents further down the road where he came from. He slowly and quietly steps out of the car with his samples, making his way to the woods line along the side of the road. He stays low to the ground, ducking down between cars to avoid being seen by any stragglers. He grabs a broken metal mile marker post for protection as he walks east. It's like a light weight axe or spade, with a particularly unlucky mile number acting as the blade. *I'm 13 miles from the Pennsylvania border.*

The runaway car that took out the sign hisses steam up a thick tree trunk. It finally stopped just a few feet into the woods line. Torn between his obligation to get the samples to a lab and his duty and oath as a medical doctor, Dr. Vogel stands in thought, staring at the crashed car. *Should I see if anyone needs help? The driver is either dead or one of them. I better not get any closer. There are probably hundreds of cars just like this one behind me and ahead of me. Why check this one and not the others? They would be easy to ignore. But what then? What kind of doctor, no, what kind of man would I be if I ignored them all? What if there's someone in there who could still survive? Or better yet, what if it's someone I know or someone that could help me in my quest to get samples to the government?*

He walks toward the car. Surprisingly the windows are still intact, and all four doors are shut. He sees the driver; a man slumped over the steering wheel. Beside him is a mess of gore, and what looks like the remains of a woman lying dead in the passenger seat. A car window ice scraper is lodged in her eye socket, handle-end in with the flat, angled scraper side sticking out. The driver's body slowly inflates and deflates. *He's still breathing. The passenger must've changed while they were driving. She likely tried to attack him, but he somehow defended himself from the woman, only to crash into a tree and get knocked unconscious.* He can't see any injuries on the man; just the stains of blood on his clothing.

After working up the courage, Dr. Vogel begins to knock on the glass. The driver stirs awake, holding his head in pain as he squints out to see Dr. Vogel. Tears fill his eyes upon seeing the dead woman next to him.

"I'm a doctor. Are you injured?" Dr. Vogel asks.

The man looks himself over, checking for wounds. "Leg," he says.

Dr. Vogel opens the door and examines his leg. There's a break just below his right knee. He carefully helps the man out of the car and lays him down on the cold dead grass. He grabs a sturdy tree branch that had been cut back from the road and snaps it down to size.

"There's a break. I need to set it and get your leg in a splint," Dr. Vogel explains. The man nods. His face is pale and clammy, as if sweating out in the cold. "Probably best to cover your mouth and nose. The debris cloud might be shifting." Dr. Vogel tears a strip of the man's pants from a small rip near his thigh to uncover the area near the break. He hands the fabric to the man to use as a makeshift mask.

Upon closer examination Dr. Vogel sees that the break is compound, with a piece of bone jutting through the skin. He also sees some slight bruising and puncture marks on his thigh. *A bite. I guess the passenger got to you after all. Setting your leg will probably prove a waste of time. Soon enough you'll seize, die and return from the dead with a hunger for rare man-steak.*

"This is going to hurt, so just hang in there, okay?" Dr. Vogel warns him, receiving a nod in return.

With a yank, a twist and a shove Dr. Vogel returns the bone into the man's skin. He groans in agony and pain, writhing and gritting his teeth. Dr. Vogel dresses the wound, tying strips of pants around the tree branch to keep the splint in place. He turns his attention to the bite, which seems to grow darker and more ominous by the moment.

"You know you were bitten?" he says.

"Yeah. It's alright. I'll be okay. Please take me with you. Take me somewhere I can get help," he pleads.

"I'm going in the opposite direction. You're welcome to come with me, but I'm kind of in a rush," Dr. Vogel explains.

"What the hell are you going that way for?" he asks through increasingly tense breaths. His leg begins to twitch.

"Take it easy. Relax. Keep that leg still," Dr. Vogel instructs. There's no response. The man's breathing becomes heavier. He sucks air in and out of his mouth furiously through tightly clenched teeth. Soon the leg twitch becomes a steady shake, spreading from his leg throughout the rest of his body. Dr. Vogel steps back and picks up his mile marker sign. He knows what's about to happen. He waits for it. When the man's eyes burst open revealing the yellow look of living death, Dr. Vogel jams the ragged end of the metal sign post handle into the man's chest to kill him. To his medical astonishment, this does nothing. The man reaches up for Dr. Vogel with bloodlust, his mouth searching for man meat. *What the hell?* Dr. Vogel removes the handle from the man's chest. He's seen a few zombie films in his day, so he tries the head next. He shoves the pointed handle down into the man's golden, bloodshot eye, piercing his brain. That does the trick.

Once his head clears, Dr. Vogel begins to put the picture together. *There are two distinct ways to change into the creatures. First is from breathing in the Lazarus meteor dust. The second is from a bite or bodily fluid transfer. The way the particles grew in the Petrie dish suggests that breathing them in causes a physical blockage in the lungs. Eventually the person dies. But that doesn't explain the seizing, the foaming at the mouth, the reanimation, the change in eye color, and the blood thirst. Something must happen in the blood. This particle from space, this organism, this living crystalline structure, must somehow take over the blood, brain and body, and alter the human state. It's not a virus, and it's not bacteria. It's a parasite of some kind; perhaps even a living, thinking being. It's certainly like nothing mankind has ever seen; an alien life form. Both the organism and its effects on mankind are beyond normal; they're paranormal. And they are beyond what*

170

could be observed in nature; they're supernatural. And it is extremely aggressive.

As he gets closer to Pennsylvania he starts to see strange yellow signs along the highway; newly erected, bright yellow pentagon-shaped signs with a black gas mask image in the center. *Do the officials know it spread beyond the quarantine? If not, the containment zone needs to be widened ASAP. All the more reason to get to the barricade and talk to someone in charge.*

He sees an exit sign for a county road that he knows runs east into Pennsylvania. Still worried about the outbreak on the highway, he turns off down the local road. It's a lonely road, dotted with farms and woods, but that means it's a safe road. Every road will be guarded, so the smart bet is to stay off the big highways, where more people are likely to jam up the roads and cause problems. He's getting close.

He hears a rustling in the woods beside him. It freezes him in his tracks. He holds his mile marker sign with two hands, with the biological sample bag slung across his shoulder. The rustling grows louder as it draws closer. He sees shadows shifting among the trees. Then what looks like moving branches emerge into a small clearing. *Antlers. It's a deer.* Dr. Vogel is apprehensive. *If the animals can change, then people are in real danger.* He steps toward it and the majestic animal fixes its eyes upon him. *They're normal, not glowing yellow with the bloodshot bloodlust of the people on the road.* Dr. Vogel steps toward it again, but the animal bolts back into the woods in fear. *If it had changed, it would've attacked me. But why didn't it change? Perhaps there's something in human blood that makes us more vulnerable, or perhaps the lungs of wild animals are strong enough to withstand the airborne onslaught of this microscopic being. That would explain Wolf's delayed and slowed symptoms. He's in incredible physical shape; one of the world's most fit. But without further study I can't know for sure.*

He wishes he never left his career in immunology. As fearful as he is, this is also an exciting opportunity to discover more about the nature of life in our world, and the nature of life in worlds beyond. *If I were still in the labs down at the CDC I might be able to study this further, to contribute, to make a difference*. But fate works in mysterious ways. His career change took him away from there, but it also put samples into his hand that might be important for the study of this microbial life form. *Perhaps I'm the first to discover that the particles from the meteor might actually be alive. I wonder if any other scientists know that.*

CHAPTER 32

After some time there's room to drive along the side of the road, so Marcus takes the pickup down from the monster truck rally on top of the highway traffic. Michael's skin seems to rattle with the lingering sensation of motion, but he can finally breathe again without feeling like he's about to throw up. Marcus keeps his speed moderate, since he doesn't want to burn through gas any more than he already has. A jacked up '86 pickup with a blown 350 doesn't do well in the whole miles per gallon arena. No doubt they'll have to stop and try to score gas at some point.

Amy turns her head to look in the truck bed; everything is still in its place, strapped down securely with bungee cords. Amazed, she congratulates Marcus on a job well done. She slides open the rear cab window and begins to climb back into the truck bed.

"What are you doing? Are you crazy?" Michael asks.

"I haven't ridden in the back of a pickup since high school," she cheers. "Do you mind?" she asks Marcus.

"Go right ahead. Just hang on," he says.

Michael glares disapprovingly. "Be careful." He watches her all the while.

They hit a small bump in the grass, giving Amy a little toss as she gets into the truck bed. She laughs it off and stands up, grabbing hold of the pipes that secure Marcus' array of high beam lights on top of the passenger cab. With her other hand she holds her mask, securing it in place and keeping it from blowing off her head in the cold winter wind. She doesn't mind the sting of frost in the air. She feels free.

"I had no idea she ever rode in the back of a pickup," Michael says to Marcus.

"Everybody got their secrets," he says.

"Yeah? And what's your secret?" Michael asks.

Marcus leans closer to Michael and whispers, "It's a secret."

The amount of stopped cars on the highway lightens as they make their way further from the city, and soon Marcus is back on the pavement. Every so often he dodges and weaves around abandoned cars or bodies.

"The concept of road kill has completely changed in meaning, eh?" Michael says.

"Indeed it has," Marcus responds. "Indeed it has."

They've entered Pennsylvania, and as long as the roads stay somewhat clear, they'll be at Amy's parents' house in a few short hours. But gas is getting low, so Marcus begins to check each car they pass. Amy helps him get the plastic tubing out from the truck bed and hops out to watch him siphon bits of fuel off from each car. On occasion he slides himself underneath the back ends of cars and punctures the gas tanks, filling a plastic gas can from whatever flows out of the abandoned or wrecked cars. They quickly notice they're getting more from wrecks than abandonments. It makes sense: the people that ran out of gas must've left their cars in search of fuel; but when people were in a crash that totaled their car, they often still had plenty of gas so long as the tank wasn't ruptured.

Amy moves back into the cab as they get closer to her town. Strange plumes of smoke rise up from alongside the highway, ruining her free-spirited ride on top of Marcus' truck. Craters dot the cornfields and farms of rural Pennsylvania. Ahead in the distance they can see the ghostly, faded shape of a massive and dispersing mushroom cloud.

Amy guides Marcus off the highway at her exit, and they slowly roll through the ravaged town that was her Main Street when growing up. Homes and storefronts look devastated, like a tornado hit the area. Some are in shambles, and others, usually the ones with sturdier structures, remain unscathed. There are more bodies and more abandoned cars. Amy begins to worry about her

174

parents. After a few quick turns they arrive on her street. The home is okay, but three bodies are flopped on her parents' lawn. She knows right away. One of them is her father, up by the glassed-in porch. His face is covered with a mask but she knows it's him. She climbs over Michael and jumps out of the truck before it even comes to a stop. Her mask fills with fog and tears as she kneels down beside her father's body. She sees the gunshot wound on his chest, and picks up his gun beside him.

"Something went wrong here," Michael says as he and Marcus approach.

"Yeah no shit! My father is dead!" Amy cries out.

Michael consoles her. "No I mean… look. He was defending the house from these two," He points at the male and female corpses in the front of the house. "They look like they changed and he shot them. But your dad still has his mask on. He was shot, not bitten or sick."

"There was someone else shooting," Marcus adds. "These bullet holes on the bodies here... they ain't from his piece. These are like rifle shots."

"How can you tell?" Michael asks.

Marcus pauses, still reluctant to bring up his past. He knew the difference between a pistol wound and something else like a rifle or a shotty.

"My mom might still be inside," Amy blurts, running inside.

"Whoa, whoa hold up!" Michael chases after her, noticing the broken windows and wide open doorway in the front of the house. Marcus follows with his scythe across his back.

"Mom! Mom!" Amy yells as she peeks her head into different rooms on the first floor.

"Okay try to calm down," Marcus says as he catches her in mid-stride between the living room and dining room. She buckles in his muscled arms and cries on his shoulder. Marcus passes her off to Michael. "Stay here," he says to Michael. Michael nods, and Marcus begins to cautiously sweep the house.

He creeps from room to room, stalking every single nook in the home, closets included. He takes notice of all the religious images displayed throughout the house; paintings of Mary, framed images of Jesus, a cross somewhere in each room. *God is watching.* He hears something fidgeting around upstairs. The ceiling squeaks with movement from above. He slowly goes up, one step at a time, silently placing each foot with care, holding his breath so as not to make a sound. The noise is coming from the right. He can hear what sounds like a woman struggling, breathing heavily. Marcus gets up to the top of the stairs and turns the corner to see an Asian woman tied to a chair on the far side of a bedroom, beside a vanity next to a window. Her face is exposed to the poisonous air that pours in from the broken windows below. Her sunken eyes glow with the dirtied amber color of piss. She drools at the mouth upon seeing Marcus, violently shaking in her chair, trying to get at him. Marcus sweeps the rest of the upstairs quickly before going back down.

"Is she okay?" Marcus asks Michael in private.

Michael shakes his head no.

Amy catches her breath and collects her emotions on a chair in the living room. Marcus pulls Michael into the kitchen and whispers to him what he saw upstairs, but Amy overhears them arguing about whether they should tell her, and she hears the noises from above. She goes up on her own as they bicker. When they hear her scream in terror at the discovery, they both run up to her.

"No! No, mom, no!" she cries. Amy's mother stretches her head so far out toward them, trying to bite them, that she nearly pulls the vertebrae in her neck out of articulation. That hunger, that rabid desire for flesh, completely consumes her.

"Hey what's this?" Michael says, picking up a letter on the vanity beside Amy's mother. It has Chinese characters scrawled onto it.

"It's addressed to me," Amy says. "A note from my mother." She opens it and reads it to herself, whimpering all the while.

"What does it say?" Michael asks.

Amy looks longingly into her mother's pissy eyes and ravenous face, trying with every ounce of her will to find a shred of humanity left in there. But there's none. She knows it.

"Baby?" Michael puts his arm around Amy.

Amy begins to read with anger in her voice. "Dearest Amy. If you should find this note, please know that your father and I love you very much. We have always wanted happiness and success for you in life. We were hiding away here. The air was safe for us inside, but no longer. We know what happens next. If you should return and find us here like those demons, please put us down. We do not wish to become the living dead."

The groans and seething hunger of Amy's mother break the tension that lingers in the air among them. She lunges at them fruitlessly from her chair. Her skin rips and tears beneath the bindings that tie her down, exposing meat and bone beneath.

"What could have happened?" Marcus asked.

"Maybe the windows broke and she started to get sick, so she wrote the note to Amy," Michael offers.

"But we still don't know where those rifle rounds came from," Marcus adds.

Ignoring the discussion, Amy holds her father's gun to her mother's head. Her mother tries feverishly to bite her hand. Tears stream down Amy's face.

"Do you want me to bear this burden?" Marcus offers.

"No. It's my burden," she says between sobs.

She fires a bullet into her mother's temple. A red spray coats everything nearby, soaking a framed image of Christ with Amy's mother's blood. A long silence follows, interrupted only by the pitter patter of brain bits and skull fragments that fall from the nearby wall and curtains like raindrops as they hit the carpet.

All momentum was drained from their cause in that moment. Their destination, their solace; it was just another nightmare. Amy's dreams of breaking her diet with a taste of the salted pork she grew up with would now remain fleeting memories of a time taken for granted.

Marcus fixes his eyes on the blood-soiled image of Jesus. He says a prayer in his head, asking for his, Michael's, Amy's and her parents' sins to be washed away in the Lord's blood. He asks that they be welcomed into God's grace. "We should give your folks a proper burial," he suggests after a moment. He beckons Michael over to him. He whispers into his ear that they should go find

177

shovels and start to dig two graves in the yard. Michael agrees, and they dig. Afterward, Marcus fashions two crosses from some wood he finds in the shed. Amy joins them outside after some time passes, after gathering her emotions.

"Thank you," she says. Michael hugs her, but the reception isn't what he hoped it would be. She's distant.

"Help Marcus with their bodies," she says to him without making eye contact.

Marcus and Michael carry Amy's parents into the backyard one at a time, and the two men bury them. As the sun sets Marcus offers a prayer, and Amy kneels with her hands folded together to join him. Michael tries not to roll his eyes or show his distaste for religion. He stands by quietly with his hands on his hips.

"Let's stay here for the night. We can pack up some things and then keep moving west in the morning. It's obviously not safe here," Amy suggests. "I don't think I can stay here any longer than that anyway."

Marcus and Michael agree with the plan, and they all head back inside to clean up and get ready for the journey ahead. They spend the evening gathering things and packing them into Marcus' truck.

CHAPTER 33

The early drive is quiet, almost peaceful. Willy pulls over and stands guard when Sheryl and Brandon have to go to the bathroom. Rocky goes as well, but he isn't concerned about taking cover in the woods.

In the distance a fast-paced thumping begins to fade in from silence. Willy cups his hand over his brow to shield the morning sun as he looks for the noise. *A chopper.* It gets louder and louder as it comes closer. Willy knows it's military just by the sound of it, and moments later it's coming right at him. It takes a sharp turn and hovers over the woods, just past where Sheryl and Brandon went in to squat. Willy feels the swirling winds as it passes overhead. A sharp pain fills his ears and a crushing migraine comes over him almost instantly. The thunder of helicopter blades gives way to the raining sound of gunfire. In an instant, he's back at war, wading thigh high in a stagnant river. His platoon is just on the other bank, making their way to his rally point but still in the jungle. An air strike was called in, so they need to hustle out, otherwise face a napalm death. He calls out to his men, shouting the last names and nicknames of brethren he's barely even thought about or remembered for 40 years. There's no answer.

The air rips overhead as fighter jets tear through the skies. A moment later the entire jungle is aflame, and the tortured screams of forgotten men fill the air behind fading war planes and the muted drumbeat of chopper blades. Charred and melting bodies emerge from the thick jungle and flop into the stale river, sizzling upon impact and leaving behind only the curled and blackened shells of men.

Two survivors, with fire still clinging to them, step out onto the water without sinking in. They run across the surface of the river toward him. A moment later they are on him, their flames consuming him. Willy screams in panic. But the river soon becomes a road, and the jungle becomes a winter forest. Sheryl shakes him back to reality, and Brandon holds a bottle of water just beneath his lips, telling him to take a sip and relax. His eyes fix on the woods at the side of the road. Smoke rises up from a short distance beyond, and there's an orange and red flicker within.

"Are you okay?" Willy asks them.

"Are you?" Sheryl responds.

"I'm fine. Just had a flashback. A relapse." His surroundings come back into focus, and in his mind he's no longer at war.

"Some helicopters just flame-throwered part of the woods," Brandon announces with excitement in his voice. "You shoulda seen it. It was awesome!"

"Shoulda seen it? Hell, I lived it, boy," Willy says with anger.

"I thought they were after us, but it looks like there's a small crater back there. I noticed a clearing when I was going to the bathroom," Sheryl says.

"They must be burnin' all the places where there was impact, trying to kill whatever's in the meteor dust," Willy explains.

A moment later the sound of helicopters fills the air again, and several special choppers with large containers attached to their bottoms hover over the same part of the woods. A thick goopy mud is dropped onto the fire.

"And that's to try to contain it," Willy says. "Could be cement, tar, or just mud. It's a wet burn."

Brandon flails his scrawny arms and jumps up and down to try to get the pilot's attention. He knows they see him, a pasty, gangly little boy, right smack in the middle of an empty highway. But they ignore him and fly off when they're done. A sense of hopelessness washes over the group. They're truly on their own.

Sheryl takes her coat off. Her bad arm is feeling cramped, so she changes from a sleeved shirt to a white tank top. They continue on, this time with Sheryl driving. But a short while later there's a string of vehicles blocking the road ahead. Sheryl eases off the gas and slows to a coast, but Willy knows in his gut that something is amiss.

"Don't slow down," he says. Ahead he sees a man scrambling into a delivery truck and starting it up. "Go 'round them. Go 'round to the right and don't stop!"

Willy reaches over Sheryl and flips on the police siren and lights. Rocky howls with the rising and falling siren blares. Sheryl accelerates in a panic. She veers off the road and onto the rumble strips along the shoulder. Then she takes the police cruiser onto the grass. But it's too late. The delivery truck rams them just as Sheryl is about to pass and drive on. The car skids on the grass, spins and tumbles. Willy, Sheryl, Brandon and Rocky are thrown around the car as they slide upside down to an almost gentle stop against a nearby tree.

"Lemme see all of yo' hands!" a gruff sounding man shouts at them.

Willy reaches back for his shotgun, but he hears a gun fire.

"Don't reach for nothin' or I'll kill every last one a y'all!" The man approaches the car, pointing a gun at Willy. "Get out. Slowly," he says. Several other men approach the car as well. A gang of marauders. Looters. Criminals.

Rocky gnashes his teeth and barks angrily out the window. Brandon shields his face and body from what he thinks is another crash soon to come. Out the busted back windshield he sees a massive black truck approaching far too fast from behind. He can hear the engine roaring like a beast. He curls into the fetal position and waits for the jolt to come.

CHAPTER 34

Marcus, knowing the mannerisms and stance of his old jail mate, sees what he thinks is a familiar person from a distance. The man points a gun at some people in an overturned police car on the side of the road. *It's Harley. What are the odds? Of all the roads I could be on right now, why did God bring me to the one he's on? Why, when there were so many other directions we coulda gone, and so many miles between here and where I left him? And why Harley and not some other criminal? This is my test. This must be. This is when I'll have to face the flaws in my vows. Kill no man. But protect the weak. Fight the wicked.* He tucks Thompson's gun in his waistband and makes a hood over his head with the black blanket.

"Hold on. This might get ugly," he says to Michael and Amy.

"Just go around. We don't need any trouble," Michael begs.

"Well, whether you want it or not, you got trouble. I know this asshole," he responds. "Get down low, so no one sees you."

Michael and Amy do as they're instructed. Marcus puts the pedal to the floor and pulls up hard and fast, screaming the engine and then ripping to a stop on the shoulder of the highway. Harley turns and points the gun toward the truck. Marcus shuts the engine and jumps out, grabbing his scythe from the truck bed.

"Harley!" he yells through his mask.

"Marcus? That you?" Harley asks, stunned by the appearance of Marcus stepping out of a skull- and flame-painted truck, donning the attire of the Grim Reaper.

"Step away from the car," Marcus says, raising his scythe in a menacing display.

Harley laughs. "You gonna defend these mutha fuckas? This is my mutha fuckin' road now, nigga. And I expect my toll to be paid."

"What do you want?" Marcus asks.

"All their shit. And the bitch," Harley says, motioning to Sheryl inside the overturned police cruiser. "It gets lonely out here. We need a good fuckin' to make it through the day. And when we run out of their shit, we gonna eat the kid." The other inmates laugh with Harley. "The zombies have it right. Once you taste man, you don't want nothin' from a can."

"Maybe we can work something else out. Take some supplies, but don't bring no harm to no one," Willy says as he steps out of the rubble with his hands up.

"This ain't Let's Have a Deal, old fool. This is I'm Gonna Steal, and I make the rules," Harley rhymes again.

Brandon stays curled in a ball, in fear, and Rocky barks nonstop. But Sheryl slowly and quietly moves her pistol into the back of her waistband, just above her ass. She tries to cover it with the bottom of her shirt as she steps out of the cruiser and puts her hands up. She positions herself behind the car somewhat, to block her hips from Harley's line of sight. It's cold outside, and her stiffened nipples show through her tight white tank top.

"Damn you look good, girl!" Harley says to Sheryl. "I'm takin' first crack at this one boys," he yells over his shoulder, receiving hoots and hollers in response. "Step out from behind the car, sweet thang, and let ol' Harley see that ass." Sheryl hesitates, not listening to the command. He snaps. "I said get the fuck over here!"

Sheryl steps out to the side of the wrecked car, still holding her hands in the air. She takes a few steps toward Harley and stops.

"Turn around, baby," Harley says with widened eyes.

Sheryl turns slowly. Without a coat to cover it, the gun is in plain view through the back of her tank top as it pokes out of her slim jeans.

"Now that's a nice piece," Harley jokes. "Lemme get that for you."

Harley walks over toward Sheryl and reaches out for the gun in her waist. Without warning Marcus flings his cloak open and draws his gun. He squeezes the trigger with a prayer on his lips. The lone bullet fires directly into Harley's throat. Harley drops his gun and falls backward to the ground with a gurgle. In an instant Sheryl pulls her gun as well, firing at Harley's men. She manages to drop one with a head shot and clip a second with a round to the shoulder. The others scatter behind the truck. A moment later the delivery truck engine starts and begins to pull away. Willy grabs the rifle from the back seat of the destroyed police cruiser. He cranks off two shots at the tires. A tire blows out and the truck yanks to the left, flipping onto the driver's side. Willy runs out after it, leaps up onto the passenger side door, and fires two shots down, killing the driver inside the cab. The final car speeds away, but not without Willy blowing out the rear window and putting a few bullets into the gas tank. All that remains is Marcus' monster truck, the busted up police car, and several dead bodies.

And Harley... He struggles to breathe, still clinging to life with all the strength he has. Marcus stands over him and looks down upon him. He kicks Harley's gun away and takes a knee beside him, preparing to put him out of his misery. He closes his eyes and prays in silence for the life he is about to take.

The pump of a shotgun beside his head interrupts his solemn thoughts. His eyes burst open to reveal Brandon standing next to him with Willy's gun pointed at Harley's face. Marcus slaps the barrel to the side just as Brandon fires. A divot rips into the frozen grass beside Harley's head. Brandon stares down, blank, emotionless. Rocky sniffs at Harley, having jumped out of the police cruiser when Brandon stepped out.

"This is my kill, little man. You don't need to be doing this," Marcus says to him as he stands up to look down over Brandon. "You got your whole adulthood to go killin' bad guys if that's what you want. But no child should ever have to take a life."

"What if I like it?" Brandon says through a haze. He stares at the gushing wound on Harley's neck.

"You shouldn't," Marcus says.

Brandon steps back beside Willy and Sheryl. Everyone stands with gun in hand. With Harley's and the other marauders' weapons there will be even more firepower to go around. But Marcus only uses his blade to kill demons. He drops Thompson's empty gun to the ground, thinking of him and how he died at the prison. *Retribution. A life for a life. An eye for an eye. But how do I do it? How do I kill Harley, how do I end it?* He thinks for a moment, and then it comes to him. *I'll let God take him…*

He kneels beside Harley and removes the mask from Harley's face. A pool of blood spills out from underneath it. If he didn't bleed to death he would've eventually drowned in his own blood. Marcus watches as he gasps for air. He begins to twitch and shake. His eyes roll back into his head, showing nothing but the whites. Rocky's hair stands on end and he starts to growl and bark viciously at the spectacle. Then every hole begins to purge; piss, shit, and bloody vomit comes out of Harley all at once. Marcus hopes it was fear of eternal consequences that caused this, but he knows it happens when people change. It happens to all of them. Marcus stands up. When Harley's yellowed eyes roll back down from their lids, Marcus brings his scythe down onto Harley's head to finish the job. He dies instantly. Marcus kneels again and says a prayer for his own soul, asking the Lord's forgiveness for all he's done. And although he prays for Harley's soul as well, he convinces himself that a demon like Harley doesn't need a burial. He takes a few moments to gather himself. As much as he didn't like Harley, he did spend a significant amount of time with the bastard behind bars. It wasn't a great loss, but it was a loss nonetheless.

"Y'all are going west?" Marcus asks.

"Past the quarantine," Willy says.

"You can ride with us," Marcus says, motioning to his truck.

"Us?" Sheryl asks.

Michael and Amy peek their heads over the dash to see the aftermath of the gunfight.

Amy waves to everyone. "Hi!"

"Marcus has some serious explaining to do," Michael whispers to her.

CHAPTER 35

Dr. Vogel's brisk, silent walk is shattered when he hears the distant sound of gunfire echoing off the empty road. *I knew there would be a military presence at the quarantine, but I didn't expect fighting.* As he gets closer he sees a helicopter hovering in the air, and a barricade stretched across the road; sandbags, a military truck, and soldiers. *It's like a war zone.* Some caution tape and street dividers are set up to prevent people from wandering in from his direction, but they aren't guarded. A lone makeshift sign reads "military personnel and citizen soldiers only beyond this point." Dr. Vogel ignores it and moves toward the closest man in uniform.

"It's dangerous here. You should go back," the soldier says.

"I'm a doctor. I can help."

"Okay come this way." He waves Dr. Vogel forward and leads him toward a tent.

"Truth is, I'm trying to get to the CDC. A man who broke through the quarantine came to my hospital and he seems to be immune to this... whatever this is. I have samples here in my bag."

"Well, the roads are pretty much all barricaded or jammed with traffic, and the air belongs to the military now."

"I was hoping I could get a lift in your helicopter," Dr. Levy pleads.

"Doubt that's gonna happen. We're short on manpower right now, and we can't afford to send our chopper off," the soldier says.

"This is vitally important. It could mean the end of the disease. I used to work for the CDC, for many years."

"Well I'm pretty sure they got samples already. Scientists are going back and forth to study the craters."

"That may be, but if the sample isn't from someone who was exposed but unaffected, then it's no use," Dr. Vogel reasons. "Is there someone I can talk to about getting my samples into the right hands?"

"Sure. I'll take you to the colonel," the soldier says.

He couldn't look any more like a colonel, Dr. Vogel thinks as he is taken to the man. He's chubby, with a big, bushy, dirt-grey mustache under his mask, and a few strings of white hair on top of his mostly bald head. He studies a paper map on a fold-out table beside a much younger, lower ranking officer.

"Get these last two areas secure. We're lucky they're sticking to the roads right now, but eventually they're gonna fan out and try to breach. We need soldiers on every inch of this perimeter. And we need radios in every group in case there's a surge somewhere else. Then we can respond quickly to any attacks with more manpower at their location."

"Yes sir," the young officer responds before slicing his hand above his brow and running off.

"Who's this?" the colonel asks.

"Sir," the soldier pauses. He never got Dr. Vogel's name.

"I'm Eugene Vogel. I'm a doctor."

"I'm Colonel Buford Wallace." They shake hands. "Let's see some credentials," says the colonel. Dr. Vogel pulls out his wallet, where he keeps a hospital ID tucked in one of the flaps. "Here to volunteer?" Wallace asks as he finishes examining the ID.

"No sir... colonel... I used to work for the CDC. I have some important biological samples that I think might be helpful in synthesizing a cure for whatever this outbreak is that we're dealing with."

"That's great Dr. Vogel, but what I'm dealing with here is the brink of war. A civil war. The entire population of the northeast is banging at my door, and I need all the resources I got to keep that door locked. I can't spare any men to lead you down in a convoy, and I sure as shit can't give you a chopper lift, if that's what you're asking."

"Understood, colonel." Dr. Vogel is visibly disheartened. *I should have known.*

"The proverbial shit is about to hit the fan out there. Our men have been fired upon, and we have a bunch of untrained, trigger happy civilians helping us out wherever possible. If it were up to me they'd be gone, but we need every man that's able and willing to help hold these lunatics back, to keep from spreading the disease even further."

"With respect, Colonel Wallace, many have already broken through to this side."

"I know. I know, damn it. It's been worse in other places, like the big highways, but I have orders. This is just where they sent me and my troops yesterday. My real opinion, this whole thing is useless. It's only a matter of time before the quarantine has to be widened. They considered it, briefly. They wanted to move it into Ohio and use the roads as borders, since they're easier to arm, blockade and defend. But it'll all be for shit when this spreads global. And that's inevitable, mark my words. It's a war we can't win, because it's not just a war against men. It's a war against nature's will, or God's will, or whatever the fuck you believe. A lot of people already got past the initial roadblocks we set up right after impact. But those were done with just a few local cops and some reflective orange saw horses west and south of the Lazarus point. We just set this one up at dawn. Heavy manpower on all the major interstates, half as much on all these other roads, and patrols in between. We've had short firefights and minor skirmishes up and down the borders of the quarantine the past couple days. They flare up at the most random times and places. It's difficult to predict, but we need to plug the holes if we want to stand a chance." The colonel strokes his moustache in thought for a moment. "Alright listen. Something's brewing over there on the other side. I can feel it. After forty years of combat experience, I can just sense it in my bones. When you can't calculate what the enemy is going to do with all your strategy and your tactical knowledge, you just have to go on gut instinct."

"Enemy?" Dr. Vogel asks.

"Something's about to happen. They're pissed." He ignores the question. "When this surge passes… and by God I'll make sure it passes if it's the last fuckin' thing I do… I'll see what I can do to get you a lift down in that direction. It may not be all the way the fuck down to DC…"

"Atlanta…" Dr. Vogel interrupts, correcting the colonel.

"Atlanta… but we'll need to send the chopper back out for more supplies, weapons, and fuel from our base. Hell, I haven't even heard from base since 0-300. Lord knows I've been trying to get them on the radio. I may be working on stale orders for all I know, but someone's got to do something. Someone's got to hold the fuckin' line! Anyway you can ride with them, but you'll have to talk your way down from there. All I can do is try to let them know to expect you. I can't promise anything."

"Good enough."

"Until then, consider yourself conscripted to the civilian army. We need medics, and a doctor like you fits the bill just right. When the fighting's done you're free to go with the supply chopper."

"Sounds like a deal," Dr. Vogel agrees.

"Sounds like a deal, *sir*. And that's an order, not a deal." The colonel nods at the soldier, motioning for him to approach. "Get Dr. Vogel some basic gear and get his ass out there. We need him."

"Yes sir," the soldier responds.

Great. Now I'm going into combat. Joanna would freak out if she knew.

The soldier hands Dr. Vogel a pistol and throws a white apron with a red medical symbol on it over his head. "You can leave your samples case with me," he says. "It'll be with the things we're taking to base."

Dr. Vogel is hesitant to part with the samples. He raises a distrusting eyebrow at the soldier.

"I'll personally make sure they're safe. And I'll label them," the soldier offers.

"Fine." Dr. Vogel hands the case over.

The soldier points. "They'll be behind the tent, over there. Chopper leaves for base in three hours, unless there's fighting."

He takes Dr. Vogel out to the barricade. There's a chest high wall of sandbags, and a few feet in front of that is a makeshift wall of poured cement road dividers, stacked three high. After that, they erected those old fashioned wood and razor wire barricades that you see in old WWI movies.

Armed soldiers and local police from the west side of the quarantine are wearing riot gear and carrying live rounds. Word came down from high up that the threat was too great to use the typical water cannons, rubber bullets, and bean bag guns. The barricades must hold. Interspersed with the soldiers and police is the civilian army; regular, average, ordinary guys in their everyday winter clothes carrying whatever guns they keep at home. A certain lack of experience drenches them, but it's wiped away by their eagerness and determination to protect the land behind them. They all wear US military grade gas masks, with singular, wide view, wraparound glass panels, and filters positioned to the left side and downward, so that their front and peripheral vision isn't obscured.

The other side of the blockade is mobbed. Some people are chanting in solidarity, others are marching with signs, or sitting in a peaceful "hunger strike" protest. One group stands side by side, linking arms to create a human wall that mocks the military barricade. Around their necks are cardboard signs displaying various quotes from the Constitution and the early founders about freedom. One man who marches up and down the blockade wears a white t-shirt with the words "Man-Feast Deadstiny" crudely scrawled onto it in black ink. He chants "Go west, dead man," over and over.

But a greater number of people are raging with anger, shouting curses and threats. Many don't have gas masks. *They're west of the impact now, where it's supposedly safe to breathe, but they probably came from the east.* They cough and hack as they try to yell and chant. *It's only a matter of time before they turn and start attacking anything nearby.*

Dr. Vogel sees a thick crowd gathering east of the barricade. He sees the barrels of all sorts of guns being raised in the air, jolting up and down with chants of "Hey, hey, we won't stay."

A scuffle breaks out in the protest. One of the protesters' gun barrels tips down and takes aim. The crowd quickly disperses from the gunpoint, and when the people clear away Dr. Vogel sees an infected woman attacking someone on the pavement. The raised voices and chants turn to screams when the armed protester opens fire upon the woman, riddling her with bullets until she flops lifeless to the road.

"Shit they're shooting at us," yells one of the civilian militia men on the west side of the barricade. He fires back, out into the crowd, dropping a few people. The men on the other side immediately open fire in response. The crowd roars and starts to surge at the wall, pushing their way up onto the cement road dividers and climbing over the wood and barbed wire fences. The soldiers dive down behind the sandbags and take aim, firing back at the rebels. *It's war. The quarantine border war. A second civil war.*

CHAPTER 36

With everyone loaded into Marcus' truck, the drive isn't quiet or pleasant. On Marcus' insistence, the women are inside the cab, and the men, including Brandon and Rocky, are out in the truck bed with the rest of the supplies. The late morning air has a bite to it that doesn't melt away with the growing sunlight. With only a half tank of gas left in the truck, Marcus is on the lookout for wrecks, but some straggling dead wander the roadside.

"I got an idea. Let's play some zombie baseball!" Brandon says. "Marcus, pull up so the zeds are along the passenger side." Brandon switches his rifle's safety on, and grips the barrel like it's a baseball bat. Marcus slows down as they pass one of the risen, and Brandon takes a mighty swing. The shoulder stock meets it's skull with a crack, sending a stream of bloody goop out into the wind. "C'mon guys, let's do it! A knock down is a single, a thick blood spray is a double, exposing the brain is a triple, and decapitation is a homerun. I have a man on second. Who's up next? Willy? Michael?"

Willy just shakes his head.

"You're a lunatic. You know that, kid?" Michael says. "Amy has a bat back here somewhere, you know."

"Look, out there," Sheryl says with her head turned toward the passenger side window.

"What are they doing?" Amy asks.

"We saw some choppers before, torching the places where meteors hit. Maybe it has something to do with that." Sheryl says.

Marcus sees them. A few men out in the field are wearing strange full body bio-suits with equipment on their backs, carrying some kind of gadget in their hands. "They look like scientists," he says.

"Maybe they can help," Sheryl suggests.

"It might be more dangerous out there. Those suits… we don't have that kind of protection on our bodies," Amy adds.

"Yeah. You're probably right." Sheryl sighs.

"You think we'll be able to get past the quarantine?" Amy asks. "Michael and I had to go through an abandoned subway tunnel to get out of New York. They had the bridges and tunnels sealed up and guarded with military."

"Got to be tough to blockade every inch of land on the border. Shit. Mexicans cross our border every day, right?" Marcus says. "The main roads'll be guarded. That's for sure. But we should be able to pass by somewhere. Like in the wilderness." *If prison walls couldn't contain me, ain't no way a fence across a road is gonna hold me back either. But what about my truck? I can't leave it behind.*

"There's more of them ahead," Sheryl says.

Marcus slows down to a crawl and pulls over, stopping on the side of the road.

"Hey what's going on up there? Why are we stopping?" Brandon yells from back in the truck bed, eager to drive in some runs.

Three scientists wander back and forth across the highway up ahead, sweeping the ground with a spray of some kind, from large tanks strapped to their backs. Their shiny yellow biohazard suits flicker and shimmer in the sunlight, and the wet road reflects their shapes, creating a ghostly mirage of golden floating apparitions.

"Everyone stay here," Marcus says. He hops out of the truck and walks over to the scientists. When they see him they become apprehensive and huddle closer together. One of them draws a gun. "Wait! Hold your fire!" Marcus yells.

Upon hearing this Willy pulls up his rifle and rests it on the roof of the truck, putting the armed scientist into his crosshairs. Brandon follows his lead. "Don't shoot," Willy instructs him.

#

"I'm unarmed," Marcus says as he walks away from his truck. "We don't mean any harm."

"Stay back. The chemicals are dangerous, and I'll shoot you if you try anything," the scientist warns.

"Okay." Marcus takes a step backward, off of the wet asphalt. The scientist lowers his gun and approaches him. The other two men continue to spray the road. "What're y'all doin?"

"Apologies for pulling the gun. It's just that we've heard about people on this side attacking scientists and taking their badges."

"Better safe than dead, I get it. But what do you mean, badges?" Marcus asks.

"We're the only ones allowed to cross back and forth. They give us these passes, like ID cards, that we show the military at the border. Then they let us back through. People found out about it and started killing us for the passes so they could go across to safety. We're always armed; at least one man per group, to fend off the dead if we have to. But now we're permitted to use them on living attackers. It doesn't even matter though. For many of us it's still a one way trip."

This disease has a worse effect on the living than it does on the dead. The old priest was right. The living are worse than the dead. "What is all this? What's happening to us?" Marcus asks.

"Still trying to figure that out. The meteors hit and the debris made everyone sick. It's some kind of parasite or organism that came in with the meteor. That's really all we know. The government is trying a few things, trying to stop it, hoping one will work."

"So what's it that you all are doing?"

"Chemical spray, and collecting samples. Ain't too many things can live in harsh chemical soup, so that's what they're having us try. A good sized meteor hit close by here, out in those fields. Some places they have choppers using flame throwers to burn the area. But us, we have to spray and collect samples. Sometimes there's not enough helicopters to spray from above, so we have to do it on foot."

"How tight is the border sealed up?" Marcus asks.

"I have no idea, truth be told, but my guess is that it's become military priority number one. Above even our mid-east operations. I just know that no one crosses that barricade without a pass."

"Why ain't they letting uninfected people cross, like us, who have masks?"

"They're worried you might be carriers if you breathed it in or if your skin was exposed. We still don't fully know how this thing works. At least they aren't telling us grunts out here, doing the dirty work."

"Y'all are the new heroes. Like the 9/11 workers who went in and did the search and rescue, the cleanup."

"Yeah. Can't wait to see all the lawsuits that come in afterwards. No doubt this chemical stew will make my balls shrivel up and my dick piss blood, despite all the protective gear. But what else can we do? We have to keep trying something, because nothing seems to be working."

"I got a feeling only God can stop this," Marcus says. "Would y'all be willing to give your passes up, for the two women and the kid I have with me?"

"No way in hell, my friend. Even if I wanted to I couldn't. It's against direct military orders. Would you?" The scientist lets out a short, disdainful chuckle.

No way in hell, he says. This is hell. Would I give mine away? That's a self sacrifice. Jesus did it for all of mankind. I'm supposed to do as he did. Orders or not, I'd have to be willing to sacrifice myself for someone in need. Maybe that's the real test for me in all of this, not Harley. One day, it might come to that. Give my life to someone else. Give up my own life to wash away my sins with Christ's blood. Maybe if I did something like that, God could find the grace to forgive me for what I've done.

"I would," Marcus gives a delayed answer. The scientist just stares blankly at him. "Aight then. You don't gotta worry about us. We're just passing through," Marcus says.

"Going to try to make it across?" the scientist asks. "Hey don't worry about me. I ain't gonna tell anyone." Marcus doesn't respond.

#

Michael hops out of the truck bed while Marcus talks to the scientists. He walks around to the side of the truck and leans into the cab through the window. "Did you see that one guy's outfit back there on the road? Underneath his jacket there was a prison suit," Michael says to Amy and Sheryl.

Amy rolls her eyes.

"I didn't notice," Sheryl says, but Michael is looking past her to Amy.

"Don't roll your eyes at me. I told you I don't trust this guy. Why did he know that other guy? How? I bet they escaped from prison together. Why'd you think he had all this money?" Michael waves a wad of cash that he had stuffed away in his bag and coat.

"You took that?" Amy asks, astounded. "What an asshole," she mumbles under her breath.

Sheryl, feeling awkward in the crossfire of a lovers' quarrel, tries to break up the tension. "I didn't notice, but he did save us. If he hadn't been there, Willy would be dead, Brandon would be eaten, and I'd be gang raped. At least that's what that asshole made it sound like. You don't really think they would've eaten Brandon do you?"

"No. Sounded more like a sick joke to me," Amy answers.

"Me, personally, I don't care what Marcus did before, because what he just did now was courageous and good. Plus I think he's kinda hot," Sheryl adds with a nudge to Amy.

Amy smiles and sighs a quiet laugh. "He saved us too, and I don't care what his past is either. He opened up his doors to us and gave us shelter just before we were about to be eaten by a pack of monsters, and then he offered to give us a ride to my parents' house. My husband seems to forget that."

"No. I haven't forgotten. I'm just telling you I was right. I knew there was something shady about this guy." He turns to the others in the truck bed and speaks louder, walking away from Amy. "He was in prison! A criminal! He's an escaped convict!"

"Just let it go. As a wife you learn to pick your battles," Sheryl offers.

"Believe me, I know. I've been picking battles and ignoring wars for too long now," she laughs. "Where's your husband?"

Sheryl says it flatly, plain as fact. "Dead."

"Oh. I'm sorry, I…"

"Don't be," Sheryl interrupts. "The prick deserved it. I shot him myself. After he turned, of course," she adds when she sees Amy's face wince behind her mask.

"Is that your son back there? Your father?" Amy asks.

Sheryl shakes her head no. "I lost my two boys." Her voice is solemn.

"I lost my parents. My dad was killed, and my mom, she turned. I had to shoot her."

"My one boy died in an accident. The other. He came at me. I just wanted to see him one last time. In the morgue, at the hospital…" Sheryl begins to cry. Amy takes Sheryl's head onto her shoulder.

"I'm so sorry. I can't imagine what that must feel like."

#

"Why can't I shoot 'em? He pulled a gun!" Brandon argues with Willy as they both train their eyes down the barrels of their rifles. They watch Marcus as he talks to the scientists.

"Cause they're talking, that's why. You shouldn't be so quick to kill a man." Willy isn't concerned about Brandon firing his gun. The safety is on, and no matter how bad Brandon may want to pull the trigger, it won't fire.

"Why not? You were, back there," Brandon argues.

"That's different. I was a soldier, you know."

"So. I cleared Body Bags in one weekend on expert mode."

"That's different too, whatever the hell you're talkin' about," Willy blows him off.

"It's a game. What the hell are you doing with a gun anyway, kid?" Michael pries as he walks back from the side of the truck.

"It was my dad's. And don't try to tell me I'm too young to have one. I already used it a bunch to save my life. I killed people you know. Killed them dead." He eyes Willy. "Saved your old ass at the gas station too, remember?"

"I do. I never said you was too young. When I was your age I used to take my own guns on a bus to go hunting with my cousins for deer and duck," Willy explains.

"They let you on a bus with a gun?" Michael asks, astonished.

"Course they did. It's my right."

"Yeah well your right, as you call it, is being taken advantage of by lunatics who shoot up schools and movie theaters, and bad parents who keep guns around mentally deranged kids. Guns should be banned from civilian hands. Just look at what's happened in the past day or two with guns in peoples' hands. Even the kid says he killed people with his gun. To me, that's a horrible thing no matter how you slice it," Michael argues. "And as for hunting… Times have changed. We have grocery stores now," Michael adds with sarcasm.

"There'll always be a crazy person willing to do anything to finish his sick deeds. Even if you think criminals like those road warriors back there won't still be able to get guns, if you take away guns then a crazy person will just use a homemade bomb and kill even more people than he could with a gun. Gun rights are s'posed to be there for us to protect ourselves from criminals, and keep an overbearing government at bay. It ain't just about hunting."

"Right, right. Spare me the gun lobby talking points." Michael turns back to Brandon. "So the tough delta force video gamer is good with real guns? Who'd you kill with your gun, kid? Some of these zombies?" Michael asks.

"Yup. My own parents. Killed my daddy with a sledge hammer, and put a bullet through my mom's head like Lee Harvey did to JFK," Brandon answers coldly.

Michael is taken by surprise with his answer. "Damn. Was she riding in a convertible, near the book depository?"

The reference goes over Brandon's head. "Killed a living guy too, at least I think so. He fired first though. Dumb chink bastard…"

"My wife is Chinese, you little twerp," Michael interrupts.

"Quit talkin' like that. You sound like a damn fool," Willy scolds Brandon right after.

Brandon ignores them and keeps bragging on with his story. "I got lucky though. I shot wild, but it got him. Dropped him right in front of his house, on the lawn, right next to the two zombies that were trying to get inside."

"Wait a second. Did the house have a glassed-in porch?" Michael asks in a panic.

"Yeah. Right on my own street too. Maybury Street. I took out a couple windows on accident when I was firing at the stinkers."

"Shit!" Michael goes back over to the truck window near Amy.

Willy pulls his eyes off the scientist at the end of his sights and puts them on Brandon. "Gimme the gun, kid."

"No. Fuck that. This is mine and I got a right to have one," Brandon snaps.

"I know you do, son. I ain't gonna keep it. Just wanna hold it for a minute."

Brandon points the gun at Willy. "I'm the one in charge here. I have the map, and I'm the one who'll get us into the compound safely."

Willy sets his own rifle down in the truck bed, and slowly puts his finger into the barrel of Brandon's gun. He balls a fist with his other hand. With Brandon's eyes fixed in bewilderment at the end of his gun barrel, Willy punches him square in the face, knocking him back onto his ass. Brandon squeezes the trigger but there's only a click. He looks down to see that the safety is still on. Willy grabs Brandon's rifle and yanks it from his hands and gives him a good hard smack to the back of the head.

"That's for aiming at me," Willy says with a stern finger extended.

An instant later Amy drags Brandon backward over the side of the truck bed and onto the street. Her hands wrap tightly around his neck, squeezing the life out of him. He struggles to breathe inside his mask. Amy fumes over him, lifting one hand off his neck and moving toward his mask straps.

"You little shit! You killed my father! Now I'm gonna rip this mask off and watch you turn into one of them. Then I'll smash your damn head in!"

Sheryl runs up behind her and pulls her off before she can get her fingers around his mask. They fall backward to the ground, rolling around and wrestling with each other. Willy comes between them, holding them at a distance.

"Calm down! You don't wanna go fighting, and pulling each other's masks off."

"Yes I do!" Amy yells, glaring at Brandon as he gets up from the street, breathing deeply in his mask to catch his breath.

Marcus runs over when he sees the scuffle on his way back from talking with the scientists. He holds Brandon back with his massive arms locked around him in a bear hug.

"What'd you do, little man?" Marcus asks quietly in Brandon's ear.

"It was her parents. I was scared. I'm not a tough guy. I'm just trying to be brave. I was trying to practice shooting zombies. I was alone, going out to get supplies. I just went inside to see if there were any more and then he shot at me. It was all a misunderstanding. I shot back just to scare him. I didn't even aim, but I hit him. Then I ran. I ran. And then I saw Willy and Sheryl. I didn't mean it, I swear! I'm sorry. I'm sorry. I'm sorry." He cries through it all. "And my parents. It's my fault they're dead. They must have been trying to get in while I was knocked out. I killed them. It's my fault. It's my fault," Brandon says through his sobbing.

Sheryl goes to him. She thinks of her boys; that panicked, gasping kind of crying that can only be consoled by a mother. It breaks her heart. She takes Brandon in her arms.

Michael holds Amy as her anger turns back into sadness. She starts to sob. "I had to kill my mother. I had to kill my mother."

"So did Brandon," Willy says. "His dad too. He's been trying to tell himself that he wanted to, that he even liked it, just to deal with the fear, the guilt, the loneliness. Believe me, I know what you guys are going through. No one should have to experience this. It was forced on me, in the war, just like it's forced on you now. You can't escape it. And I've had to live with what I did ever since. Don't go killin' each other. What Brandon did to your daddy was a mistake, Amy." He turns to Brandon. "And what happened to your parents was out of your hands." Brandon hugs Sheryl tight. "I believe what he says now, because I saw through his tough guy braggin' right down into his soul. Lots of young guys just like him came over in the draft. That bull headed, macho attitude is just one way of dealing with the stress, the fear. Another way is goin' crazy, or turnin' to drugs and booze, and worse; suicide. I feel like I've dabbled in all of it, and the only way to get past it is you gotta first recognize that it's happening."

There's silence. After a few moments Marcus relays everything he learned from the scientist, and they solemnly move on.

CHAPTER 37

"Hey! Stop the truck, you gotta see this!" Brandon wraps on the cab window.

Marcus pulls over. "What is it?"

"Look. Through the clearing there. See it?" Brandon points.

A mushroom cloud towers up into the sky from where the largest meteor impact struck the earth. The black soot that once stood in solid contrast against the bright sky behind is now dispersing, blurring the image of the monstrous plume of deadly debris. Everyone takes in the horrific sight.

"We must be getting close," Brandon says. "That means Pittsburgh isn't too far. We should get off the highway soon. It's going to get dangerous as we pass by the city."

"He's right. We barely got out of the New York City area alive. We ran from a swarm of these monsters, and then all the roads were in gridlock."

"Could be fun though." Brandon smiles.

"We ain't got much ammo," Willy says. "Anyone got a map?"

"I do," Brandon says.

"We need more detail than that computer printout. Need to see a road map," Willy explains.

"I think I have one in the glove box," Marcus answers. "Let's see where we can turn off."

Amy approaches Brandon. She holds the note that her mother wrote to her. She's been reading it over and over on the drive. "Hey. I'm sorry I tried to kill you," she says, almost playfully.

"It's okay. I'm sorry I killed your parents," Brandon returns the light hearted attitude.

"But seriously. I've been thinking about it, thinking about what this note said that my mom left for me. They may have both started to get sick even before the windows broke. When you shot my dad, you might have been putting him out of his misery, and stopping him from changing too. When I got there, my mom was tied up in a chair. She already changed. Maybe my dad was just trying to keep her alive in case there was a cure."

"But your dad was fine. He had a gas mask on, right?" Brandon asks.

"Yeah, but something tells me he put it on too late. I don't know. The way this letter is written, it's like they knew they were both about to die."

Michael walks over. "What are you doing talking to this psycho?"

"Michael, just stop it, will you?" Amy says.

"Stop what? Telling the truth?" he sarcastically replies. "About Brandon? About Marcus?"

"No just... stop being a fucking dick to everyone," she mumbles. Michael rolls his eyes and there is silence between them.

Marcus walks over, having heard his name. "Found some county roads that might be a little safer. We can try those, but it still might be rough as we get close. I bet all the roads are patrolled and barricaded."

"Hey you guys should come with us to the compound," Brandon offers Amy.

"Compound?" Michael asks.

"Yeah. My girlfriend's family has this big farm where they've been preparing for a doomsday scenario. They've got water, food, shelter, weapons, and probably power too," Brandon explains. "She said I can bring whoever I wanted."

"Thanks but we'll just go our own way after we cross the border. I'm fully aware of what those kinds of places are like, and the kinds of people who do that shit. No way. They're fucking crazy people," Michael says.

"We don't know how dangerous it is over there. This could've spread. Who knows, it could be worse," Marcus adds. "Might be good to have a destination. A place we can settle into. A new beginning. Or even just a place to take a rest and figure out the next move. I'm up for it."

"I'd rather take my chances fending off an occasional infected person on my own in flyover country than to willingly lock myself into some mid-west, lunatic fringe, gun crazy, ultra-conservative, Christian cult compound."

"Ay man, why you gotta be so hostile against Christians?" Marcus fights back. He's finally had enough of Michael's intolerant remarks.

Michael snaps. "Oh please, Marcus... Don't get all self righteous with me. Why don't you tell us all who you really are? Huh? Why not tell us about how you knew those animals on the road earlier? Tell us about the stash of 'blood money' you had hidden away in your warehouse from 'before you went away.' Why not tell us the truth?"

"Michael..." Amy tries to cut him off.

"Because it's none of your damn business, that's why!" Marcus answers with widened eyes.

"No? I'd say it's right within our damn business, seeing as though we're travelling with you. I think we have a right to know who we're riding with," Michael argues. He turns to the others. "Don't you guys?" No one answers.

"You're welcome to walk," Marcus retorts.

"Just tell us! What are you hiding?" Michael pushes.

"Fine. You wanna know? I'm a convict. The jail turned into a madhouse when this plague hit, and a bunch of us got out. That's how I knew that fool on the road," Marcus explains.

"That fool? Seemed to me you were his friend. What'd you do to get sent to jail, huh?"

"I was selling drugs. Someone tipped off the cops, and I..." Marcus hesitates.

"Go on. The truth shall set you free!" Michael mocks him with laughter.

"It was murder." There's silence for a moment. "I did other bad things too. Things I never got caught for. But I'm a changed man now. A new man. Harley wasn't my friend, neither. Sometimes in jail you just get stuck rollin' with people, or groups of people, whether you like 'em or not. It's a hard thing to explain. I tried keeping to myself though, because I am a changed man. Reformed in Christ's image, as best I can."

"Yeah sure. That's what they all say, isn't it? How typical and hypocritical. He found God in the jailhouse chapel, and now he's saved! The murders of the past are wiped clean!"

"I never said that," Marcus says.

Michael folds his arms across his chest, standing proud and satisfied, as if he won some great victory. "You still want to ride with this guy? A drug dealing murderer? A man whose peers deemed him unfit for society?"

"I killed people. Lots of people. In the war." Willy says. "Also got stuck runnin' with groups of bad people despite my better judgment. Maybe it's not the same, but I can understand what it's like to make changes in your life. To reform, as you say."

"I killed Amy's dad," adds Brandon.

Sheryl puts a motherly hand on Brandon's shoulder. "I wanted to kill my husband. So many times. I was happy when we found him turned into one of those things," she says. "No. I don't care what you did, Marcus. You saved our lives. Every one of us here. He saved your life too, Michael. I don't care what he did."

"I don't care either," Amy says. She glares at Michael. "You're the only one who does. And I'll go to this compound or farm or whatever… with or without you."

"I'm not going anywhere without you," Michael says.

"Then I guess you owe Marcus an apology, and you should consider yourself lucky if he still lets you ride with him." She goes back into the truck.

CHAPTER 38

The slower drive on the county road feels more personal than the highway. More real. There's a story behind everything. The body draped over the wooden split rail fence; the half eaten child sprawled out in the middle of the road with a stuffed teddy bear next to her finger tips, just out of reach; the farm house torn in half, with a crater where the proud colonial once stood with decorative Christmas majesty. Every one of them is a tragedy; a nightmare come to life. They slowly pass by with solemn, grim thoughts.

But the soulless cannibals get no reprieve. Marcus parks the truck and slashes their heads in half any chance he gets. He sees it as his mission, his duty. Brandon quickly becomes enamored with him, and helps him with each kill.

Soon they come upon a string of cars blocking the road. Marcus drives up around the side for a closer look. It's not just a snarl of frozen traffic. They've reached a roadblock; the border barricade. They hear gunshots and fighting in the distance. Groups of people huddle close to the barrier, trying to get over, only to be gunned down. They see men and women hidden behind cars and makeshift walls. Local police, military personnel, and armed gunman are positioned behind barbed wire fences and concrete barricades on the other side, squaring off against westward travelers.

Michael gets angry when he sees a seemingly innocent person get shot down while holding nothing but a picket sign. He opens the cab window so Marcus and the women can hear him. "Those people are just protesting up there! We need to help them! They're being slaughtered!"

"Whoa whoa whoa, hold up. That's a lot of firepower on the other side there," Willy says. "Now look. A helicopter like that can be armed with turret guns that shoot bullets the size of beer bottles. You sure you want to go rushing up there? Besides, check out what's happening on this side." Willy points off to a small storefront building along the right side of the road where civilians are hiding. Two men carry what look like rocket launchers around the back, and other men with guns are scattered around in various hiding places, shielded from the view of the soldiers. "Something going on here. A rebellion or something. Best we stay back and avoid it."

Michael becomes indignant. "Screw that. You may be tired of war, but when I see shit like that I can't just sit back and do nothing. I want to help. We're gonna need to get through this blockade anyway if we want to make it to safety."

"I'll go. I kicked ass at Domestic Warfare III. I know what I'm doing," Brandon says. Willy shakes his head with disappointment again.

Marcus allows the truck to creep slowly toward the action. "Michael's right. We need to get past this. But maybe we can go around if the fighting is concentrated to the road." He turns left and starts to drive across some property that stretches back to a tree line, parallel to the blockade. Suddenly the helicopter rises up and turns its guns toward the truck, and nearly every gun on the barricade puts them in its sights.

"Shit. Get out! Run!" Sheryl yells. "They're going to shoot us!"

Marcus pulls the parking brake but leaves the pick-up running. Everyone bolts from the truck and sprints back the way they came; even Rocky. Bullets start raining down like a hailstorm. Marcus turns his head to see his beloved truck being riddled with holes. They dive behind some farm equipment as the gunfire penetrates the engine block. Marcus' jaw drops when he sees it explode. His pride and joy is engulfed in a massive flame, and it shatters into shards of flaming shrapnel and twisted metal. His heart sinks for a moment. *No matter. It's for the best. It was made with blood money, and now look: it burns and crumbles. The last remaining piece of the old me is finally gone.*

The rebels return fire, drawing the soldiers' attention away from the group. One of the rockets lets loose from behind the storefront building, blasting a gory hole of blood and rubble through the concrete road partitions that blocked the way. A moment later a stream of gunmen pop out all over the place from in hiding. Suddenly the fight looks evenly matched, except for the helicopter. The sound of its armament firing is deafening. The drone-like, mechanical whir of death fills the air with dread as people are mowed down by the dozen.

The rebels fire a second rocket. It erratically snakes its way up into the air. The helicopter sharply tips to try to avoid it, banking up and away. But the rocket finds its target and ignites the chopper into a fiery explosion. The heat that comes off the airborne fireball nearly singes their eyebrows off, and for one brief moment their icy skin is warmed by the burning fires of battle. The remains of the chopper crash down onto the soldiers standing along the barricade, crushing them and burning them alive.

"You know… I think I might actually be buying into your point about the second amendment, how it's meant for people to push back against an overbearing government," Michael says to Willy with a smile, winning a short chuckle from the old vet.

"Without those rockets and guns, we'd be sitting ducks right now," Marcus adds.

The rebels gained the upper hand, but the protesters and travelers are starting to change into bloodthirsty demons. It's mayhem. As if normal warfare wasn't chaotic enough, there are zombies to fend off as well. Soldiers and rebels alike are attacked and eaten. The bloody faces of the dead glow a bright crimson as a gentle snow begins to fall on the battleground.

Rocky starts to snarl and growl. One of the undead made its way over to them and lunges for Sheryl. He barks in rapid fire, and before anyone could hold him back, he darts out at the beast. Rocky leaps up and locks his jaws around the zombie's neck, sinking his teeth deep into its dead flesh and knocking it down to the ground before it can grab Sheryl.

"No! Rocky!" Sheryl yells, but Rocky ignores the command. He rips the flesh off the monster, burying his snout deeper into the

209

beast's neck. Sheryl walks up and puts a bullet into the zombie's head. Rocky looks up at her and releases the zombie's neck from his clutch. His ears go back and he whimpers. His breathing quickens and his eyes seem to fog up. He lies down and begins to shiver.

"Oh no! No Rocky, no!" Sheryl starts to cry. The only part of her family that was left alive is now dying. She wants to pet him, but she's frightened of him, and bullets are whizzing by all around them. "He's turning," she says as his mouth begins to foam up. "I can't do it. I can't," Sheryl whimpers.

Brandon loads his rifle and takes aim. Sheryl steps behind him as Rocky struggles back onto his feet. His hair is stiffened on end, and the skin on his snout is pulled back to reveal a furious set of teeth. The golden glow in his eyes means he has changed. Brandon squeezes the trigger, and Rocky is no more.

"Come on. Let's make a run for it now. There's an opening," Amy suggests.

"And plenty of dead bodies to keep the zombies busy," Brandon adds.

"Y'all go ahead. I'm going to run back to the truck and see if any of our supplies survived," says Marcus. "I think I see my scythe, believe it or not. I'll be right behind you."

Gunfire fills the air as they run. Willy leads them to strategic spots along the way; first along a fence line, then crouching and crawling near some bushes, and then sitting behind a car.

"Why are we stopping?" Sheryl asks.

"I'll give you some cover fire," Willy says. The others look confused. "You know what that is?" Blank stares come back at him.

"He'll fire his gun, so the enemy ducks. While they are ducking, we move forward," Brandon explains.

"That's right. Then you guys give me cover fire while I run up to meet you. Got it?" Willy asks.

"Got it." Sheryl nods.

"Okay now make for that truck up ahead like there's no tomorrow. Move, move, move!" Willy starts firing at the soldiers behind the remains of the barricade.

The soldiers take cover, and the group runs toward the truck. They dive behind it to safety and look back to Willy. Then Brandon and Sheryl begin firing at the barricade. Willy darts out into the open. But when he's about halfway across he meets with a bullet to his gut. It knocks him off his feet.

"Willy!" Sheryl screams as she stands up. Bullets hiss and zip by her ear, hitting the truck they're hiding behind. She ducks back down to safety.

"Shit! Keep shooting! He can make it to us," Brandon says.

Willy struggles to his feet and trots the rest of the way over. His body is bloodied. He flops back to the ground, and Sheryl takes his head into her lap. "We need to get him some help," she says.

"There's a guy over there with a red cross on his chest. Look. He's like a doctor or something," Michael says as he points across to the other side of the barricade.

"Let's go," Amy says.

"Michael. Take my gun," Sheryl says. "You and Brandon give us cover fire. Hopefully if they see two women with an injured old man in their arms they won't shoot."

"Okay," Michael says. A sense of power and purpose washes over him as he grasps the pistol grip.

Sheryl and Amy stand Willy up between them. His arms hang across their shoulders.

"On three," Brandon says. "One... Two... Three!"

CHAPTER 39

Dr. Vogel does his best to patch up the bullet and shrapnel wounds of fallen soldiers up and down the barricade. Things are looking pretty grim for the west though. First the highway was breached, and now this county road. The quarantine is falling apart, and that means the disease will spread.

Dr. Vogel's hopes were destroyed when he saw the chopper go down in flames, crushing the command tent and the supplies where his samples were stored. *The samples are ruined. I've got to go back and find Wolf. Maybe I can slip away without anyone noticing.*

The barricade is almost completely overrun. The rebels somehow managed to get their hands on a couple of RPGs and blew a hole through the barricade. They're crawling under the barbed wire fences, climbing over the cement dividers, and blasting through the sandbags. All the while more and more people are turning into ravenous beasts and eating each other. Three times already Dr. Vogel had to pull his piece and kill zombies that were rushing after the bleeding soldiers he was tending to.

This is fucking madness. I gotta get out of here.

"Help! Please help us! Are you a doctor?" a woman calls out for him. She and a younger woman carry an older man between them. He bleeds from his stomach.

"Was he bitten or shot?" Dr. Vogel asks.

"Shot," they say in unison as they set the old man down before him.

Dr. Vogel presses his hands around the wound to feel for the bullet. He takes out a long clamp-like pair of tweezers and plunges it into the bullet hole. It's deep, but he feels the tweezers make contact with it. The old man moans in agony.

"Just hang in there. I have to get this out, and then try to stitch you up quick because you're losing too much blood." Dr. Vogel explains.

"Is he going to be okay?" a young man asks as he runs up beside them.

"Vogel, what the fuck are you doing?" Colonel Wallace yells from just behind a toppled row of sandbags. "You're supposed to be helping the soldiers, not the rebels!"

"I care for *all* people. I took an oath to be a doctor, not a soldier!" Dr. Vogel nervously insists. His craft is no good under the incredible stress and pressure of a battlefield.

"And we're *Americans*, you asshole! Not rebels!" the young man yells.

"No. What you are is in violation of the quarantine," Wallace says as he raises his sidearm and takes aim at the young man.

The young man tosses his pistol aside and puts his hands up. "I'm unarmed."

"It don't matter," Wallace says as he squints one eye down the sight.

Just then Wallace's head jerks back and a mist of blood bursts out from behind. He falls to the ground, lifeless. Vogel's skin jumps at the sound of the gunshot, despite all the sounds of war going on around him. He turns to see a young boy with his eye trained down the barrel of an old rifle.

Jesus Christ, a kid? What the fuck is happening. In shock at the sight of a kid holding the weapon, he can't concentrate on the old man. It's a mess. The old man's skin is ice cold, blood is pouring out all over the place, and he can't seem to get a hold of the bullet. Frustrated, he tosses the tweezers aside and tries closing the wound. But his fingers are too cold and numb to feel anything. Sticky yet slick with blood, they're pretty much useless. He can't fix the wound, and the old man is slipping away, shivering. He can't help but feel responsible for the old man. *This might have gone better if the circumstances were different. Just a few degrees warmer, perhaps. Or if I had gotten a hold of that bullet.*

A roar of cheers erupts all around them. The barricade is completely down, and the soldiers are in retreat. Floods of people barrel over the rubble and into the west, to freedom.

"I'm sorry. I'm so sorry." Dr. Vogel looks the old man right in his eyes as they slowly roll back into his head. Soon the shivering stops. He lies motionless, cold and dead. Dr. Vogel slams his medical kit to the ground in frustration, stomping it under his foot.

"Willy!" The woman drops to her knees beside him. Her mask fills with tears.

CHAPTER 40

"What the hell happened here? Who are you?" Marcus asks. He's nearly out of breath from running, but his scythe is slung across his back once again.

"I'm Dr. Vogel. I tried to help this man. Willy. Was that his name?"

They stand in silence, looking down upon Willy. After a few moments Marcus introduces himself and the others.

"Willy was a good man," Marcus says.

"He was, or at least he seemed to be. I only knew him, what, half a day? But he already got me to think about guns differently. In fact I think I'll take one of these handguns to keep on me. I feel bad that I was harsh towards him," Michael offers as he tucks a dead soldier's sidearm into his waistband.

"He reminded me so much of my dad," Sheryl adds. "He really tried to hold me together, you know? He could've just left me to fend for myself. He would've survived on his own, no doubt about it. It's like he came out this way to help me. Totally selfless. And now he's dead because of me."

"Don't say that," Marcus consoles her. She hugs him.

"I feel terrible about this. If it wasn't for all the insanity that was here a few minutes ago, he'd still be alive," Dr. Vogel says.

"I'm sure you did your best," Michael says.

"Well, let's give him a proper burial," Marcus suggests.

"I'll help," Dr. Vogel offers.

They dig a hole and find some rocks to use as headstones for Willy's grave. They lower him into the grave as the sun begins to fall. After they cover him up with stones, Marcus gathers them for a prayer. He finishes with: "and you shall return unto the ground; for we come from dust, and we return to dust. Amen." Silence follows for a few moments as they stand and pray.

Brandon smirks as they walk away. "Ashes to gashes, dust to dead."

Marcus smacks him on the back of the head.

"Oww!"

"Knock it off little man. Show some respect," Marcus sternly reprimands him.

"What, I'm just trying to put the 'fun' in 'funeral.' Jesus!"

Marcus smacks him again. "Don't call him unless you mean to talk to him."

"Oww! Alright, already! Alright!" Brandon rubs his head. "Sorry."

"Ain't nothin' to be sorry to me about. Be sorry to God. Be sorry to Willy," Marcus says.

They all walk down the county road, away from the battlefield. Bodies lay strewn all over the area, staining the yellowed grasses red with gore. The lingering zombies feed on the bodies, paying no attention to the living.

"Ah, now isn't that clever?" Michael remarks. He picks up the crisped remains of the picket sign that reads "Man-feast Deadstiny."

"The guy holding it was chanting 'go west, dead man' over and over. I wonder if he made it." Dr. Vogel adds. "This is horrible. I know you guys must have been struggling just to get here, and fighting to get across, but a busted quarantine means bad news for the rest of the world. You shouldn't be here. And I'd try to stop you myself if I thought it'd make a difference. But the truth is it's too late. We're fucked." *Unless I find Wolf…*

"Think the military will be back to plug this hole?" Marcus asks Dr. Vogel.

"Maybe. I'm not sure. I came here today just to deliver some medical samples I collected from a patient. He seemed to be immune to the airborne version of this disease."

"Deliver to the military?" Michael asks.

"I thought maybe I could get an escort down to the CDC. The guy your son shot promised to help get me on my way but I guess that isn't happening. The military retreated, the chopper is destroyed, and so are the samples," Dr. Vogel explains.

"He's not our son," Michael corrects him.

"After a ways this road runs up and hits the highway, and the highway is like a whole other kind of war zone. I think you're better off going through the woods to wherever it is you're going," Dr. Vogel continues.

"West," Brandon says.

"Me too," says Dr. Vogel. "I need to go back and find Wolf, so we may as well walk together a while."

"What you need to find a wolf for?" Marcus asks.

"Not *a* wolf. Wolf. Wolf Camden. He's my immune patient," Dr. Vogel explains.

Brandon's eyes widen. "Are you serious? I love Extreme Naturalist. It's like the coolest show ever!"

"Yeah, you and my kids too." Dr. Vogel chuckles. "Greatest show to ever happen to the Boy Scouts."

"What do you mean he's immune? I watched him breathe the smoke right in! I hadn't thought about it since, but he should be a zombie right now. How awesome is the idea of a zombie Wolf Camden?!" Brandon bounces with excitement. "He'd be like, totally invincible."

"I dunno kid. He came to my hospital and was having trouble breathing. He told me what happened, so I took some samples. I heard the emergency broadcast, so then I locked him up because he was west of the quarantine. I tried getting in touch with the CDC. No luck. And then he broke out. Escaped."

"Stupid ass. Wolf can escape anything," Brandon brags.

"Apparently so," says Dr. Vogel. "So where are you all heading?"

"The Branch Davidian Compound. Our happy new home awaits!" Michael says sarcastically.

"You can go your own way now if you want. We're past the quarantine," Amy snaps back.

219

"About 70 miles from here," Brandon says as he pulls out one of the many printed maps he has with directions on it.

"Shit. How long is it going to take to walk 70 miles?" Michael asks.

"Where are we now, let's see..." Dr. Vogel looks over the map. "You're gonna have to cross the highway anyway, looks like. And a river, too. Good news is we're still heading in the same direction for a while. Let's just hope the highway isn't too badly mobbed when we have to cross."

"There are some military tents lying around back there." Brandon points. "We should go as far as we can before nightfall and then sleep in those."

CHAPTER 41

After an uneasy sleep in the cold, they try to put down some MREs they found near the border. The morning is darker than the previous evening. The woods and a creeping set of black storm clouds block out the sun. They walk on and on. It's so dark that most of the day goes by without a change in brightness overhead. Dawn bleeds into day, and day bleeds into dusk. And all the while it's snowing.

Brandon sings. "I'm dreaming of a red Christmas, with every zombie that I fight. May your days be dreadful with fright, and may all your Christmases be bloody."

Michael shakes his head. "You're a crazy person. That doesn't even rhyme."

"Who cares, it's funny," Brandon says through a laugh.

"There's a road up ahead. It's the highway I was telling you about. We have to cross it, but when I was there it was a madhouse. We better be ready for the worst," Dr. Vogel cautions. He glares at Brandon. "And be quiet."

The trees thin out ahead of them. The road sits silently beneath frozen, snow covered traffic. Marcus scans the area looking for demons. "I don't see any," he whispers.

"They're covered in snow, laying on the ground," Sheryl answers. She sees the snowy bumps in the road and knows that there must be people underneath.

"Those are dead people though, right?" Amy asks. "Wouldn't the zombies be up?"

"Who knows. Let's find a place to cross with less bumps. Better safe than sorry," Sheryl says.

"I think we should set up camp before it gets too dark," Brandon says.

"We can't do it here. We're too close to the road. I'm telling you it's bad," Dr. Vogel says.

"Yeah we should get as far past the road as we can before we stop for the night," Marcus says.

"I don't like it," Brandon says.

"It'll be alright little man. Have some faith," Marcus says.

"Opiate of the masses, kid. Soothes all your worries," Michael retorts. Brandon's face is blank. He doesn't get it. *Must be nice to be so ignorant*, Michael thinks.

They step out of the woods onto the shoulder of the road. A cold shroud of snow covers the whole scene like a white sheet draped over old furniture in an abandoned mansion. Snow drifts pile up alongside flipped and crashed cars, hiding God knows what kinds of horrors beneath. The wind pelts them with icy bits of snow as it blusters down the empty highway. There are eerie snow bumps almost everywhere. Some are big, and some are small. Some are faintly reddened with blood, and others are yellowed with piss. Some are on cars, and some are on the road. The cars are all covered in snow too; it's even managed to pile up on one car that's still running but stuck in place, jammed into an accident and overturned along the center median. A few moments later the engine sputters to a stop, and the air is filled with only the sound of wind, and the quiet tinkling of icy snowflakes as they silently shatter on every surface they fall upon.

"Move quietly," Sheryl whispers. But the squeaky crunch of snow beneath their feet sounds so loud compared to the unnerving silence of the road. So loud it could wake even the dead.

The wind blasts them as they reach the middle of the road. The snow sticks so fast that their masks get covered and need constant wiping. Dr. Vogel shields his eyes and tips his head down as he plods on, not looking where he's stepping. One wrong step topples him over the edge of a bump in the road. He falls on top of it with a grunt. "Fuck," he utters as he tries to regain his footing. But the bump stirs. He hears a moan and then sees the snow fall away from the bump as it rises to its feet. "Run!" Dr. Vogel yells. The others turn back to see what happened. Other bumps are rising now; three, five, eight… "Run!"

They bolt across the rest of the road with reckless abandon, stepping on bumps, tripping, falling, getting back up, fending off cold dead grasps, and heading fast for the woods on the other side. They run, and run, and run, until the silence of the woods surrounds them once again. They stop to catch their breath. Night has fallen.

"Anyone bitten?" Marcus asks. No one answers.

CHAPTER 42

After dragging the bodies of several dead zombies outside his living area, Wolf settles in for a bit of crisped squirrel and some hot birch bark tea. He flips on a small battery powered radio and twists the knobs until the static clears. He hears a new emergency broadcast.

"Weather patterns are preventing debris from moving west of the impact. The debris cloud is settling, and isolated parts of the northeast have safe air, however it is best to continue using air filtration systems and breathing masks to be safe. The Lazarus condition is now spreading more violently in the form of aggression; specifically by bites from the infected. Remain indoors, and avoid contact with anyone who may be infected."

Thanks for telling me what I already knew. They're not even letting people know how you can stop these things with a blow to the head. Typical politically correct garbage. They don't want to encourage people to kill each other.

Next he gives the CB radio another try. To his surprise he hears the familiar voice of Spider yammering away with another story of vanquishing the undead. Cough Drop's raspy voice pokes in with questions here and there.

Wolf jumps into the mix. "Breaker one nine, this is Wolf."

Spider howls like a wolf. Cough Drop laughs, and so does Wolf. "How you doin' old buddy?" Spider asks.

"Barely surviving, you know. But tomorrow…"

"There's always tomorrow." Cough Drop and Spider deliver Wolf's tag line in unison.

"You got it," Wolf responds. "I set up a home camp a little ways off the highway. Close enough to poach supplies if I need any, but far enough not to be detected by anyone. Only problem is every once in a while I get some stragglers, some poisoned people wandering around in search of flesh."

"Not too shabby, considering," says Spider.

"Any news since we spoke last?" Wolf asks. "I've pretty much been living in the woods."

"Well it looks like we got ourselves another civil war brewin' up at the quarantine," Spider answers.

"How do you mean?" Wolf asks.

"A bunch of people from the east were mobbing up and trying to break through the barricades just west of Pittsburgh. Folks on our side are helping the government keep 'em at bay," Spider says. "But now it's gotten pretty serious. No more rubber bullets and water cannons, and every road that goes west out of the quarantine has fightin' brewing up. It's a border war, and the good guys are losing to the dead guys."

Cough Drop chuckles. "It might be the only time in history that the mid-west conservatives are on the side of big government."

"Sometimes you got to protect the homeland from the people at home," adds Spider. "Get your guns ready, cause the west just got wild again."

"Might not be worth fighting anymore. I heard there were some meteors further west too, near the Rockies. Unconfirmed though. But I say these borders ain't going to hold. Better off just holing up and protecting our own now. Pretty soon no place'll be safe," Cough Drop adds. "Glad my family and I have been preparing for something like this."

"Any more info about the disease itself?" Wolf asks.

"They callin' it Lazarus, named for the meteor," Spider says. "Lazarus A for airborne, and Lazarus B for the bite kind."

"Did they identify what it is? A virus?" Wolf asks.

"Don't know. But another guy on the CB said that he heard some older house pets can turn; weaker domesticated types, but not the younger ones or wild animals. Seems if you're in better physical shape then it'll take longer to make you change, at least for breathing it in. When people are bitten I guess it all depends on how severe the bite is," replies Spider.

"Yeah we thought you'd have changed, being you breathed it all in," says Cough Drop.

"I did feel quite ill, but then it passed," Wolf says. "I'm a wolf, so I guess I'm immune since I'm a wild animal. What happens if a wild animal gets bitten by one of the undead?" Wolf laughs.

"Hell, you got me there boss. I got no idea," Spider says through a laugh.

"Me neither," Cough Drop adds.

"Say... if we're close by we should meet up and have ourselves a bar-b-que!" Spider suggests. "I still got about a dozen cases of beer. I prepared myself real good."

Wolf laughs. "I'm going to ride it out in the woods until all of this passes. At this point it seems more dangerous to be around others than to be alone in the wilderness in winter, no offense."

"I reckon it'll be a long while before this one passes," Cough Drop warns.

"Let's hope you're wrong about that one, mate. But if it does pass that bar-b-que sounds like a great idea," says Wolf.

"Is it true, you know, about Australians puttin' shrimp on the bar-b-que?" Spider jokes.

"Only when we run out of kangaroo meat," Wolf says sarcastically.

The three of them laugh.

"I'd better turn in for the night," Cough Drop says.

"Yeah me too," says Wolf. "Time to climb up into my tree bed."

"There's always tomorrow. Spider out," he says.

Wolf shuts the radio and disconnects the battery. The silence of the winter's night fills his ears once again. He puts the fire out and climbs up his tree for another cold, uneasy sleep. A light snowfall coats the sparse oak canopy above. Wolf hears a light rustling in the distance. A few of the dead leaves that still cling to their branches moisten and fall to the ground below. But it's not that. *Footsteps. People.* He hears their voices as they approach. Then the car keys jingle. They've set off his trip wire.

CHAPTER 43

"Jingle bells. Dead guys smell. Shoot zombies in the head. Oh what fun it is to die in a zombie apocalypse. Hey! Bleeding on the snow, with the dead piled on a sleigh. Through the woods we go, killing zombies all the way. Hey! Shells from shotguns ring, making brains fly. What fun it is to laugh and sing in a zombie song tonight. Ohh… Jingle---"

"Oh man. Here we go again," Michael interrupts. "Christmas is over!"

Brandon suddenly goes silent. "Shit, did you hear that?" he asks.

"Yeah, ADD boy. We're trying *not* to hear it," Michael adds, winning laughs from the others.

"No, it was a jingling sound," Brandon explains.

Michael stares at him blankly, expecting it to be some kind of joke. "Maybe it was Santa Claus. His sleigh got knocked out of the sky by meteors," Michael adds.

"I think I heard it too," Marcus says.

"I knew we should've set up camp while it was still light out," Brandon mutters.

"Hold it right there!" a voice booms from the darkness. They stop dead in their tracks. "The whole place is booby trapped. You'd better go back the way you came."

"We don't want any trouble. Just passing through," Marcus says as he looks around for the source of the voice.

"Well, pass through somewhere else," the voice answers.

"Is that Wolf?" Brandon talks to himself. He recognizes the voice, the rustic Australian twang. "Wolf Camden, is that you?" he asks louder. There's no response.

"Just the man I need to see," Dr. Vogel adds. "Wolf, it's your doctor. Dr. Vogel."

There's silence for a few moments, then the rustling of tree branches followed by the crunching of snowy footfalls. Wolf emerges from the darkness. "You've got some set of stones showing yourself to me," he stares at Dr. Vogel as he walks closer. "Locking me up like some kind of wild animal?"

Brandon's jaw drops in awe. He's star struck. Dr. Vogel bumbles his words, trying to figure out an excuse that might satisfy. But before he can spit out anything coherent, Wolf decks him in the face with a right hook. The blow knocks him off his feet. Wolf stands with his fists clenched in anger.

Marcus tightens his grip on the scythe. "Take it easy now. We said we don't want any trouble." Wolf pays no mind to Marcus' menacing mannerisms. He just stares at Dr. Vogel.

Dr. Vogel spits out some blood in his mask. The shot made him bite his tongue. "You're right Wolf. I deserved that. But I don't think you realize how important you might be."

Wolf takes a few steps forward and stands over Dr. Vogel, fuming as he looks down. Marcus squares up his feet, ready to defend his flock with the flash of his blade if needed. *The living are worse than the dead*, he thinks again, wondering if this is another test. But then Wolf extends an open hand to help Dr. Vogel stand up.

"Holy shit, it's fucking Wolf Camden!" exclaims Brandon.

"Let's keep a lid on it, shall we?" Wolf suggests. "Otherwise they'll find us."

#

Against his better judgment, Wolf lights another fire for his guests. They're cold and wet, and he figures the benefits of company and social interaction outweigh the benefits of a good night's sleep. He's still leery of them, but after a quick assessment he sees no real threat. They're just passing through, after all.

"So where are you all headed?" Wolf asks.

"A prepper compound west of here. Not too far either," Brandon answers. "Would you help us get there?"

"I'm staying here. Going to wait it out until this whole thing passes, and do what I do best," Wolf says.

"I don't think this place will be safe for much longer," Sheryl adds. "The barricades are breaking, and people are carrying the disease west. I mean, we're all okay. None of us breathed it in or were bitten, but we were there when the quarantine broke. We were only on a small road and it was still bad, so I can't imagine how insane it is now on the main ones."

"It's safe to breathe here, or so I've heard," Wolf says. "I'm doing fine without the mask."

"You're a special case, Wolf. It might be safe to breathe but I certainly wouldn't take any chances. By the way, the samples I took from you were destroyed. I was trying to get them to the CDC. I thought maybe we could figure out a way to stop this disease."

"How's that?" Marcus asks.

"Well, I used to work for the CDC. If we were to get down there with someone who's immune, they might be able to make a cure," Dr. Vogel explains.

"That's a long hike," Wolf says.

"But a noble one," Dr. Vogel says. "Worth the risk, I'd say."

"Aye. I'll give you your samples then," Wolf says. "But don't you need some medical equipment?"

"Yes. We could go back to my hospital, but…"

"Bad idea," Sheryl says. "Hospitals aren't safe. Trust me."

"They've got medical supplies where we're going," Brandon says. "You could come with us." There's excitement in his eyes. The idea of traveling with Wolf is right up there with his thoughts of Apocalypta in lingerie. He has no idea what she looks like, but in his mind she's a hot pin-up or a porn star. And she'd be all over him if she knew he was hanging with Wolf.

231

"Well, what I was going to say is that samples are one thing, but if I could get *you* to the CDC with me, then we'll have a better chance at solving this thing," Dr. Vogel says.

"You have any idea how dangerous a trip like that can be?" Wolf says.

"I can imagine," says Dr. Vogel.

"On foot no less. The roads are death traps. And you don't think they'll try to lock me away just like you did? Stuff me in some windowless room 12 floors underground behind decontamination walls? No thanks, mate. I'll help you get to this compound and give you your samples, but that's as far as I'll go."

"I'll take what I can get," Dr. Vogel says.

#

Marcus leafs through the Bible beside the fire, taking note of passages that mention the dead coming back to life.

Michael eyes him and walks over. He scoffs. "You went back to the truck for supplies and this is what you came back with? The Bible and your threshing blade?"

"It's a miracle. Completely unscathed," Marcus holds up the Bible to show him.

"A miracle, eh? So what does your book tell you about what's happening to us all? Is it the end of the world?" Michael asks sarcastically.

"Isaiah says: 'Your dead will live. Their bodies will rise. Hide yourself until this wrath passes by. The Lord is coming to punish the sinners.' And Jeremiah says: 'I will make them eat the flesh of their sons and daughters.' Jesus rose from the dead. Lazarus rose from the dead. Only God can do that... can make people come back."

Michael rolls his eyes. He can't even begin to get into it with Marcus on this stuff. "Ridiculous," he says. "You know... I look at this from a scientific perspective. Zombies aren't fit, as a species. It's survival of the fittest out there, and they're on the path to extinction. They can't use tools or weapons. They don't think. Their method of reproducing is also their food source *and* a dangerous predator. Humans. Thinking, intelligent humans. Just imagine if every time you wanted to fuck or eat, you needed to fight a tiger that was smarter than Einstein first." The group laughs.

"So then we're in agreement," Marcus says. "The Bible says to wait for the wrath to pass. And you say the zombies are doomed for extinction anyway."

"Yeah but isn't this the end of the world for you?" Michael asks.

"I don't know. Revelation is the book about the end times. It says a beast will come from the abyss and kill us. Our dead will sit in the streets for three days and then rise and strike fear into the living," Marcus explains.

"And you believe this stuff? Like in a literal sense?" Michael asks, this time more sincerely.

"These are prophetic visions. They're not meant to be taken so literally. If you read some of the other zombie passages in the proper element, then nothing really predicts any of this. They're about specific things in the old days. I just look to it for guidance. I recognize that some things are too powerful for me to control, and that there are things bigger than me at work here."

"So you'll just sit around and wait for things to get better? To hell with science trying to find a cure?" Michael asks.

"I never said that," Marcus responds.

"You know what we should do," Brandon jumps in. "We should get suits of armor, so the zombies can't bite us. Imagine how sick it would be to have a full suit of armor? The knights of the apocalypse... That would be a totally kickass video game concept."

"That would make you too slow and noisy," Wolf reasons. "Better off with something like bulletproof vest material, so you can move quieter, quicker, and be more agile."

Brandon nods his head in agreement. "Yeah... we need to get that. Sweet."

The sound of clanging climbing hooks breaks the conversation. Then the sound of pebbles rattling in a can, then car keys.

"Anyone wander off?" Wolf asks. Everyone looks around at each other but no one is missing. "Get ready, or climb a tree.

They're coming from both sides. Silent weapons only. No guns," Wolf whispers.

Sheryl and Amy climb up into Wolf's tree. Dr. Vogel grabs a medium sized hunting knife that was plunged into the dirt close to the fire. Marcus stands alert with his scythe in hand. Michael, Brandon and Wolf each grab one of the nearby spears that Wolf sharpened out of branches. They can hear the beasts groaning and shambling through the dead leaves and snow.

Three of them appear out of the darkness. Their eyes glow with pissy bloodshot luminance. Brandon is eager to vanquish them. He plunges his spear into the lead zombie's face, killing it instantly. The other two reach for him, but Marcus slashes one clean in half at the waist and then stomps on its head. Dr. Vogel jabs his knife down into the top of the other's skull.

Michael and Wolf fend off two apiece from the rear. One has a busted leg, a twisted torso, and its arm is shorn off clean at the elbow. It was clearly in some sort of car accident. Michael takes that one down first. He clubs it with the spear, knocking it down to the ground easily. Then he steps up and jams the spear down with two hands into the beast's right eye. Marcus and Dr. Vogel come over to help with the rest.

Brandon takes in the scene. "Awesome."

"Look out behind you!" Sheryl yells down from the tree top. A zombie runs toward Brandon from further back in the woods.

A loud snap echoes off the trees. Then the woody zipping sound of rope being yanked tightly across tree bark fills the forest. Brandon turns to see a zombie dangling in the air by its feet, hanging upside down from one of Wolf's snares just a few strides away.

"It worked! Excellent," Wolf says. "Too bad I didn't get you in one of my traps, eh?" He nudges Brandon with his elbow. Brandon laughs. "Whew! Smells like shit, doesn't it?" Wolf holds his nose in disgust.

"The mask blocks most of it, but sometimes I can smell them anyway," Brandon says. "They piss and crap themselves when they turn. Throw up too. Nasty."

"Come on then. Let's go put him out of his misery, shall we?" Wolf suggests.

"Wait, wait!" Dr. Vogel says just before Brandon skewers the dangling beast. "I'd like to examine him first."

"Be my guest," says Wolf. "Best to tape his mouth shut, just to be safe, yeah?" Wolf rummages through a pack by the campfire and flings Dr. Vogel a roll of duct tape.

Dr. Vogel manages to wrap the tape around the zombie's head, covering its mouth. He binds its hands together too as a precaution. First he checks for a pulse. There is one; steady and fast. He presses his ear against the zombie's chest next, listening for any blockage in breathing. There is none, but the body is cool to the touch. "It's as if they're completely rebooted after they die. They breathe, and have a heartbeat. But they're cold as ice." Just then a stream of warm liquid courses over Dr. Vogel's hands as he rests them on the zombie's stomach. Piss. "Ugh! Digestive system still works too," he adds as he plunges his hands into some fresh snow to clean them.

"Dude, you just got pissed on by a zombie?" Brandon bursts into laughter. The zombie writhes and struggles as it hangs there. "Can we kill it now?"

"Sure, go ahead. I'm completely baffled," Dr. Vogel says. Before he can even finish, Brandon has his spear lodged into the beast's brain.

"They have a keen sense of smell too. For blood. They're like sharks," Wolf adds, pointing at the bottom edge of Dr. Vogel's mask. A line of blood trickles down his neck from under the mask.

Dr. Vogel wipes it away. "That'll teach you for hitting me."

"It was worth it." Wolf smiles. "We have to get out of here at first light. Sheryl's right. It's getting too dangerous because of the barricades failing. Get some rest, everyone. I'll take first watch. If anything happens I'll wake you up."

CHAPTER 44

Sheryl wakes early, as the darkness fades back into the light of morning. She smiles as she watches Brandon sleep underneath the tarp of his military tent. She knows she's slipping from herself, attaching a mother's love to this bizarre child. But she lets it happen. It's the only way she can cope. Her eyes play tricks on her in the dimly lit grey woods, turning his face into Stephen's, then BJ's. When Brandon's eyes burst open her skin jumps at the memory of seeing BJ's eyes glimmer with evil in the dark morgue.

"Jesus, lady. What the fuck are you looking at?" Brandon mumbles as he turns over and gives his back to Sheryl.

One minute he's giddy like a child, and the next acting like an adult, Sheryl thinks. *He's going through an extremely awkward phase. This whole meteor thing isn't helping either.*

Soon everyone is up. There are arguments about trying to take Wolf's truck from the nearby highway, but Wolf assures them they're more likely to survive out in the wilderness, off the road. They just have to make the long hike to the compound. Wolf says it'll be a couple of days, depending on terrain and weather conditions. They pack up some gear and start walking.

Brandon sings more morbid versions of Christmas songs as they crunch through the icy leaves in the woods. "Later on, we'll expire. As we're gnawed beside the fire. We're all so afraid of what the meteor made. Walkin' in a zombie wonderland."

"Shh... Don't want to make any more noise than we already are," Wolf says.

"Hey check it out." Amy points. "There's a clearing up ahead." The woods trickles away in the distance and opens up to a frosty dead grassland that stretches out and slopes downward.

"Quiet. Everyone stop moving," Wolf says. A moment later their creaky footsteps give way to a quiet rush of water. "A stream. Just down that slope no doubt. If we follow it up a ways we can probably cross it without having to get wet. There'll be a bridge eventually," Wolf says.

"What difference does it make? We're already soaked," complains Michael.

"Not down to your skin. Believe me. If you step into that stream and the water goes up to your chest, you can go into cardiac arrest from hypothermia within moments in this cold. Especially if you don't warm your core back up fast enough and put on dry clothes."

"He's right," Dr. Vogel adds.

"Yeah. Duh." Brandon scoffs at Michael. "Don't you watch his show?"

"I don't watch television at all. It poisons the brain," he responds. "Just like video games and comic books."

"Friggin' hippie fag," Brandon utters under his breath.

"Stay quiet," Marcus says.

"Yeah, and keep close to the woods line, not out in the open," Wolf adds.

#

After a few miles they see a huge patch of black grass up ahead in the clearing. They start to speculate about what it could be as they draw near.

"Burned. I bet they did one of those flame thrower things there like we saw on the other side of the barricades," Brandon says.

"No. Look. It's moving," Amy says.

"I hear them squawking. It's birds. Crows," Marcus says.

"I think you're right," Wolf adds.

"Only one way to find out," Brandon says as he hurls a stone toward the cluster with girlish form.

The rock lands well short of the black mass, but the sound startles them. A thousand crows instantly take to the air, blackening the morning sky. The sound of flapping and screeching fills their ears. Several birds flop back down to the ground in death, while others fly erratically. Still some are more aggressive, crashing into others mid-flight and pecking at their bodies.

"Holy shit. They're infected," Michael says.

"You think?" Amy asks.

"Of course. Crows are scavengers. They eat the dead. Then the meteor shit gets into their bodies and they turn," he explains.

"We'd better hide. If they make for us it'll be like a Hitchcock film out here in no time," Wolf suggests. "Back into the woods. Now!"

A swarm of undead crows spirals in the air, chasing down a flock of those still living that tries to evade them.

"They're heading for the woods!" Amy shouts as the birds make a turn in their direction. Some crows disappear into the canopy over their heads.

"I see a bridge," Sheryl says. "Look past where the birds were on the meadow, up ahead."

"Run for it and hide underneath. Now! Go!" Wolf says, and they all sprint out across the meadow toward the bridge.

A flickering shadow hovers over them as they run. The birds are everywhere; in the air above, zipping by their sides, dead underfoot, and dropping from the sky all around them, peppering the ground. They reach a vacant dirt road and a lonely wooden bridge that spans the stream. They crouch under the planks along the river bank, staying on dry land as the birds soar and screech overhead.

"It's like watching fighter planes in a dogfight," Amy says.

"This is bad. Real bad. See? This is why you don't eat meat. This is why you go veggie. Man wasn't meant to eat meat," Michael says.

"What the hell are you talking about, mate?" Wolf asks.

"Think about what this does to the food supply. If birds, why not chickens, or fish, or any other animal that can get infected from eating the virus? And then if we eat the animal, what happens to us?" Michael asks.

"It's not a virus. I've studied it. And if it alters animal cells then why not plant cells?" Dr. Vogel asks. "I mean let's be truly open minded about it, rather than just try to shove a food agenda down someone's throat, no pun intended. And cooking it might kill it, whatever it is."

"Plants have rigid cells, right? I bet this stuff can't penetrate them, so it'd be as easy as just washing the dust off. It's not like plants can bite people, or have blood," Michael argues.

"Yeah but they have plenty of fluids. And would you want to be the first person to try eating a plant that was just covered in zombie dust? It's not worth the risk. Safer to just stick to canned goods for now, until we know more."

"That shit is just as toxic for your body," Michael retorts. "We're not meant to eat preservatives and industrial chemicals."

"Maybe. But they don't turn you into a cannibal, and they'll keep you alive if you're starving." Dr. Vogel fires back.

"I like canned beans," Brandon adds out of nowhere. They all stare at him curiously for a moment, not having any idea what the hell he's talking about. "The good news is that the compound has a closed greenhouse, so no dust will hit the vegetables. And they probably knew to move the chickens and rabbits they breed for food indoors," Brandon says. That seems to settle the argument. "I'm telling you; these people are no joke."

"Yes, yes. We know. They're Apocalypse Preppers. Thank you, Education Channel, for spreading that plague," Michael says.

"I thought you didn't watch TV?" Brandon asks.

"I don't, but I know about the lunatics on that show," Michael answers.

"You're a lunatic for only eating vegetables!" Brandon argues. Amy chuckles.

"Looks like they're all heading back into the woods," Marcus says. The sky is clearing out over the meadow, giving them a chance to cross the bridge safely and move on.

CHAPTER 45

They continue along the dirt road for a while. Flanked by wooded areas on either side, they feel safe, and Wolf assures everyone that they're heading in the right direction. A heavy breeze picks up. It blows directly into their faces and blusters through the woods beside them, making an otherwise silent walk hiss with the white noise of leaves in the wind.

"Do you think they sleep?" Brandon asks.

"What, the zombies?" Michael asks. "Like when they got up on the road in the snow?"

"Yeah. When I found my parents, I could swear they were dead, and not undead. They weren't moving or breathing, and they had no pulse. I even dragged their bodies away from my bomb shelter. Then they got up while I was doing something else. It's like they were asleep," Brandon explains.

"Maybe. When I took the police car I might have woken one up," Sheryl adds. "A cop was dead at the wheel. Or I thought he was dead. I moved him out of the door, and after I got his keys from his pocket he got up. He had to have already changed, otherwise I would've seen or heard it happen, like with Rocky."

"You'd know it if he changed right there on the spot," Marcus says.

"It's not a pretty sight," Dr. Vogel adds.

"So then maybe they do sleep, or go dormant or something," Brandon concludes.

"Their pulse is very fast when they're active, so maybe when they're inactive it slows down, like when an animal hibernates," Dr. Vogel suggests. "That could be why *you* didn't feel any pulse when you checked your parents, but *I* felt a fast one in Wolf's trap. Either that or you somehow found them just when they died, before they changed, and then they changed after you dragged them away."

"I think they were there all night. They must've been asleep," Brandon answers.

"The amount of snow covering the ones on the road yesterday suggests they were laying there for at least a few hours. So maybe they do go to sleep when they're not feeding. It's like some kind of short term hibernation," Dr. Vogel muses.

The dirt road begins to twist and meander, and the grey sky above grows darker as night approaches once again.

"Come on. We should try to find some cover in the woods. This wind is bone chilling," Wolf waves them off the road and back into the trees.

After a few minutes of searching for a good spot to shield themselves from the elements, Sheryl spots an old structure. "Is that a barn?" she asks.

"Looks like it," Dr. Vogel says. "Has to be abandoned."

"That'll do," Wolf says. "Just need a place we can dry off and warm up."

"What if it's somebody's property?" Marcus asks.

"Come on, we're in the middle of nowhere, and this place is falling apart," Michael says.

The spongy rotting wood of the wide-planked shack splinters in all directions like thorns on a rose. The roof is caved in on one side, but on the other side it sags down to form a slope. Underneath it's dry, and just big enough to fit everyone.

"A little tight, but it's better than being soaking wet," Wolf says. "I'll work on getting a fire going. Here. Eat." Wolf unzips his pack and tosses out a few travel sized bags of peanuts and trail mix.

"Is this organic?" Michael aks.

"I don't know, mate." Wolf chuckles a bit. "Read the label."

"I don't think it is," Michael holds the package at odd angles to try to read it in the fading light.

"If you want organic, I'm sure we can dig up some frosty worms around here," Wolf jokes.

"What about you?" Amy asks.

"I've got some squirrel," Wolf says as he whips out a hunk of charred meat from his pocket. "Organic."

Michael screws up his face. "Sick!"

"Had some rabbit too, but I already ate that."

"Can I try a bite?" Brandon asks.

"You ain't gonna like it kid, but be my guest." Wolf pulls off a small shred of meat for Brandon.

Brandon yanks at the piece and gnaws at it, chewing vigorously before swallowing it down. The others look on, waiting for his response. "Needs salt. Tastes like chicken."

#

Sheryl finds herself lying beside Marcus. He reads through his Bible by the campfire light. She glances at the musculature of his body as the flickering flames create harsh shadows across his dark skin. Everything but his pants drape over some fallen rafters on the other side of the fire, drying out from the day's wet walk. Her eyes fixate on the goose pimples that spread across his skin with each icy gust that whistles through the fraying wood walls surrounding them. Sheryl hasn't let herself be attracted to someone since the boys were born, and after finding out about her husband's affair, she lost all sense of what intimacy was.

"What part are you reading?" She pulls her eyes off of his biceps to meet his eyes.

"Exodus," he says, keeping his eyes glued to the text.

"How fitting."

"You read the Bible?" Marcus asks her.

"Not for a long time. My father used to read parts for me when I was a kid. It was always a few Bible passages just before the bedtime story." She smiles thinking of it.

Marcus closes his Bible around a finger and looks over at her. She's undressed down to her bra and underwear, but covered by a dry blanket that Wolf had rolled up in his bag.

"May I?" Sheryl reaches for the Bible. As she stretches her arm out the blanket slips down off her shoulder, revealing her breasts to Marcus as they sit firmly in her wet bra. Her stiffened nipples cast shadows in the glimmer of the campfire. Marcus averts his eyes, and Sheryl has to suppress her smile. As he hands her the Bible he notices the ring on her finger. Sheryl quickly retracts her hand and removes it before taking the Bible.

"He was no good," she says plainly as she flings the ring into the fire. "And now he's dead." Sheryl leafs through the Bible until she finds the page she's looking for. She reads. "'Love must be sincere. Hate what is evil, and cling to what is good.' That was always one of my favorites. Remembering it got me through tough times."

"How so?" Marcus asks.

"Well instead of dwelling on what a bastard my husband was, I just focused on what I loved between us; our children." Tears start to glisten in her eyes.

"They also say you should hate the sin but still try to love the sinner. We all fuck up in some way or another. So don't hate your husband when you think back. Instead, hate what he did and try to forgive."

"That's difficult. But it's good advice." She wipes the tears from her eyes before they fall.

"No one said forgiveness is easy. I just hope the people I harmed can think the same way about me. I doubt it though. Some things, people can't forgive. Or they won't."

"Well you've done nothing but good around me," Sheryl says with a smile. "Whatever your past was, all that matters is what you do from here on." She thinks of what Willy told her; the thing he said that reminded her of what her father used to say. "Anyone can be a good person in good times. But doing the right thing even in bad times… that shows character."

Marcus smiles. "Amen, girl."

Sheryl leans in close to Marcus. "Thanks for saving my life," she whispers just before kissing him on his mouth. He puts his arms around her and she falls into his embrace.

#

Amy hangs some of her clothes to dry and zips herself into a sleeping bag along the shack wall. The movements of the others sitting by the fire flicker into a macabre shadow dance on the ragged planks beside her. She watches it, letting her eyes blur the shapes into memories. Shadow puppets with dad in her childhood bedroom. Her nightlight always shined up from the bedside table toward the closet door. She was afraid of what lingered in there. Who knows what kind of monsters lurked behind, waiting to steal her away in the night. Her dad folded and twisted his hands to make hopping bunnies, barking guard dogs, and flying birds to watch over her on the closet door. But now the rabbits are being trapped and roasted into campfire jerky, the guard dogs are eating the dead and turning into rabid beasts, and the birds are dropping from a poisonous sky. There are real monsters behind the wall now.

Michael approaches and sits beside her, rubbing her back through the thick padding of her vinyl sleeping bag. She pretends to sleep, but he saw her eyes open just a second ago.

"I don't think we should be distant from each other now, not with all that's happening," he pleads with her. "Babe, I know you're awake."

"I need you to stop being so serious and combative with everyone. Enough with the politics and religion bull crap," Amy says. "We need to get along with these people despite all that."

"I know, I know. You're right. I just… you know I hear these things and I can't just let them be. I feel like I have to respond otherwise I get pissed off."

Amy faces him and props herself up onto her elbow. "Well it pisses *me* off! I've generally kept my mouth shut in the past about this, but things are different now. This is why my friends are all weird around you, and why they have to walk on egg shells and bite their tongue during normal conversation. If a zombie plague isn't reason enough for you to try to play nice with people, then I don't know what it would take."

Michael hangs his head. "I'm sorry. The last thing I want is for me to be driving us apart. Will you forgive me?" Amy nods her head yes after a moment, and they hug. "Is there room for me in that sleeping bag?" he asks.

"No. But you can snuggle up next to me if you want."

Michael lays down a blanket and folds it over himself on the floor beside Amy, where they doze off from the long, uncomfortable day of hiking.

#

"So why didn't it change me?" Wolf asks Dr. Vogel.

"I really don't know. Without the benefit of a true lab, the only thing I could come up with is because of your physical fitness."

"So if that's the case, then there could be others like me, unaffected by the dust?"

"Yeah, there could be."

"What about all the scientists we saw in suits collecting samples?" Brandon asks. "The military is sending them over to study this."

"They may not know there are people who are immune. That's why I want Wolf to come with me. It may just be a physical fitness thing, but it could be a genetic thing, or even something else."

"Like what?" Wolf asks.

"When we first met, you said you picked up all sorts of exotic bugs in your travels. I assume parasitic, or one of those conditions that leaves a trace behind for the rest of your life. Could be that something in your body is preventing this parasite from changing you. Maybe one of our parasites is fighting this space dust parasite. I call it a parasite but I really don't know what it is. I just know it's not like any other form of life we've seen on Earth."

"What makes you think it's even alive?" Wolf asks.

"It multiplied in a Petrie dish, but you're right. I don't know for sure. It could be anything, and maybe it's not even alive."

"So you think something in my body, or DNA, is preventing it from finishing me off?" Wolf asks.

"Maybe, but not just that. You're apparently done fighting it off. Your symptoms are gone. You essentially killed it. That makes you scientific gold if we ever want to try to work on a cure."

Brandon's eyes gleam as he smiles up at his hero. "Badass."

"Will you reconsider coming with me to the CDC, now that you understand how vital you are?"

Wolf strokes his hand through his silvery blonde hair. "I'll think on it, mate. After we get everyone to safety, we'll talk."

The conversation lulls for a moment, and everything is quiet except for the hissing and popping of the fire. Brandon sings a somber tune as everyone fades to sleep. "Silent night, zombie night. All are gone, none alive. Round the meteor living will die. All infected will shamble and rise. Sick with hellish disease, sick with hellish disease."

CHAPTER 46

"Horses! They're eating too, so I guess the whole 'dust on food' thing doesn't create a problem," Brandon says as everyone approaches them. Four horses huddle up near a gate on a split rail fence. A few troughs of grains hang off the aging posts.

"We don't know if the debris made it out here yet," Michael says.

"Yeah," Dr. Vogel affirms. "Winds are shifting though, now that the storm passed. Things could get very different out here if any of that crap is still suspended in the air. My guess is the snow knocked a lot of it down."

"There's no way I'm taking this mask off, that's for sure," Brandon says.

"Maybe we should take the horses," Michael suggests.

"That's stealing," Marcus says.

"Says the convict," Michael retorts. Amy jabs an elbow into his side. "Sorry Marcus."

"What do we need horses for? We're almost there anyway, right?" Amy asks.

"Not too much further up this road," Wolf says.

Michael unlatches the gate. The horses walk out and stand along the roadside. "I thought we'd use them to pay our way into the compound. You think they're going to just let a bunch of strangers in?"

"I told you, it's going to be fine," Brandon urges. "Everyone in her family is allowed to bring whoever they want. I was invited, and she told me I could bring whoever I wanted, and it would be okay with her father."

"How well do you know her? Do her folks like you enough to let that happen?" Dr. Vogel asks.

"Pssht…" Brandon blows off the questions. "Who knows... I never met them."

"What?!" They all say it in unison.

"How the hell do you know these people then?" Michael asks.

"From the web. A message board. Dude we talk every night; it's not like she's a stranger," Brandon argues.

"Yes, it's *exactly* like she's a stranger." Michael scoffs at him. "This is fucking perfect. We're following a goddamn kid around…"

Just then there's some yelling from across the horse pasture. Two men carrying rifles run out towards them from a barn at the far end of the field. Gunshots shatter the cold morning air.

"Shit!" Dr. Vogel exclaims. "Now we *have* to take the horses."

"Go, go, go!" Michael yells.

Wolf quickly mounts a horse and starts up the road. Dr. Vogel and Michael fire back in the direction of the two gunmen. One of them drops, and the other runs to his aid. Dr. Vogel gets on the second horse. Sheryl and Brandon share another. Amy and Michael take the last one, and Marcus follows behind at a sprint.

Amy sloppily hangs onto the horse's neck as it trots, and Michael hangs onto her with his hands around her waist. The ride is painful, bumpy and uncomfortable. Without a saddle, they're slipping all over the place, and without reins, Amy has to wrap her hands around the horse's hair.

Marcus can barely make out the distant, fading shape of Wolf's and Dr. Vogel's horses way up ahead, just reaching the crest of a hill in the road. Sheryl and Brandon are about halfway there, and Michael and Amy are moving slowly, within speaking range. *Four horses. It's like the Four Horsemen of the Apocalypse, bringing plague and death. Maybe this is all wrong. Maybe my place was back on the other side, finishing out the rest of my punishment in hell. I was given freedom… Freedom from jail, from the consequences of my past… Freedom from disease, and freedom from the quarantine lockdown… and I still failed. I broke my vow. I brought harm to the living, to the innocent. It may not've been me who fired those shots, but it was the people I was with. If we hadn't stolen those horses...* His mind races through all the scenarios that could have been as he runs. He wears down and begins to tire as he struggles just to stay at half pace. The mask is restricting his breathing, and fogging up like crazy. *Fuck it. I'm taking off this mask. If God wants me dead then so be it.* He peels off the mask, bathing his face in the fresh, icy air. It feels like freedom.

"Are they following us?" asks Amy.

Michael frees up one hand and aims his gun backward nervously.

"Easy man!" Marcus yells as he trails behind on foot.

"No. Just Marcus," Michael says. "The crazy bastard took off his mask." Michael puts his hand back around Amy's waist and feels wetness. He sees the red on his hands. She's bleeding. "Oh fuck! Were you shot? Are you okay?"

There's no answer. Amy's grip on the horse loosens. The horse slows to a walk as she slips off its back. Michael hops down and catches her in his arms. He lays her on the ground.

"Help! Stop!" he yells. "Dr. Vogel!" But Dr. Vogel can't hear him. He's too far ahead, just over the hill. Sheryl and Brandon turn to help them. "She's still breathing. This is all my fault. This is all my fault, isn't it?" Michael whimpers.

Marcus doesn't answer him. "Lay her over the back of the horse."

"We're almost there," Brandon says. "She can make it."

"Why didn't you guys shoot back? Why didn't you help?" Michael asks with tears in his eyes.

"We were in the wrong for stealing," Marcus says. "Those guys were just defending what was theirs. You might've done the same."

Blood trickles down the horse's hind legs, oozing from Amy's side. They make it over the hill. Wolf and Dr. Vogel are stopped up ahead in the distance. When they catch up, Dr. Vogel tends to Amy's wound. Michael hovers over him nervously.

"Is this it?" Marcus asks.

"I think so," Brandon says as he looks over his map.

An overgrown path winds its way backward from behind a tall, bush-lined chain-linked fence. They can't see anything through the padlocked gate before them.

"She's alive, but I can't stop the blood loss without some medical gear," Dr. Vogel says. "You said they have stuff inside?" he asks Brandon. Brandon nods yes.

Wolf rustles a roll of duct tape out of his pack, along with a small tube of instant glue. "This'll help."

"Not for long." Dr. Vogel dresses her wound, squeezing out the entire tube of instant glue into the bullet hole. Then he wraps her waist with duct tape.

"Instant glue?" Michael asks.

"One of its many early uses was on the battlefield," Wolf says.

"I need real supplies or else she's gonna die. I need to get the bullet out and close her up properly," Dr. Vogel says. "I can't lose her the same way I lost Willy."

Michael turns wily in the eyes. He starts to roar at the fence. "Hey! Let us in! Let us in, damn it!" He picks up a big rock near the fence and smashes it against the padlock over and over. He kicks it and thrashes about, wrapping his ice cold fingers around the metal fence. Suddenly he feels a jolt go through his body, and a screaming pain runs from his finger tips down to his toes. He flails backward and falls to the ground. "Ahh! What the fuck!"

"The fence is electrified," Wolf says as he scans the delicate wiring that snakes its way up from the ground through the fencing. "They've got power, and you're lucky you aren't dead," he says to Michael.

Another gunshot rings out and everyone scatters along the road except for Dr. Vogel. He stays with Amy. One of the gunmen from the horse pasture makes his way up the road, firing wildly in their direction. He's old, and has a crazy look in his eye. He grumbles under his labored breaths. "Gimme those dang horses. I stole 'em first, fair and square."

"Are you fucking kidding me?" Michael steps out into the road to meet him. He raises his gun at the old man, filled with righteous anger. "You're the one who shot my wife?"

"Da… da… damn right I did," he stammers.

"Don't you think it's a little extreme to fire at someone just for taking a horse?" Michael asks.

"Four ho… horses!" He grins an ornery black and yellow, semi-toothless smile back at Michael. He spurts out a wad of chewing tobacco in Michael's direction and coughs repeatedly. Spittle and drool dangle from an overgrown, unkempt reddish beard.

"Still… The punishment doesn't fit the crime. You could've fired a warning shot or just told us to stop. Instead you tried to kill us. And are these even your horses?" Michael asks.

"They are now. To… to... took 'em from some border jumpers like you." The man twitches and ticks between stuttering words and coughs.

"Border jumpers? Man. I guess what they say is right. It's not the guns that do the killing; it's the people. The fucking morons and psychos!" Michael catches himself before going on a rant. "Listen. I'm sorry. You can take the horses back. Just leave us alone. My wife needs help."

"Sorry ain't gonna help you, bo… bo… boy. It's only fair. You took one of mi… mine, now I'm gonna take one of yours."

"It was self defense," Michael argues.

After several throaty hacks the old codger cocks his rifle and takes aim at Michael. Michael quickly raises his gun and pulls the trigger, but there's no shot. Just a click. Without thought Marcus leaps up from behind Michael and dives out in front of him as the hick pulls his trigger. The bullet hits Marcus square in the chest as he passes in front of Michael.

"No!" Sheryl yells. She and Brandon open fire and drop the old man with a hail of bullets. But Brandon keeps cranking out round after round, loading single bullets into his bolt action rifle over and over until the anger fades. A tear falls down his cheek as he sees Marcus dying on the ground.

"Marcus!" Sheryl runs to him.

"Put pressure on the wound," Dr. Vogel instructs her.

"What business you got here?" A raspy voice seems to come from nowhere. Everyone turns, but there's no one there. "What do you want?"

"I'm friends with Apoc… I'm friends with Jilly," Brandon says. They traded names at some point, but he'd almost forgotten. He's attracted to her avatar, and her avatar is called Apocalypta. The name Jilly means nothing to him. He doesn't even know what she looks like, but he knows every damn pixel of her Japanese anime-inspired icon.

"Please help us. My wife was shot, and this guy just pulled a Jesus and jumped in front of a bullet to save my life for the *second* time. They need your help. They *deserve* your help," Michael pleads. He kneels down and grasps Marcus' hand, giving it a good squeeze. "Hang in there," he says under his breath. Marcus squeezes back to acknowledge, but he's weak.

"Pulled a Jesus?" Marcus asks with a confused whimper.

"Sacrificed yourself for a sinner," Michael explains with a whisper. "Come on Marcus. You didn't get that? I expected more from a man of your spiritual intellect."

"We're already full up here, and you're too many," the voice says.

Wolf emerges from the side of the road where he was hiding with a puzzled look on his face. He cocks his head like a canine as he listens to the voice. His eyes dart all around looking for the source.

"Jilly asked me to come. Said I could bring friends. Ask her yourself, sir," Brandon pleads, mustering up his best rendition of respectful Sunday school manners.

"Doesn't matter what my daughter said. I'm the boss here," the mysterious stranger says.

"I know that voice," Wolf says. "It's unmistakable." Wolf points beyond the gate. "You there; I can see you… Cough Drop? Damn good ghillie suit, mate. Only reason I saw you was because the filter on your gas mask is poking out."

"Wolf?" the man asks as he steps out from the brush and reveals himself. He's draped in a netting that's covered with natural foliage, twigs, and branches from the area. It's a military style sniper or recon camouflage.

"You guys know each other?" Brandon asks, confused.

"No shit…" Michael is stunned. His mouth drops open in shock.

"This is incredible!" Wolf exclaims. "I knew we had to be in close range with the CB, but this is downright unbelievable."

"No," Michael says. "It's fate."

"Fate," Marcus utters. *Maybe he's coming around. It's no longer a dirty word for him. He's starting to see it. Every connection we've made in these past few days; it's all fate, part of God's plan. It's no mistake, no accident, no freak coincidence. It's providence.* "I've done my duty." Marcus struggles to get the words out. "I've been like the shepherds of old, leading a flock to the promised land." He turns to Cough Drop. "Now it's up to you, the father. Show grace as the heavenly Father does. Let them into your kingdom despite their flaws. I'm ready to face judgment and pay for mine." Marcus manages a smile before slipping into unconsciousness.

"I'm not letting you pay for shit, Marcus. You stay with us. Stay with us!" Michael turns to Cough Drop with a pleading look in his eyes. Tears well up behind his mask.

Cough Drop signals over his shoulder. There's a fading buzz noise, and a moment later he unlocks the gate and lets them in. He closes it behind them once everyone is in, and signals again. After another buzz sound the electrified fence is powered back up.

"Come on. Let's get them inside and see what we can do. And get a mask on him," he points to Marcus.

"Thank you Cough Drop," Wolf says.

"Name's John Reynolds." They shake hands.

CHAPTER 47

Dr. Vogel is with Michael in another room, tending to Amy and Marcus. Sheryl, Wolf and Brandon sit around a table inside the home with their masks off, breathing freely for the first time in days. Their senses of smell seem to overwhelm them. The oddly familiar scents of a stranger's home fill their noses; the lingering farm fresh food from this morning's breakfast, the sweet pine sap oozing from the wood paneling on the walls, the mustiness of old fabric covered furniture draped with grandma's quilts... And they can smell themselves, badly in need of bathing; almost as pungent as the wretched dead, whose odors were so potent that they even managed to traverse the filters on their gas masks at times.

"Jilly will be around in a few minutes. She's feeding the chickens and rabbits in the back barn," John says to Brandon while pouring hot coffee for Sheryl and Wolf.

"I'll go help her out," he says, excited to finally meet his internet girlfriend in person. He bolts out the door so fast he almost forgets to put his mask on. Visions of double-D tits dance in his head.

"Is the air bad here?" Sheryl asks.

"I wouldn't take any chances after hearing that old hick coughing," John says.

"I mean *you* were wearing a mask out there," she points out. "I thought it was safe to breathe out here."

"I wear one for the same reason you all do I suppose. Better safe than sorry," he explains. "Only a matter of time before it spreads, or there's word of more meteor impacts in the US. Already hearing rumors of that, matter of fact. Could be raining down all over the world and we wouldn't know it, just pelting different parts of the globe as we spin through our days. No telling how big that cluster of meteors was."

"What else have you heard? Anything more from Spider?" Wolf asks.

Just then Dr. Vogel and Michael walk in. Sheryl immediately stands up. "Is he okay?" she asks about Marcus. "Are they alright?"

"I think Amy's going to pull through. No vital organ damage. I stopped the bleeding on both of their gunshot wounds and removed the bullets, but Marcus is in bad shape. He's still unconscious. I don't know if he's going to make it. Right now it's just a wait-and-see thing with him. Good news is he can't get much worse. And he's a tough son of a bitch, I'll give him that," Dr. Vogel explains.

"Can I see him? Sit with him?" she asks.

"Sure, go right ahead," Dr. Vogel says. He sits down to a cup of coffee with Michael, Wolf, and John. "Now let's talk about this trip to the CDC," he looks over at Wolf.

"Boy you don't waste any time, do you? Mate, whatever is in me is gone, dead," Wolf says.

"You don't know that. We need to get under a microscope to know that," Dr. Vogel explains. "Besides we don't necessarily need the parasite. I'm sure the government has samples of it if they were sending scientists into the infected zone. What we need is you, what's in your body; whatever it is in you that fought back and won. *That's* the key."

"There's an old hospital close by," John offers. "I'm sure they have microscopes somewhere, some lab equipment. Could try to see if they're up and running on generators before you go all the way to the CDC."

"Maybe. But most hospitals don't have the sort of things I need, or the safety equipment to properly study something of this virility," Dr. Vogel says. "Besides Sheryl was right; hospitals are probably the most unsafe places right now. People get infected and rush to the ER, then the ER becomes hell on Earth."

"You're dead serious about this, ain't you mate?" Wolf asks. "We've got a safe place to crash and you're gung-ho to leave already?"

"I left my wife and kids at home in the middle of this to fend for themselves, and I set out for the CDC with your samples. That's how determined I am. That's how serious this is, and that's how strongly I believe in you. We *need* to get you to the CDC, otherwise this thing might never stop," Dr. Vogel argues.

"You realize what you're asking me to do? They might lock me up once we get there! You're asking me to give up my freedom, possibly my life, everything, for this cure," Wolf says.

"Willy gave his life for us. Now maybe Marcus too. It's the least we can do. We'll all go. All of us. It's too important," Michael says.

"No, no, no," Dr. Vogel says. "You need to stay here with Amy. She'll need you during her recovery. And I'm sure Sheryl will want to stay with Brandon and Marcus. It'll just be Wolf and I."

"The less people we have with us the better," Wolf says. His survivalist brain already mulls over scenarios and situations, calculating the best way to go about taking the journey. "More bodies to feed will only slow us down. Wait, what the hell am I saying? I didn't even agree to this yet!"

"Neither did I," John jumps in. "Tell you what. I'll make it easy for you, Wolf. I'll let everyone stay here if you agree to help Dr. Vogel. You just have to do what you do best. Get yourself and Dr. Vogel down to the CDC with your survival skills. Seems like everyone sacrificed something just to get here. I'll tell you right now; this place ain't no paradise. It's hard work. Everything we do, all day, is aimed just at surviving, making it to the next day, preparing for the one after, and so on. I don't know what the hell that boy told you to get you all to follow him here, but you seem like good enough people. And Wolf, this isn't just some favor you'd be doing for Dr. Vogel. This is a service to humanity. If you think about it like that, the decision you have to make might start looking pretty clear, regardless of whether they lock you up."

Wolf runs his hand through his hair in thought. *Maybe I should've just stayed in the woods. Now look what I've gotten myself into.* "Bullocks. Alright. But do we have to go right now?"

"No. Of course not. We'll need to plan a route, gear up, all that. I'm sure you need time to figure out the best course of action," Dr. Vogel says. "Tomorrow."

"Tomorrow, then." Wolf nods his head. "There's always tomorrow."

EPILOGUE

PFC James Reynolds is on his first tour in Afghanistan. A country boy, his home is in central Ohio; a small town with one street light in front of the general store, and great pride in their local high school football team. Everyone knows each other. He met Jennie Linker when they were both six, and he's had a crush on her ever since. They write each other every day, the old fashioned way. They vowed to stay together, and give their relationship a shot at long distance. He was deployed three months ago.

A bad dream wakes him early in the morning; Jennie left him for someone else. The day before was another nightmare too; she was sick and dying. He hasn't heard from her, and worries if everything's alright. He steps out of his bunk and into the frosty morning air. The sun is already starting to burn away the dead chill that lingers from the night as it rises over the rocky ridge in the east. He shakes the nightmares from his mind, and reaches up for the orange ball just beginning to peek over the mountains in the blue-grey sky. He stretches his entire body as he yawns.

"That ain't gonna make you any taller, Junior," Bucky, one of Reynolds' bunk mates, jokes with a light slap to the shoulder. Reynolds laughs it off. He's short, and his initials are JR. Naturally he became Junior to the guys. He would've been a real junior too if his parents named him John, after his father.

Bucky, a ginger with big buck teeth, got his name because all the guys used to say "What's up, Buck?" to him in basic training, in reference to the old cartoon character Bucky Rabbit, who had huge front teeth. Rabbit is even thrown about sometimes as a nickname too.

"Let's go, short stack. We got good government work to do today!" Junior's buddy Vice joins in, having faintly heard Rabbit's comment. Donny Johnson, or Florida Vice, as he's called, is a Florida native, always tan, and always wearing frog sunglasses pulled right out of the 1980s. Usually it's just Florida, or just Vice, for short. Fitting too, because all he talks about are the hot chicks and beaches back home.

Reynolds gives some sarcasm back to Bucky and Vice. "Wow. Two short guy jokes in one minute! You guys deserve a medal of some kind."

They're part of a small team with orders for a humanitarian mission. The plan is to bring supplies to villagers who might have been cut off due to recent violence, skirmishes on the roads, and security lockdowns in the area. Travelling by road is dangerous, but it's the only way now. Choppers aren't being used. They load two humvees with essentials like sacks of rice, bottled water, and gas masks.

"Aight, let's move 'em out!" Captain Davies shouts from the lead vehicle, and a moment later they're off.

#

They're on a dusty and rocky dirt road, 50 klicks north of base in southern Zabul province, Afghanistan. Reynolds is in the rear vehicle with four of his brothers. Florida drives. Then there's Celery sitting shotgun, who got that name because he's tall, skinny and green – green as in a total clueless newbie. Reynolds gets a reprieve from short jokes when Celery is around. Rabbit sits bitch in the back seat. Behind Celery is Tackleson. He got that name because he's a hair trigger, blast happy, wild-eyed lunatic hick, just like the character from a 1980s police comedy movie franchise. Reynolds is positioned behind the driver's seat.

"What are all the gas masks for? Usually see a couple on these kinds of missions, but not this many," says Celery.

"Something to do with meteors that hit back home. Rumor is that no one's been able to make contact with anyone from back home for a while," Reynolds answers him.

"Where do you get this shit? No one tells me nothing," Celery asks.

"I don't know. Just hearing things," says Reynolds.

"We should've been in a chopper. The roads are too fucked," Tackleson adds.

"The last contact our high-ups got from home was to ground all air transportation. That's why," Vice tells him. "Ain't heard from the old Commander in Chief since."

"So communication sats are down? But not ours?" Celery asks again.

"Don't know. We have radio though. Also heard that it's poisonous to breathe the dust from the meteors. Guessin' that's what the masks are for," Vice responds.

"So what about us?" Celery continues.

"We got our standard issue masks, and there's a bunch more in crates at base just in case. It was the last supply shipment we received. Davies told us to bring 'em if things get crazy," Bucky explains to a dumbfounded Celery while holding up his own mask. "You brought yours, right?" There's a long pause of silence. "You stupid, goony-ass bastard. Celery, you forgot it didn't you?"

"Fuck you, Rabbit. You guys don't tell me shit," Celery whines.

The other guys laugh.

"Now now, don't get your panties in a bunch. Buck's just nibblin' on your celery stalk a little bit. Ain't you Rabbit?" Florida looks over the top of his shades in the rearview mirror with a grin fixed on Bucky. Bucky flings an extra gas mask in Celery's direction.

"That's fuckin' gay, Vice. You must've spent too much time down in faggy ass Miami Beach watchin' homos nibble on each other's celery stalks." Tackleson laughs.

"Man, oh man. What I wouldn't give to be back home on the beach in Miami right now."

"Gaybot!" Tackleson cuts him off, earning laughs from the others.

"Nah man, I'm telling you. The chicks down in Miami are like nothin' you've ever seen. Think of it like spring break every day, man," Florida explains.

Tackleson moans. "Here we go again. Should we pull over so you can jerk off?"

"Sounds nice. Why'd you leave?" Reynolds asks.

"That's a good question Junior. One whose answer I've totally forgotten. Tell you what... my new year's resolution... go back home and bang as many of those sexy ladies in bikinis as I can while I'm still young enough to pop wood."

The guys laugh.

"What about you, Buck? What's your resolution?" Celery asks.

"Shit, I don't know. Quit smokin' I guess," he says.

"Oh come on man. You gotta make it something good. All of us, you know, we risk our lives out here... and your resolution is to quit smoking? Pick something better than that Bucky. Pick something like 'have a three way' or 'blow coke off a hooker's tits' or something," Florida suggests.

"What about Tack?" Celery asks.

"Two thousand confirmed kills," Florida answers in his best Tackleson impersonation, which is a cross between an Austrian body-building robot and a toothless hillbilly. Everyone laughs but Tackleson.

"I can make that happen," Tackleson says, all straight faced and serious.

"What about you, Junior?" Celery asks.

He thinks for a moment. "I'm gonna ask Jennie to marry me."

"Oh that's just precious," Florida says though a laugh.

"What can I say, I'm in love. Being apart just makes me want it more," Reynolds says.

"I'm in love too. And being apart from all my Florida ladies makes me want them even more too. Variety is the spice of life, my man. One day you'll remember me when you're sick and tired of Jennie's saggy tits and cottage cheese ass." Vice looks at Junior, fixing his eyes on him in the rearview mirror, not watching the road ahead. "You'll be thinkin' of old Vice, sittin' on the beach with one lady bringing him drinks, two ladies rubbing his feet, and three ladies…"

A deafening explosion outside cuts Vice off mid-sentence. Captain Davies' hummer jolts up into the air and lands on its side, as if it were bounced by a boy with a toy car. The ground thunders all around them. A short, angry rain of dirt and rocks pours down onto the hummer, nicking and cracking the windshield. Vice slams the brakes, but their vehicle slides and slams into the rear end of Captain Davies' hummer. Smoke pours from Davies' hummer across to theirs, and they can't see shit.

"What the fuck, dude?" Rabbit complains. He struggles to sit himself up, having been thrown into the front of the vehicle.

Celery puts his gas mask on immediately. He shakes his head nervously and the loose rubber straps fling around the side of his face like streamers dangling off a balloon. "Was that rocket fire?" he asks. No one answers.

Vice opens the door cautiously with his weapon in his hand. He steps out to get a better look at Davies' humvee. "Holy fuck," he says. Reynolds opens his door too, and a moment later they all step out of the vehicle.

Davies' body is hanging halfway out of his windshield. His right arm is a burnt stump sheared off just below the shoulder. A hole is ripped through the hummer, with seared, charred edges. A small flame flickers within a crater on the dirt road, and smoke rises up from the hole. There's screaming from inside the vehicle, along with the sounds of vomiting and coughing.

Vice and Reynolds run over to Davies to check his vitals, but it's obvious he's dead. They open the rear door and drag the other men out from the back seat. Two are dead, and the other is coughing and throwing up like crazy.

"Can you stand up, Ghost?" Vice asks the guy between his vomiting. He notices a pretty bad gash on his side too; it's not mortal, but it certainly inhibits Ghost's breathing. Vice applies pressure to the wound. But when Ghost winces in pain and gasps several short, ineffective breaths, Vice thinks there might be some broken ribs or a collapsed lung.

Ghost is so white that he's almost clear. That's how he got his name. But now it's worse. He's lost some blood, and he's so sick that he's turning yellow in the face. Even his eyes look a little yellow. Reynolds gives him his mask, and he begins to breathe a bit easier. Eventually he stands.

The last guy in the front seat won't stop screaming. Bucky and Tackleson pull him out of the wreckage. It's Peters. He never really got a nickname because he was just too normal. They tried calling him Average or Regular for a while, but neither stuck for too long. His left hand is missing. They try to calm him down, but he's bleeding out. Rabbit ties a tourniquet around his arm, just below the elbow. That's when Bucky notices the hole in Peters' stomach, ripped clean through his body and cauterized the entire way, like a smaller version of the hole through the hummer. Peters flops to the ground and dies moments later.

Celery stands in the road confused and scared, trembling like a frightened mouse. He creeps close to the rubble and looks down at the steaming, flaming crater beside the vehicle. A piss yellow smoke curls up from the hole, and a greenish glowing rock sits in the center; a burning pitch, an ember of space rock. Celery smells a faint scent of burning plastic and sulfur coming through the mask.

The radio inside their hummer is rattling off like crazy, but the voices are either inaudible or muffled and distorted by static. Tackleson tries to communicate back to base on several channels, but there's no coherent response; only panic, distress, and confusion.

"Look, out across the hills," Reynolds points. A flaming shower of debris falls from above. The glowing orange hail is trailed by emerald-tinted black soot and accompanied by a distant but descending whistle sound. Then more fireballs sail overhead, this time much closer, right on top of them. Flames streak across the sky, ripping through the morning air with ear piercing shrieks. The ground shakes when they hit the dusty earth, nearly knocking the men down. The debris continues to pelt down on them, and they take shelter in the hummer.

"Holy shit! They're coming down all over the place!" A hail of flaming rocks rains down on the desert all around them.

When the barrage of brimstone and hellfire settles, they step back out into the sun. In the windless dead calm of the desert, a strange, thick, piss-milk smoke snakes its way up from each impact, all around them and in the distance. Just like the smoke coming from the busted hummer and the crater in the road. Behind them, far in the distance, a small mushroom cloud lingers out in the desert.

"Looks like base was destroyed. Gotta be. Ain't nothing else that close by," Bucky says.

"Try the radio again," Vice suggests.

"I did. It's dead air. Nothing," says Tackleson as he steps away from the hummer.

"Could it be missiles? Rocket fire?" Celery asks.

"No those are meteors you damn fool! Or debris from one," Vice explains.

"But what kind of explosion makes a cloud like that? Could it be an attack?" Celery continues, pointing to base.

"I don't know. I doubt it though. Meteors could've hit the fuel supply, generators, or munitions storage." Vice eyes Celery for a moment. "Everyone, do like Celery and put your masks on."

"I gave mine to Ghost. I'm taking one from the supplies in back," Reynolds says as he runs.

"You know the Bible says God will bring the end of days upon us," Tackleson muses as he stares off into the distance.

"Yeah but ain't that a flood or something?" Celery asks.

"No. He already flooded us once. The next time he promised fire from above." Tackleson begins to quote. "I will show wonders in the heavens above, and signs on Earth below. Blood and fire and vapor of smoke…"

"You actually believe that bullshit?" Rabbit jumps in.

"That 'bullshit' is believed by lots of people. And not all of 'em ignorant hayseeds like Tack," Reynolds adds.

"Thanks, I guess?" Tackleson responds.

"You too, Reynolds? And that still don't mean it ain't bullshit," Bucky presses.

"Look I don't know what I believe. Just saying don't mock the man for his religious beliefs, and nobody'll mock you for *not* believing in anything," Reynolds says. "Whether or not it's true is a whole 'nother story."

Ghost walks around in a stupor as they argue. He throws up in his mask and then sluggishly pulls it off to let the sick spill out onto the dirt to clear out the stink.

"Nasty dude," Celery comments.

Ghost struggles to put his mask back on. His eyes start to roll back in his head. Then his body goes limp and he drops to the ground.

"You said the debris is poisonous. What kind of poisonous?" Celery asks.

Ghost starts to violently convulse and foam at the mouth. Vice tends to him after putting a mask on his own head, but moments later Ghost fades. He's dead.

"Shit. He's gone," Vice says. He looks around at the others. "Damn it Tack, put your mask on already."

Tackleson shakes his head. "Leaving mine off. It's too late anyway. God's plan can't be stopped with masks."

"That's an order," Vice says. "Seeing as though I'm the next highest rank after Davies, I'll be taking over here."

"I believe the order of things is God, country, corps," Tackleson retorts.

Vice twists his face in frustration. "Yeah well until God comes down from the heavens and says otherwise, I believe putting your mask on won't infringe on your religious duties and revelations."

Tackleson reluctantly complies.

A gurgled growl escapes Ghost's foamy throat. Vice looks down at him as his eyes burst wide open. "Ghost? Ghost, you okay?" Vice hooks his hands under Ghost's arms and tries to pull him up to a sitting position. "Come on, you pasty old fuck. Let's get you some water." Vice puts one of Ghost's arms across his shoulder and helps him to stand up.

"I thought you said he was dead?" Celery asks.

"Well, apparently I was wrong," says Vice.

"He don't look too good. Looks like a wild animal, you ask me," Bucky adds.

"I didn't ask you. Grab me a bottle of water, would you?" Vice commands.

Vice slowly walks him toward the hummer. Ghost turns a snarling face toward Florida's arm. It dangles across Ghost's shoulder and hangs down near his face like a sausage in a butcher's window. Ghost opens his fouled mouth and gnashes his teeth with a vicious hiss. He tears off a chunk of flesh from Florida's arm, taking bits of ripped desert camouflage into his mouth with it. Vice yanks his arm away and screams in pain as the remaining connected skin stretches and snaps from the wound. He immediately presses his other hand on the wound and backs away from Ghost, still facing him. Ghost chews at the chunk of meat in his mouth and runs after Vice.

"What the fuck?" Reynolds yells as he draws his weapon. "Hold it right there, Ghost!" Ghost keeps chasing Vice. Tackleson and Bucky train their sights on Ghost as he runs after Florida. Celery stands in shock. "I *will* shoot you, Ghost! Stand down now!" Reynolds warns him again, but Ghost doesn't listen.

Vice backpedals, but stumbles and loses his footing on a rock along the side of the road. Ghost catches up to him and tackles him the rest of the way to the ground. A cloud of dust puffs up around them as the scuffle continues. Ghost gets on top of Vice, and Vice struggles to keep Ghost's bloodied mouth away from him. He claws and scratches at Florida's clothes like a wild dog.

Reynolds runs over to them. "Last warning, Ghost!" He aims his weapon at the back of Ghost's calf. "You have 'til the count of three! One…"

"Shoot the crazy bastard already!" Vice yells from under the beast.

"Two…"

"Don't kill him, Junior! Don't kill him!" Celery whimpers.

"Three!"

Reynolds fires a round into Ghost's leg. Ghost twists his head upward and roars at him. Reynolds is shocked by the horrific look on Ghost's face. He steps backward in fear, but keeps his weapon aimed at Ghost. Ghost stands up, focused completely on Reynolds. Florida scrambles out from under him and gets back onto his feet.

Ghost drags his wounded leg behind him as he shambles toward Reynolds.

"Sorry buddy. I didn't mean to hurt you but you weren't listening," Reynolds pleads with Ghost. "Stand down, soldier!"

Ghost presses forward, his mouth dripping with blood and saliva. His chest heaves up and down with breathy grunts and growls. He reaches his arms up toward Reynolds, his hands grasping at the air as he moves forward. Reynolds squeezes several rounds out at the ground in front of Ghost to scare him, but it's no use. He keeps coming. He fires another shot into the same leg, this time up on Ghost's thigh. Ghost is knocked back a step, but he limps on hungrily, unaffected by the gunshots.

"What the fuck?" Tackleson utters, completely baffled by the sight. "He's a goddamn zombie."

Florida steps up with his sidearm and presses it to Ghost's temple. Ghost turns and lunges at Florida. Vice squeezes his eyes tight and squeezes his trigger finger. With one loud pop, Ghost is silenced. He falls to the ground, dead again.

"Oh fuck, Florida. You killed Ghost! You fucking shot Ghost!" Celery yells in panic.

"That wasn't Ghost," Tackleson says. "It was some kind of fucking hellish demon monster come back from the dead. A devil."

"Quit talking your crazy religious shit again, Tackleson." Bucky's voice shakes with uncertainty. "It is crazy, right?"

"Tack is right," Florida says. "That wasn't Ghost. I could see it in his eyes. He was like a rabid animal."

"Your arm okay?" Reynolds asks.

Florida sucks air through his teeth in pain. "Ahh, should be. Stings like hell. Burns actually. Like it's infected." He rolls up his sleeve to reveal a bruised, festering wound. Streaks of black extend outward on his skin from under the surface of the bite, as if the veins in his arm are poisoned with death.

"Let's get you taped up." Reynolds sits Vice down and dresses his wounds.

"We gotta get out of here," Celery says after a few moments.

"We can still press onward. We have orders. We still have one humvee that's operational. Let's pack the remaining supplies from the crashed vehicle into ours," Reynolds suggests.

"We've got wounded and dead men. We can't just leave 'em here. Remember 'no one gets left behind?' We need to get back to base and let them know the mission failed," Rabbit says.

"There is no base. There is no communication. That means there is no command." Tackleson adds.

"We don't know that for sure," Bucky responds.

"Something happened back there. No one is answering the radio. We're safer going forward instead of backward," Reynolds says.

"Or AWOL," Florida blurts it out. The others look at him with screwed up faces, clearly confused by the idea. It goes against everything they believe in, everything they've trained for. Other than treason, it's the worst thing they can do. It gets quiet for an uncomfortably long moment.

"What do you mean, AWOL?" Celery breaks the silence with incredulity.

"I mean I just shot a fucking fellow marine in the head. I ain't going back anywhere. You shot him too, Junior. Twice. How we gonna explain this? You think people are gonna believe a man came back from the dead and attacked us? How the fuck are we gonna explain that? Why not any of the others?" Vice points to the other bodies that lay still. "They'll court marshal us, and lock us up in a mental institution if not in jail for the rest of our lives."

"That's crazy talk," Celery says. "We could..."

"No it ain't," Bucky interrupts.

Tackleson laughs and looks up to the heavens. "Lock us up? We're already dead."

"Tell you what, Celery. The mission is all yours. I'm leaving." With his bandages finished, Florida stands up. "Who's with me?"

"I am," Rabbit says with a stony nod.

"Shit. Me too, I guess. End of the world, right? Might as well make it count," Tackleson says. They all look to Reynolds.

"I'm not doing anything unless we all do it together," Reynolds says after a pause. He fixes his eyes on Celery.

Celery looks around at all the carnage. His gaze stays with Ghost, and in his head he replays the horror they all witnessed. He's made up his mind. "Shit. Alright. AWOL."

#

They quickly bury the bodies of their fallen marine brothers in shallow cratered graves along the side of the meteor pelted road, but there's no time for solemn words or prayers. They need to move. Reynolds speeds off with the remainder of his team, peering through the humvee's cracked windshield and struggling to see the dirt road in front of him. When the midday sun hits it from high up, it almost blends in with the surrounding desert. But it doesn't matter. They need to get off the road and hide somewhere. As if the meteors weren't bad enough, there's also the very real threat of roadside bombs and insurgent attacks to worry about. Reynolds keeps a breakneck pace heading north with the gas pedal floored.

Bucky fruitlessly fiddles with the radio in shotgun. Tackleson, sitting behind Bucky, stares wide-eyed out the window at the blasted lands. Celery shakes nervously behind Reynolds. Florida sits bitch, complaining about his arm and growing dizzy with pain from Ghost's bite.

Vice groans with agony. "It burns. Ahhhh, man it burns!"

Bucky turns from the useless radio and eyes Vice's bandage. "Let's see what it looks like under there."

Vice squeals. "I ca... I can't,"

Rabbit nods at Celery. "You do it."

Celery shakes as he peels back the bandages that Reynolds put over Florida's wound. A stringy yellow mucus comes up with it. He wipes the pus away to reveal a deep, amber-black bite mark with ripped, dead skin surrounding it. It's like his arm already turned gangrenous.

"Ah shit," Vice whimpers, seeing it for himself. His breathing quickens almost instantly, and his brow moistens with a cold sweat above his gas mask. "That's bad, isn't it?"

"We're at the end. My dearest friend, the end," Tackleson sings a popular haunting and trippy 60s hippie song as he stares off into the distance.

"Fuck off Tack," Bucky says. Tackleson doesn't listen.

Dust sprinkles the humvee, like they've pulled behind someone who's kicking up dirt from the road in front of them. But Reynolds doesn't let up on the gas, and moments later the dust becomes a rain of pebbles and debris. Then rocks. The road is useless. There is no road, none that Reynolds can see. He just drives, doing his best to keep the wheel steady.

"Of our special plans, the end," Tackleson continues.

"Vice... Vice!" Celery nudges him but there's no response. His head is tipped back, and his eyes are rolled into his head.

"Of all that ever stands, the end..."

Bucky shoves Tacklberry's head back viciously. "Fuckin' shut up asshole!"

Tackleson ignores it completely and keeps singing. "It pains to see you free. You'll never be with me..."

"Fuckin' douche bag," Rabbit utters under his breath.

"Florida?" Celery pokes at him. "Guys. Something's wrong. He was just shaking like crazy for a minute and now nothing."

Vice groans and a stony stare rolls forward as he lifts his head, revealing bloodshot, bile colored eyes.

"The end of smiles and soft eyes..."

The humvee lurches down and back up, jostling everyone from their seats.

"Shit!" Reynolds yells. "I hit a fucking crater!" The dust settles for just a moment, and he sees an RPG vapor trail zipping toward them from a distance.

"The end of days, we try to die..."

Reynolds yanks the wheel hard to the left and floors the gas pedal. Florida's head ends up squarely in Tackleson's lap, but Tackleson still stares off with his face pressed against the window.

"We're at the end... RPG!" Tackleson yells when his gaze fixes on the white stream of smoke darting right for them.

Vice rips a massive chunk of thigh, dick, and pelvis from Tackleson's groin. A deafening blast drowns out Tackleson's

screams as the RPG detonates in front of the hummer. They flip
into the air, and white-hot light fills the vehicle.

\#

A camcorder video screen fades in from black to reveal
Reynolds in his US military fatigues sitting on a rickety wood
chair. Piss, shit, blood and vomit stain his desert camouflage. Rope
binds his hands behind him, and a burlap sack covers his face.
Behind him stand two men in ski masks wearing filthy white
linens. One holds a saber and the other a banana-clipped
machinegun. Behind them is a haphazardly draped banner showing
the ominous symbol of their violent jihadist organization; one the
free world is all too familiar with. The man holding the saber
speaks Dari Persian to the camera as it sits on a tripod. He makes
wild and threatening gestures. The gunman holds the barrel of his
weapon to the back of Reynolds' head.

"Allah has made himself known. He has fired his missiles
down from the heavens upon the Great Satan in the places where
he occupies our holy lands. The United States military has bent the
knee and bowed before Islam. Allah has delivered them to us,
diseased and ill. They choke upon the poisonous words they have
spoken against us for so long. The desert has risen up and taken the
air from them. Allah rewards the martyrs who have given their
lives to the cause of Jihad. But my brothers, we are victorious!
Look and see. Look how Allah has snatched the very breath from
their lungs."

The terrorist with the gun pulls the covering off Reynolds'
head. He's bruised and battered, bloodied and beaten. His gas
mask is gone. He labors in his breathing, wheezing and coughing
repeatedly. Every gasp of air between heaves seems to sap what
little strength he has left in him. No more energy to vomit, no more
energy to plead for help, no more energy to fight. He struggles to
keep his head upright, and his eyes roll back into his skull. On the
brink of death, he stares up at the earthen ceiling. He thinks of
Jennie, the farm back home, his family. He closes his eyes. His
breathing slows, and then finally stops.

The two terrorists begin to cheer and chant praises to Allah upon his passing. But moments later he begins to violently twitch and convulse in death. A frothy white foam oozes from Reynolds' mouth as the seizures cease. The terrorists stop their praises and look strangely upon the ungodly sight. Reynolds lifts his head up. His eyes burst wide open; they're wily, yellow and bloodshot. He stares off and looks all around the room until his eyes meet the terrorist holding the saber. The jihadist steps back in fear, whispering prayers of desperation with panic beneath his breath.

The one holding the gun asks what's happening with a quivering, shaky voice. But before the other can answer, Reynolds shoots up from the chair and gnashes his teeth at the terrorist's neck. With one massive chomp he rips out the terrorist's throat, and then continues to ravage him. The terrorist's shocked, yelp-like scream quickly turns to a bloody, bubbling gurgle as they both hit the floor. The other begins to fire his machinegun at Reynolds, knocking him off his dead comrade. But Reynolds continues to eat, unharmed by the hail of bullets.

Frantic, the jihadist runs past the camera, leaving the dank commode in which they intended their execution and victory celebration.

"Allah has lifted the dead from their slumber. Allah has set the dead against us!" His screams fade in the distance.

Reynolds continues to gnaw at the flesh of the dead terrorist. Blood smears across his face and chest, bathing evil with evil.

TO BE CONTINUED

ABOUT THE AUTHOR

Vincent Todarello recently returned from the first manned space mission to the moons of Saturn, where he covertly provided aid and leadership to a fragmented but determined rebel force which later dislodged the entrenched, tyrannical Zang Jankfu regime in a bloody coup.

Next, he plans to descend deep into the Marianas Trench and return to Sea Lab Alpha-437 to continue his study of bioluminescence and bioelectricity in giant squid populations. He left this vitally important work largely unfinished, despite major breakthroughs and new discoveries, to pen *The Lazarus Impact* for his devoted audience.

Actually, he is working on transforming his mysterious noir style screenplay into a novel. Mr. Todarello's other published titles include *The Return of the Fifth Stone* (epic fantasy), and *Mindscape* (a short collection of poetry and lyrics). Mr. Todarello does his own graphic design, illustration, and cover art. His work can be seen at www.vintodphotography.com.

When not working, writing, or shooting photos, Mr. Todarello is usually eating steak in and around Manhattan with his lovely wife. He's eaten so much steak that he has created a thorough review website (www.johnnyprimesteaks.com) which ranks steakhouses on a rigorous 100-point scoring system according to 10 categories.

23350120R00153

Made in the USA
Lexington, KY
06 June 2013